ALONE

Edie Melson

Copyright 2016 Edie Melson
ALL RIGHTS RESERVED
Cover Art by Joan Alley
Edited by Susan M. Baganz

This book is a work of fiction and any resemblance to persons, living or dead, or places, events or locales is purely coincidental. The characters are the product of the author's imagination and used fictitiously.

Warning: The unauthorized reproduction or distribution of this copyrighted work is illegal. No part of this book may be scanned, uploaded or distributed via the Internet or any other means without the permission of Prism Book Group. Please purchase only authorized editions and do not participate in the electronic piracy of copyrighted material. Thank you for respecting the hard work of this author.

Published by Prism Book Group
ISBN-13: 978-1539893233
ISBN-10: 1539893235
First Edition, 2016
Published in the United States of America
Contact info: contact@prismbookgroup.com
http://www.prismbookgroup.com

DEDICATION

In loving memory of my father, Jim Mahoney,

Daddy, you shared your love of books with me and fed my soul.

You encouraged me to follow my dreams and helped me find God's path for my life.

I miss you every day, and I'll love you forever!

PART ONE—FREEDOM

CHAPTER ONE

Only the chimes, oddly sweet, told the passing of time. This far beneath the surface, day and night were arbitrary, dictated by necessity, not nature. Bethany looked around at the other workers, some in standard issue coveralls and others, like her, in the tunics of slaves. Only she and Elisheba carried the mark of Seeker. They were the last two left in this worker block, both of them female, one too old to bear children and herself just entering adulthood.

Slave or free, the designation didn't really matter. Their lives were all governed by someone else. She tried not to fidget as she waited for the supervisor, and Elisheba gave her a half smile from the opposite end of their shared station. The refuge of the chest-high worktop provided a place to lose herself in the tedium of work. Bethany nodded back at her friend, unwilling to speak and draw attention to them.

"I'm no seeker-slave." The old woman at the next workstation glared in Bethany's direction. "They shouldn't force *me* to stand here waiting."

Elisheba tapped the hardened steel worktop with her broken fingernail three times. It was their personal code for patience. Bethany didn't need Elisheba's caution. She wouldn't answer the angry woman. She might have laughed had there been any energy left in her body. These people could label her anything they chose. She wasn't here to please them. Her purpose was to endure—until the One finally called her home.

Elisheba edged closer. "We've little output to show today. The supervisor won't be pleased."

Bethany frowned at her. Conversation was strictly forbidden. Once they'd been dismissed and reached the safety of their sleeping cells, they'd discuss the day.

"The Behavior Board called me in for another hearing. It's my seventh." She looked up and met Bethany's eyes. "I won't deny the One."

Bethany reached out and covered Elisheba's hand with her own. They didn't need words. The board had summoned Elisheba a few days earlier. They both knew what happened at the seventh inquisition. Bethany had been called before the governing board four times herself. No, there'd be no discussion tonight. This would be their final time to await inspection together. Tomorrow, Bethany would stand alone.

She stiffened her spine and searched for the strength to continue. Controlling her emotions at the end of any day was a struggle. Now this? The cavernous environment didn't help. Intense task-lighting and poor circulation led to the ever-present odor of sulfur mixed with leaching compounds. Few chose to remain in these conditions long. The agonizing headaches and recurring respiratory problems ensured a short, miserable lifespan. At almost two klicks beneath the metropolis, the noxious haze, unable to dissipate, burned the throat of any unfortunate worker. Wrinkling her nose, she remembered the smell of earlier times, when she roamed above ground in the sweet rasoon fields of Sintue.

The supervisor stopped at their table. "Worker 456, is this your total for the day?" Simon, always correct in his address to Bethany, had adopted a strange formality that denied the fact they'd grown up together. He didn't even glance at Elisheba.

"Yes, sir." Bethany kept her head down, unwilling to be drawn into his game. She concentrated, determined to keep the tears that pooled in her eyes from falling. She couldn't afford to irritate him. Early on, she believed he'd found her in the slave pens and recommended her for this job, in spite of her Seeker affiliation, because of their past bond. Now she wasn't so sure.

Simon inspected the small amount of assembled electronic components on Bethany's workstation. It didn't matter that the tedious work called for intense attention to detail, with almost two hundred different connections required for each tiny unit. Every worker's quota was based on the need of the talarium dealers—and nothing else.

"And once again, your output falls short."

Bethany could feel his lingering look as his pale hand brushed hers. An accident or on purpose? His height had never bothered her before, but now, he always seemed to loom over her, dark eyes flashing with an avarice she tried to ignore.

"We must come to an understanding." Simon stepped closer, and she tensed her muscles to keep from taking a step back. "I would consider it a personal favor if you'd see that your totals are a little higher in the future." His voice, though low, contained the hint of a purr underneath.

She willed herself not look up. "Uh…yes, sir." Why didn't he leave? Give her a moment with Elisheba. They must solidify their plan. They needed time. Elisheba must not attend the hearing.

"All right, then." Simon turned, slapping his hands together and rubbing them. "All workers in this section may leave." He held up a finger. "Except, I wish to see numbers 142, 301, and 456 in my office." He strode back down the aisle, workers making room for him to pass in the tight space.

"He called you." The urgency in Elisheba's whisper colored her words. "Number 456 is your number."

Bethany shook her head. Her inadvertent gasp at hearing her name called had given her lungs a large concentration of harsh fumes that made her throat close and eyes water. She grabbed Elisheba's hand. "Wait for me." She glanced around. "Go to the designated place. I'll meet you." She'd do whatever it took to save Elisheba. In spite of the older woman's pushy ways, her friendship had been just what Bethany needed, fresh to the rank of slaves. She'd never have survived those first few months without Elisheba and her managing ways. She owed this woman so much and she'd do everything she could to ensure her safety.

She sensed Elisheba's whispered prayer following her as she dodged through the throng of dismissed laborers to answer Simon's summons.

"Hope they're getting rid of that snotty Seeker."

"Thinks she's better than us, does she? I'll wager the supervisor will soon change her mind." An ugly laugh followed.

Other, similar remarks dogged her steps as she crossed the immense workers' block to the area of cubes reserved for those with rank and authority. It would be so easy to hate, but the Text, the Book of Truth, stated clearly what her response must be. *Love your neighbor. Turn the other cheek. Love your enemy.* Such simple instructions, but so difficult to follow. Times like these made her wish she'd never heard the Truth. But she had, and now, those responsibilities outweighed any temporary difficulties. She shook her head. Temporary difficulties indeed. What cruel, cosmic joke labeled her fight to survive in such an innocuous way? When would the One have mercy on her and just take her home?

She hurried down one cramped gray row and into another. This particular block contained almost five hundred workstations, designed for maximum speed of assembly and not the comfort or needs of workers. High-yield light fixtures, necessary for the detailed work, hung low over the tables and left the ceiling in hazy darkness, giving the area an oppressive ambience. Was this her future, a world always in shadow?

Inside his office, Simon consulted the chrono set in the cuff on his arm. All those associated with the Organization were presented with one. The tiny keypad allowed them to reach necessary information almost immediately. Of course, ordinary supervisors like himself weren't allowed access to the upper levels of the database.

That little Seeker was too stupid for words. But she always had been. His father had offered her father an honorable arrangement when she was still a child—a chance to become his lifemate. But the "oh-so-important" Dr. Amariah Randolph would have nothing to do with him. The Randolph's had judged him and his family and found them wanting. But that wouldn't stop Simon now.

These religious fanatics had no idea what actually went on when one of their number disappeared. But Simon did, and he'd found a way to cash in on their ignorance. Thank the One for the Organization. He snorted at the irony—the One had nothing to do with this Organization.

For a substantial fee, this enterprising group supplied personal workers to the luxury class on Sintue. The arrangement benefited many. The Organization quietly took care of the government's problem with the Seekers and, in the process of getting rich, fulfilled a need. Simon, and everyone else, knew exactly what these servants did. He wasn't wealthy enough to own one himself, but his supervisors didn't mind if he sampled the merchandise before delivery.

He settled behind his desk. Everything must be perfect when she came in. Bethany had seemed pathetically grateful after he searched her out and offered her this position. The little simpleton had even tried some of that Seeker jargon on him, spouting something about the Creator using him for the Creator's own purpose. Simon let her know right away what he thought of that. At first, her blue eyes had flashed in a hint of anger, but she had quickly lowered her head and thanked him for finding her—nice and humble.

Bethany was a pretty one, always had been. Her tall frame with dark auburn hair set her apart from the crowd and was a perfect fit for his own unusually tall frame. Now, she kept her hair short, as required in this position, but he often wondered what it would have looked and felt like heavy and long against her neck. He'd even gone so far as to offer her his protection when he first found her. Of course, taking her as a lifemate had been impossible by then. But again, she refused his generous offer. Not this time. This time, she'd have no choice.

He looked up, glaring when 142 and 301 entered his cube.

"Yeah, boss, what do you want?" The Organization planted employees like these at all their facilities to keep track of the workers—and the supervisors.

"Watch outside the door after 456 comes in." Simon raised a black eyebrow. "I don't want to be disturbed for anything short of a true emergency."

The men exchanged looks and left.

Two workers stood outside Simon's door when Bethany approached. "He's waiting for you." The taller of the massive men turned and winked at his partner.

Their attitude added sand to the rocky lump Bethany tried to swallow as her wariness crystallized into certainty. It was time—her time had come. Simon was about to demand something she couldn't—wouldn't—relinquish. Only the One could provide escape. But she had to hang on long enough to let Elisheba make her way to safety first.

Please…protect me…give me strength to see this through.

She raised her chin and pushed open the door.

"Bethany." Simon came around his desk, smiling. "Have a seat. I know you must be tired."

Her nerves turned to pin-pricks, racing up and down her body as she struggled for control. She must give Elisheba time to get away—then she could make good her own escape. Her lips tightened as she lowered herself into the offered chair. Reticence would be her best ally.

"We go a long way back." Simon perched on his desk in front of her, swinging one foot. "And I've always thought of you more as a cousin than a friend."

"You've always been in my prayers." Bethany kept her hands clenched in her lap and her gaze on him. "I do appreciate this job and will try to increase my production. I don't want you to get into trouble with your supervisors because of me."

"Oh, don't worry about me." He stilled his foot. "I know how to handle the higher-ups." He winked at her. "But it's you I'm worried about. Are you still sold on that Seeker nonsense?"

She teetered on two levels, forced to carry on a civil conversation while waiting for the right moment to flee. "It's not nonsense." She fought the urge to explain, to tell him all that being a Seeker meant. He had warned her against that. The world only saw what she'd given up. Besides, Simon made his position clear when she began working for him. "And yes, I am still completely sold out to it."

"I really hate to hear that." He came to his feet, towering over her in an instant. "Because it means you're out of a job."

Bethany's nails cut into her palms as she fisted her hands tighter. Had she waited long enough—or too long?

He circled around behind her. "The word came down from my supervisor today. He gave me no choice but to terminate all employees with known Seeker affiliation. I wanted to offer you one more opportunity before I let you go, just for old-times' sake." Bethany flinched as he put his hands on her neck and began massaging her shoulders. "I wish you'd give up this insanity. There is no future for you as a Seeker."

"My future comes later." A sense of peace from another time and another place rushed through her.

"No." He pulled her tight against the back of the chair. "Your future has been decided, and it's about to begin now."

Bethany gasped, but before she could speak, the room filled with noise. The screech of the emergency sirens amped up the adrenaline already flooding her system. Simon flinched back from her and rushed toward the door. Before he reached it, one of the guards exploded into the room.

"What's going on?" Simon pushed the man aside, peering out.

"Sir, we're under attack. The boards are flashing '*no drill.*'" The man gestured toward the surface. "It has to be an invasion."

Simon stood immobile, and Bethany sprinted from the chair to the door. She pushed through the men to freedom.

CHAPTER TWO

Bethany forced her way through throngs of people to the main exit in the corner of the underground block. It opened onto a dark corridor leading to the trams that carried the workers up or down several levels to the many substantive living quarters and sleeping cells. The passageway rang with questions as tension played on the faces of the people surrounding her.

"Why are the sirens going off?" A woman rushed by, one hand covering her mouth and nose, the other outstretched, pushing through the crowd.

A man, obviously searching for someone, tried to stop people as they ran past. "What's happening?"

"Is this a riot?" Another woman's voice crescendoed and broke, ending in a wail.

Bethany bumped into the man in front of her as he came to an abrupt stop. Most of the time, she tried to hide her taller than average frame, but today, she used it to find the bottleneck.

That's when she saw them.

They jogged in from a little-used tunnel. The beings became a line of warriors, each at least seven feet tall, loosely cradling powerful weapons. Full body armor left them invulnerable, while opaque face-plates rendered them anonymous. Their lack of expression brought Bethany's breathing to a stop as her blood turned cold. These were the nightmares from her childhood. She remembered the tales so well. The Book of Truth told of a future populated with such beings before the end of time.

The crowd became a mindless sea, intent on escape, forcing Bethany to move with them or be trampled. She fought against the relentless current of their panic as they surged toward the express tram. Fighting to free herself, she elbowed those nearest. She must not enter that train.

But the hysteria of the crowd was too much, and they swept into the open maw of the nearest tram. Once inside, their panic became hers. Slaves, especially Seekers, weren't allowed on the express cars, and yet here she was. To be caught on one meant severe punishment or even death.

Her heart thundered in her chest as she forced her way back to the door. *Stay open. Please, stay open.* She was close enough to freedom to hear the whisper of the mechanism as the doors slammed shut, trapping her inside.

As the train began its ascent, Bethany froze, unwilling to draw a breath lest she bring attention to herself. Surely, in their fear, those around her wouldn't notice she was there. The crowd shifted, still restless, but with the rise to possible safety, individual voices began to babble. A couple standing close to her voiced her own thoughts aloud.

"Who are they?" The woman wore the orange of a tech worker.

"I don't even want to imagine." The man, barrel chested and more of a size for an on-ground worker, put his arm around her. "They'll probably be waiting on the tram topside. I'll try to cause a distraction when we get nearer to the surface. Keep close and follow my lead."

Discussions broke out as the crowd's panic receded and those in the tram settled into small clumps of individuals. Bethany held her collar high on the side of her neck, careful to hide her Seeker's mark.

What had happened to her world? She'd known the Book held Truth, but the idea that it pictured a literal future? No, surely not. She searched her memories for details, specifics about the coming times. It had foretold a race of giants. But these? The urge to sink to her knees almost overcame her resolve to stay hidden. Could the monsters she'd seen been the ones foretold to *save* Sintue? Surely not, they looked more like planet-devouring R'hobans than something the One would have provided. *Save us...please save us.*

The tram continued its ascent and Bethany began to breathe, her heartbeat settling into a normal rhythm. Only seconds remained until the car arrived at the surface and she could escape.

The barrel-chested man to her right stared at her. In her reverie, her hand had relaxed and her mark been exposed. He smirked, and his look told her she'd become the diversion he'd been waiting for. "Hey, what's a Seeker doing here?" The crowd, already nervous and agitated, began to morph once again into a beast with no conscience as their pent-up tension found release.

The first blow caught her in the stomach. She couldn't keep back a cry as she doubled over with pain. Bethany fought for breath and tried to straighten, feeling the tram slow as it reached the surface. Angry words came at her from all sides, but there wasn't time to react as another fist connected with her head. She reeled from the force of it, light and stabbing pain exploding through her temples. Only the crush of people kept her upright.

The tram doors opened, and the sound of a stunner firing rang in her ears. Had she been hit? The acrid odor of a weapon filled her nostrils as those inside the tram froze. Several of the giants entered the tram and surrounded her. One of them took her arm and shoved her behind him. She wanted to sink to the ground, but he gripped her arm like an iron band. *No, please. Just let the crowd kill me.*

"The next one to move will die." The stranger delivered his threat in a low voice but with such authority, no one moved. He'd quieted the agitators, who were now more afraid of his weapon than upset by a Seeker in their midst. Other strangers waited outside the tram. They herded the now docile crowd—including the barrel-chested man and his companion—toward makeshift pens that stretched across the rockcrete commons and into the dirt fields as far as Bethany could see. Immense cruisers hovered everywhere, casting insect-like shadows on her world.

Bethany gasped, and the warrior who still held her arm gave her a shake.

She twisted her head to gaze up at him.

"Are you a Seeker?" The man's voice, though still low, seemed kinder somehow.

"Yes, I am." She raised her chin.

"Then you have nothing to fear from us." He led her from the tube, slowing his long stride, and signaled to another captor. "Manaen, see to her wounds and take her to the captain's holding area to await processing."

Manaen removed his helmet, and Bethany saw that he was a she. The warrior's height, along with the helmet, had misled her. But as she caught sight of the giant's eyes, surrounded by sooty lashes, Bethany knew no one could never mistake her for anything but a woman.

"Yes, Josiah." Manaen brought her fist to her shoulder in a gesture of respect. Turning, she touched Bethany's arm. "What is your name, child?"

"I'm Bethany." She looked up at this strange warrior woman. Bethany's head didn't even reach her shoulder. "Who are you, and why are you here?"

"We are the R'hobans, and your world has been chosen."

Bethany's terror returned in waves that threatened her sanity. She closed her eyes, her stomach roiled, and her center of gravity tilted. R'hobans. She'd been right, but hearing the name gave the nightmare life. Everyone in the galaxy knew them by reputation. They were monsters, conquerors that overtook worlds and enslaved the inhabitants. They left few alive to recount the stories of their domination. Why had the One chosen now to abandon them? Abandon her?

"Don't be afraid." Manaen caught her before the dizziness took Bethany to the ground. "Things, for you, are going to change for the better." She set Bethany upright. "Let's get you patched up."

Manaen loaded her into an aircar, the engines purring to life before they lifted off to another part of the city. As they rode, Bethany looked down on Sintue. The landscape sped by, sunset illuminating the inside of the aircar with a reddish glare. Just above the horizon, a deep haze hung like an invasion force of darkness, threatening to obliterate her world. She closed her eyes against the dark omen in the sky and the nausea building in her throat.

"Tell me about your personal dwelling. Is it close by?" Manaen's voice held no threat.

Bethany opened her eyes, glancing at her captor. "I live below the city, in a block of housing ten klicks down."

"Have you always lived in such a place?"

Bethany's mind raced through her memories, to a place of light and air. She swallowed back the pain and subdued the images. Difficult, because her captor's eyes were the exact color of the grass that once grew in abundance on Sintue. "I've been there for nine years. Ever since my parents died."

"What happened to your parents?"

Could this monster actually be interested, or was there another reason for her questions? "They were killed during the Seeker cleansing in 2580." She kept her voice even, practiced at keeping all emotion at bay. "I was away at the time."

"And the authorities?" Manaen's amazing eyes widened. "What did they do?"

"They didn't *do* anything." Wasn't she aware of how the government had ruled their beliefs an act of terrorism? Did these invaders learn nothing about a world before they conquered it? "The government doesn't sanction Seeker beliefs."

Manaen frowned and sighed. "I knew of the Seeker persecution here on Sintue, but didn't realize it occurred to such a degree or with the government's blatant approval."

Once again, her Seeker affiliation had set her apart. For better or for worse?

A sad smile played across Manaen's lips before she turned her attention to the outside. The aircar landed, and Bethany arrived at an unfamiliar destination—silence and worry her two familiar companions.

CHAPTER THREE

Simon swore under his breath, even as his thoughts raced. A clear head and logic were his best weapons. A quick glance at the panic-stricken looks of his companions made his first decision simple. "You two follow that sniveling Seeker." He needed to distance himself from them as fast as possible.

They hesitated, exchanging looks.

"We'll meet later, at the usual place." At his emphatic nod, they turned and ran from the room.

Watching them from the doorway of his office, Simon weighed his options. The two enforcers disappeared from view as he chose his next step. He almost grinned as he remembered the tunnels. Put in place by his superiors, he'd been informed of their existence and warned against their use except in extreme emergencies. Well, at least these circumstances fulfilled the emergency criterion.

He darted through the now empty workrooms, made all the more unnatural by the claxon that continued to screech. In a supply area, he moved several plastic drums, sneezing at their acrid odor. The dark ring on the floor beneath one of them evidenced a slow leak of an unknown and surely toxic substance.

Simon tried to protect his nose and mouth in crook of his arm as he bent to loosen a vent set low in the wall where the barrels had been. He squatted, flashing a handheld into the damp space. The light illuminated only a few feet, but it was enough to verify this was the tunnel's entrance. He stood for another quick look around the vacant workspace, unwilling to risk exposure. He inhaled deeply. It was important to keep his wits and be prepared for anything. Simon ducked his head and crawled into the dank darkness.

Bethany's captor piloted the aircar toward an area well north of Laol City and landed it in the courtyard of a compound. Manaen helped Bethany from the aircar before turning her over to an older woman dressed in white tunic and leggings. Perhaps the uniform of a healer? The large compound she entered was not unlike the one where she'd grown up, although her family's home had been southeast of the city.

The ache in her head was real enough, but everything else seemed unreal, like she watched the unfolding events happen to another person. At first, she scarcely noticed her surroundings as the white-clad captor treated her wounds. They were cleansed, medicines applied, and even some kind of inoculation administered. While the woman cared for her, Bethany began to catalogue her environment in more detail. The room where she lay had windows, and she could actually see the outside. Her eyes were drawn to the out-of-doors. The sun had set, but the afterglow brightened the window well enough for her starved senses. As her eyes drank in the sight, she started when the woman tapped her arm.

"What is your name, Seeker?"

Bethany pulled her eyes from the window and focused on the healer's features. This R'hoban, too, was tall, but less than the seemingly-average seven feet. The silver in her hair and the lines on her face mapped her maturity. "I'm Bethany…uh…ma'am."

"I'm no ma'am." The woman laughed, a silvery sound, contagious with joy. "You may call me Casiphia."

Her response puzzled Bethany. Could this be some elaborate act to get her to lower her defenses? Why would they do that? She was less than nothing. Why treat her as though she had worth?

"How does your head feel now?" Casiphia patted the last bandage into place on her temple.

Bethany turned her head slowly back and forth. The pain had diminished considerably. The inoculation must have contained an analgesic. "It feels better." She took a cautious breath. "My ribs aren't as sore either."

"That's good." Casiphia began to gather the debris from her treatment. "I'll get someone to escort you to your quarters. You'll be able to rest."

Quarters? Were there quarters in a medical facility? Could it be a prison instead—or worse? Bethany flinched as images of dark, damp places populated with unimaginable horrors flooded her mind. "Where will they take me?"

Casiphia grey eyes filled with concern. "Don't be frightened. You're safe now."

Bethany shook her head. Casiphia was the second to reassure her on this issue. "I don't understand. Where am I? What do you want with me?" She hesitated, then finished in a rush. "The other one said you were the R'hobans."

"You're at a retraining center. Don't worry, we'll explain everything tomorrow." She patted Bethany's hand. "The injection I gave you will take effect soon, and you won't remember much from now until you wake. I'll be close by to answer all your questions. I promise." She turned to the doorway. "Nathan, Bethany's ready."

A young man in a white jumpsuit stepped into the room and helped her from the cot. He seemed to be in his early teens and while he still towered over her, the fact of his youth kept his height from intimidating her as much. Perhaps the medicine had already affected her mind.

The corridor he led her down was familiar. The layout was common in the private compounds that dotted the surface of the planet. They normally ran from one building to another, allowing for ease of travel no matter what the weather conditions. It had been years since she'd been in such a dwelling. The walls glistened a pale yellow and had been recently cleaned. They smelled of something she couldn't quite place, a pleasant memory from her childhood.

"Almost there." Nathan kept a soft grasp on her arm since she was wobbly on her feet. Her head felt too big for her body, and she gazed at everything as through a haze. The corridor ended in a large room. The simple furnishings were arranged in several inviting conversation areas. Oversized wooden chairs, softened with pillows in shades of blues and green, as well as cushioned benches, were scattered about. These were broken up with low wood-and-metal tables, dotted with candles and bowls of freshening herbs. Numerous doorways, leading to other parts of the compound, were set into walls tinted a softer amber. They took the first hallway, and he stopped outside a spacious sleeping room. "Here you go."

She peeked inside and couldn't help the way her heart leapt. "Oh—a window."

Nathan laughed. "And a bed." He helped her to the inviting cot heaped with blankets and pillows in cheerful greens and yellows. "Sleep as long as you want. Someone will be here when you awaken." He made a face of exaggerated disgust. "If I'm not mistaken, Casaphia will insist on the duty. She seems quite taken with you."

She smiled at the young man. The presence of her captor no longer distressed her, but she was too tired to analyze why. Perhaps the One hadn't abandoned her after all. "Thank you."

Nathan stepped to the door. "Good night. Sleep well." He dimmed the lights and pulled the door closed.

Simon heard low voices before he noticed the light. He doused his own feeble beam and froze, allowing his ears to ascertain the level of danger at the end of his journey.

"I can't imagine we're the only ones who've escaped detection." The voice seemed to move, as if the speaker paced in the room beyond.

"Give it time, there will be others."

Simon let out the breath he'd been holding. He recognized the nasal twang of the first speaker. It could only be Loenne, his supervisor—or to apply her accurate title, his controller. He grimaced at the all too appropriate designation. Whoever directed the Organization, they wielded the power of life and death over those who served them.

He crawled out of the tunnel into a dimly lit room and stood, his attention focused on snapping the handheld back onto his belt. "You're not the only ones who've survived." His almost cheerful tone evidenced his relief at leaving that slimy environment. He looked up when she didn't answer, and instead of Loenne, found himself looking at a stranger pointing an accelerator pistol directly at him. "Hey now." Holding up a hand, he backed slowly away from the man with the weapon. "Tell him who I am." He risked a quick glance around the room and settled on his controller. "Tell him."

"It's okay, Aven." The slim woman put a hand on the barrel of the weapon. "He's in my cadre. I vouch for his identity."

Aven lowered the weapon, his eyes still locked with Simon's. "Are you alone?"

"Of course." Simon didn't try to hide the defensiveness of his tone. "I made certain no one followed me." Who did this man think he was, one of the Overseers?

Aven turned from Simon. "Loenne, you haven't introduced us."

"So sorry, sir." She dipped her head. "Simon is our handler at plant 1291." Her ingratiating tone surprised Simon. Her manner with him had always been imperious and condescending. Perhaps he should re-evaluate this man who insisted on respect.

Aven returned his attention to Simon, holstered his weapon, and raised his hand, palm facing Simon, in a gesture of friendship. "I greet you in the name of the Prince."

The formal salutation took Simon by surprise. He'd only heard it on a few occasions. The controllers he dealt with were more relaxed in manner. "May the Prince rule forever." Simon rubbed his chin. "Do you have any word on what is actually happening?"

Aven took the only seat in the room, a metal bench beside a wall. "We've been invaded." He cocked his head. "I'm sure you've heard that much."

"That's *all* I've heard." Simon also relaxed, leaning against the opposite wall. "Do we know *who* invaded?"

"It's the R'hobans." Loenne began to pace, rubbing her hands together. "We're doomed. There is no hope."

"Shut up." Aven stood. "It's merely a setback." His lips twitched with almost a hint of a smile. "It might even work to our advantage, if we're clever enough to make the most of this opportunity."

Simon relaxed, this was a man who knew how to evaluate and exploit a situation. "I think you're correct," Simon said. "The Overseers could definitely turn this to our benefit." Loenne's histrionics grated on his nerves. These circumstances called for quick thinking, not wallowing in fear.

"I'm glad to see not everyone I serve with is an imbecile." Aven glanced at Loenne, and she blanched.

"I meant no disrespect." She swallowed convulsively.

Simon ignored Loenne and began to inspect the room. No windows and only one plain metal door. The illumination grate inset in the ceiling grid looked as if it hadn't been cleaned in years. He cocked his head and listened—either the sirens had quit or the room was well insulated. "Where is this place?"

"We're four klicks below the administration complex." Aven seated himself again, resting his hands on his knees. "This is part of a former group of offices sealed off years ago. We should be safe here for quite a while."

"What about food and water?" Simon addressed Aven directly, ignoring Loenne. "What do we have in the way of supplies and facilities?"

Aven waved a vague hand in the general direction of the door. "It's all been taken care of. We'll receive word when it's safe and then we'll join the others."

Simon's heart rate increased. The Organization had always been careful to keep identities and numbers secret. He only knew as much as needed to accomplish the goals set for him in his position. Obviously, the time had come to share more. With careful planning, he could turn this situation to his advantage. A former supervisor had once likened him to a feline—no matter the circumstances, he would always land on his feet.

CHAPTER FOUR

Josiah sighed, tossing his helmet on the smooth-surfaced table just inside the entrance of his city quarters. It skidded across the top and came to rest beside a stray order tube. He hadn't slept in thirty-two cycles, not an uncommon occurrence during the beginning of an occupation. At this point, sleep was an inconvenience and not yet unavoidable. He continued into the briefing area of his assigned dwelling, ignoring the plush furnishings of its previous owner. His rank of Commander for this mission entitled him to this elegant city dwelling, as well as a compound outside Laol City. His brother had the same largess when… No. He had to stay focused on the job at hand.

He strode past his desk, littered with order tubes, to the window, gazing out at the ugly sights before him. Dawn had broken, but instead of beauty, a dank haze hung over the city. He could still taste the metallic bite in the polluted air. The city seemed to go on forever. Try as he might, there wasn't a hint of anything green or growing. Why would a people destroy themselves in this fashion? Hadn't they seen that the One had blessed them with an abundance of beauty and resources? An abundance that would have lasted forever with only a small bit of stewardship? He shook his head. They'd just liberated a world populated with fools and unbelievers.

The unbelieving were almost all that remained on this planet. He sighed again. What had been the purpose of waiting so long to rescue Sintue? The hope they brought seemed almost too little, too late. From what he could tell, there were few Seekers left on this desolate world. Here he was again. Once more, too late to accomplish the things that needed to be done.

"Josiah, you look troubled." His sister entered from her sleeping quarters on the opposite side of the dwelling. They often shared a domicile since neither had chosen lifemates. It used to be the three of them, until...

Manean carried a pot of qua. The subtle fragrance of this traditional tea concealed its powerful stimulant, and they usually shared the first pot of the day.

He turned and smiled at her. She was the light of his life as well as a formidable warrior. "I'm disturbed by the condition of the few remaining Seekers we've found." He ran his fingers through his unruly hair and looked back on the cityscape outside. "The one I handed off to you nearly died before I intervened."

She joined him at the window, her hand resting lightly on his forearm. "That isn't our concern. You, of all people, know better than to dwell on the what-ifs of life."

"So how is she?" He didn't turn from the window until his sister's silence forced him to face her.

"How is who?" Her striking green eyes held his.

"Manaen, don't tease. That Seeker took several hard blows." He'd never before inquired about an individual on the planets they freed, and they both knew it. But this one small woman had touched something he thought long dead.

"She was shaken and scared out of her wits, but she will be fine. She'll carry no permanent damage."

"That's good." Josiah could still see the woman he'd rescued in his mind's eye.

Manaen cocked her head. "I have to admit, her courage and calm in spite of her circumstances struck me also." She settled on a low couch covered in yellow silk with bright blue pillows. "I bypassed the captain and took her directly to Casaphia's training compound myself. She seemed taken with the girl, and I'm certain she'll see to the girl's medical treatment herself."

"Casiphia's insightful. And she takes her duties to heart." His sister knew him well. "She's the perfect choice to see to the little ones' training. Her sort of courage and faithfulness should be rewarded." He joined her on the sofa. "What else do you know of the Seeker?"

"Her name is Bethany." Manaen paused and bit her lip. "Her name means house of misery."

His face froze. "How does that signify? Did you find out what had happened to her?" He took a deep breath—where had this rush of emotion come from? "I don't know why it matters to me, but it does."

Manaen's surprise at his frank honesty showed on her face. "I know her parents were killed in the Seeker cleansing of 2580." She closed her eyes and paused. "By this world's reckoning, that would have been almost nine years ago."

"A long time to live without a family."

"We don't know that she's without family, only that her mother and father are dead."

"True enough." He walked to the desk, picking up an order tube. "We've missed a sizable number in our initial occupation of this world."

"That's unexpected." Manaen sat forward. "What happened?"

He frowned as he reread the report. "Our intelligence report left out the existence of an extensive tunnel system."

"We've been on other worlds with underground systems…what's different this time?"

"The tunnels appear to be lined with a special composite of talarium impervious to our sensors."

Manaen got up and joined him at the desk. "That is odd. Talarium is exceedingly hard to manufacture and very few know how to make it resistant to scanning." She tapped her chin. "Although we knew this planet was a major talarium supplier."

He gestured to the scene out the window. "As the condition of their world can attest. The manufacture of that stuff is deadly for an ecosystem if it's not done correctly."

Her gaze followed his gesture. "And it obviously hasn't been. Since so many escaped into the tunnels, do you think they had advance notice of our plans?"

"That's the most reasonable conclusion." He banged the tube on the desktop. "How did they find out? They must have infiltrated the spies we had on-planet somehow."

"It is possible." She picked up the offending message carrier. "But have you considered the possibility of a traitor within our own ranks?"

He turned to face her. "How can you suggest such a thing?"

"It's something we should consider." Manaen looked down, but not before he caught the glint of tears in her eyes. "Especially since the outcome of our last mission."

He knew how much she missed their brother. He covered her hand with his own. "Impossible. We are the chosen. Who among us would even consider denying that grace?"

Manaen laughed. "You know we are not a perfect people."

He began sorting through the tubes littering the table. "Of course I know that, don't be stupid." He looked up, caught her reproving look, and half-smiled an apology. "I fight my corrupt nature constantly, as you see. But a rebellion of this magnitude? I can't begin to imagine it."

"There are many things you don't understand, big brother. And I fear the One is about to make them known."

Bethany awoke with a start. The injuries she sustained ached, but not as much as she'd expected. She slowly turned her head, afraid of the pain, but only felt a slight echo of the intensity from yesterday. It had been so long since she'd been treated by a healer, she'd forgotten the benefits of real medicine. Yes, she'd be sore for a few days, but nothing more. She sat up, unfamiliar with her surroundings. Light filtered into the room, and she caught the odor of…no, it couldn't be. She glanced at the table by her cot and sure enough, there sat a vase of Fayro flowers. It had been years since she had seen the vibrant purple petals. She stroked one, barely touching it, afraid it was only a dream.

"You're awake."

She jumped as Casiphia rose from a chair across the room. She still wore her white tunic and leggings. Was that a healer's uniform or just her preferred colors? "What time is it?" Bethany rubbed her eyes and looked at the bright window.

"Almost midday." Casiphia walked to a gray wooden storage chest and pulled out a green tunic and deep purple leggings. She brought them to the bed for Bethany's inspection. "Your clothing had seen better days."

That was an understatement. Bethany took the proffered garments, her fingers stroking the soft fabrics. She flinched as the roughness of her hands caught on the delicate nap. "Thank you."

"I'll be right outside. Let me know when you've changed." Casiphia stopped in the doorway. "There are other necessities in the chest. Feel free to help yourself."

As the door closed, Bethany crawled from the sleeping cot, hoping Casaphia meant the chest had fresh underthings as well.

Opening the lid, she let out a deep breath. It contained everything she could possibly want, even several pairs of supple ankle boots in different sizes. It had been years since she'd had such luxuries.

Looking around, she noticed the smaller door on the wall to the left of the window. Opening it, she found a compact room, complete with a bathing unit. She took full advantage of the facility. Then, fresh and relieved, she donned her new clothes, luxuriating in the feel of soft fabric next to her skin. She dug through the small chest again and came up with a hairbrush. Her short hair responded quickly and the tangles disappeared.

Casaphia's bright smile met Bethany when she opened the door to the corridor. "I believe I'm ready." For what, she couldn't imagine.

"This way." Casiphia gestured in the opposite direction of where she'd come from last night. "You must be famished."

She hadn't noticed before, but at Casiphia's suggestion, her stomach made its requirements public. Heat suffused her face at her body's noisy betrayal.

Casiphia laughed. "Come on, dear, the dining hall is this way."

They entered a large room occupied by only two women. The smell of freshly prepared food gave the luxurious room a comforting aura. A wooden table, easily able to seat twenty, dominated the space. Chairs and benches punctuated its length.

The women sat at the end closest to them. One appeared to be about her age and Sintuen by birth. The height betrayed the other woman's R'hoban origins. Both looked her way as she and Casaphia entered. The Sintuen looked down at her untouched bowl when Bethany tried to make eye contact, but the R'hoban gave a welcoming smile. A slight tremor raced up Bethany's spine, and she swallowed back the bile that rose in her throat. She mustn't forget what had happened, no matter how well they treated her. She'd learned well the lesson that everything had a price.

"Have a seat." Casiphia pointed to the long table. "I'll bring something to break your fast."

Bethany slipped onto the bench facing the Sintuen and the beautiful, large window behind her. The girl was also dressed in a soft tunic and leggings and didn't meet Bethany's eyes. She seemed as puzzled and nervous as Bethany felt. That shared feeling made her brave. "I'm Bethany, what's your name?"

The girl glanced at the woman beside her who nodded encouragingly. "I'm Keturah."

Casiphia returned with a steaming bowl of spiced gruen and set it in front of Bethany before turning to the other R'hoban. "Come, Leah, we'll leave them to get acquainted."

Bethany sat silent and still until the two women left the room. Then, with a quick exchange of glances, she and the other young woman attacked the food before them. The rich nuttiness of the gruen answered a craving Bethany had almost forgotten. She finished every bit and began scraping the bottom of the bowl before she ventured a question. "Do you have any idea what's happening?"

Keturah's eyes darted to the doorway. "No, I hoped you might."

"Where are you from?"

"I live in Laol City now, the Balstrop section, eight klicks down." She took sip of tea, the bowl in front of her as empty as Bethany's. "What about you?"

"I'm from Laol City, too." Bethany stretched, her stomach finally full of something delicious instead of just the usual synthetic mix of nutrients that had sustained her for so long. "I live in the Soroked district, ten klicks down."

Bethany saw Keturah's eyes narrow and focus on her neck. The mark. How could she have been so careless? Now, she'd been identified. She started to cover her neck and stopped. What was the use? She kept her eyes on Keturah, every nerve on alert as she waited for Keturah's reaction. She hoped and prayed it was only verbal. Her poor, sore body couldn't take another physical attack.

CHAPTER FIVE

Josiah unbuckled his helmet as he strode into headquarters, the chaos of the morning apparent in the nervous chatter which ceased with his appearance. Without breaking stride, he pointed to his second in command and rounded the corner into his private ready room. He was pulling up the latest reports on his personal plasscreen when Bezek entered and saluted.

"You wished to see me, sir?"

Josiah slammed another tube into the reader. "What I wish is that we'd had more accurate information on this place before we landed."

"Sir?"

"Sit, man. I know you're as exhausted as I am." Josiah pointed to a chair and took a deep breath. He grimaced, as much at the lingering odor of sulfur they'd brought from outside as at the situation. It wasn't Bezek's fault the advance intelligence had proved faulty. "Do you have the numbers from the outlying areas?"

Bezek eyed the small chair nearest the desk and slowly eased his bulk into it. It creaked, but held. "I do, but you won't like 'em."

"Of course I won't. I haven't liked anything about this liberation. Nothing has gone as it should." Josiah leaned back and raked his fingers through his hair. "Give them to me anyway."

"Only three of the twelve outlying districts are reported fully secured. Five of the remaining nine are close." Bezek scratched at his red beard. "I've never been on a freedom mission that fell this far below expectations." He caught Josiah's look and shifted his gaze. "Well, almost never."

Bezek was more than a second. He'd been there when…but Josiah refused to even think of that time, much less speak of it. And he wouldn't begin today. "Stay on top of it, and keep me updated." At Bezek's glower he waved him out of the office. "I know you will. Get out of here so I can try to salvage what's left of this operation." He raised an eyebrow when his second didn't move. "Is there anything else?"

"I'd like to—" Bezek's voice squeaked. "I'd like to ask your permission to court your sister."

Josiah's mouth dropped open. Manaen with a lifemate? Bezek and his sister? Bezek asking for his approval? "I hope Manaen never finds out you asked permission to court her."

"I'm not asking you as her brother." Bezek's face reddened. "I'm asking you as my commander. I didn't want you to think…I mean I didn't want things to appear…." He shook his head. "You know what I mean."

A chuckle burst from Josiah's throat, answered by a grin from Bezek. "I do, and I appreciate your candor. Things will be fine here, no matter what my sister decides." He sobered. "I assume this means you haven't broached the subject with her?"

"No. There hasn't been a good time yet."

Josiah bit back another chuckle. "I'd have to say sooner rather than later would be the place to start."

"Obviously." Bezek got up from the chair and began to pace, an almost comic endeavor in the cramped space.

"You know her well. Why the sudden indecision?"

"Because it's so important." Bezek stopped in front of his desk. "Some day, you'll find someone and you'll understand."

Josiah's mind flashed with a picture of the young Seeker. "Nonsense!" He leaned forward. "Just tell her. You know as well as I that Manean values plain speaking. I'd never thought you fearful of anyone's opinion."

Bezek's eyes narrowed. "And I never thought you foolhardy with accusations."

"It's not an accusation, it's a warning." Josiah blew out a breath. "Nothing is going right, and you know as well as any of us how brief our time can be." He motioned Bezek out of the office. "Go. You're officially off-duty for the rest of the day. Find my sister and speak your heart."

The room was silent and, after an interminable pause, Keturah's lips quivered. "I'm a Seeker too." She pulled her thick, dark hair away from her neck, exposing the mark to Bethany. At Keturah's revelation, Bethany's heart resumed its normal rhythm.

"How did you come to be here?"

"Do you know where we are?"

They spoke in unison, then giggled. Keturah motioned Bethany to speak first.

"How did you get here?" Bethany's mind raced as her questions tumbled out. "Do you know what's happened?"

Keturah leaned close to Bethany. "They are the R'hobans. You knew that?" At Bethany's nod, she continued, "A group of these giants burst into our section, ordering everyone from their assignments." She dropped her head. "I'm ashamed to say I went with them willingly. The drudge work I'd been assigned was almost more than I could bear." She glanced at Bethany. "How about you?"

"At our facility, we heard the alarms and rushed to the trams." Bethany lowered her voice. "I got caught in the crowd and was forced onto an express tram. When it reached the surface, the R'hobans were there, waiting."

Keturah touched the bandage on Bethany's temple. "Did you get this from riding the tram or from the R'hobans?"

"Not the R'hobans. They protected me. I couldn't believe it. In truth, they saved my life." Bethany wrapped her arms around herself, remembering the terrifying ride above ground. "After the rescue, they separated me from everyone else and brought me here."

Keturah nodded knowingly. "They isolated me, too. It's almost like they were searching for Seekers." She looked down at her hands knotted in her lap. "They checked everyone for the mark."

Bethany leaned forward to catch her eye. "Do you have any idea what they want from us?"

A tear traced a damp line down Keturah's cheek. "I wish I did." She brushed at it with the back of her hand. "They've treated me well, but no one will tell me anything."

"I know." Bethany got up and went to the window, drinking in the midday sun. The polluted air seemed lighter here, outside the city. On the far horizon, she could just make out a single green field. "It's been almost two years since I last saw the sun." She turned, clasping her hands. "It's as beautiful as I remember."

Keturah joined her. "It is glorious." She sighed. "I wonder how long we'll be able to enjoy it."

The door opened and Casiphia and Leah came back into the room. Bethany and her new friend exchanged looks and returned to their seats at the table.

"I'm sure you both have a lot of questions." Casiphia's smile seemed sincere, but it didn't stop the quiver in Bethany's belly. "I want to first reassure you that we mean you no harm."

Leah leaned forward. "Our race is here to save your world, not destroy it."

"How can that be?" Bethany couldn't hold the questions in any longer. "I've heard of the R'hobans, and I know you annihilate the worlds you take over." She hid her face in her hands. "What is His purpose in this?"

"His purpose?' Casiphia pulled Bethany's hands away from her face. "If you mean the One, He has sent us to save you."

Keturah gasped. "You know about the One? How? You're destroyers, not creators." At her outburst, Keturah covered her mouth with her hand.

"Oh, child. We're not destroyers, we serve the Creator. And our Creator isn't just the creator of Sintue. He created everything." Casiphia's outstretched arms took in their surroundings. "Your world has become corrupt beyond measure, and the One sent us to you to redeem what is His."

"It's a sad day when even His own don't know much about Him." Leah shook her head. "Those of you who are Seekers already know Him a little, but a great deal of His truth has been lost through time."

"You're here with us to begin the process of learning that truth, a time of retraining, if you will." Casiphia laughed. "I think you'll enjoy getting to know the One in a safe place."

The thought stunned Bethany. Practice her religion openly? She looked to Casiphia and back at Keturah. Her parents had dreamed of this very thing, of a land where they could worship openly. They said it had once been this way. Could it be again—was this the intent of the One? She opened her mouth to speak, but her tongue was dry. She swallowed and tried again. "May we really do this?"

"Of course you may learn about the One." Leah wrinkled her nose, then smiled. "We'll begin right away."

Casiphia held up a hand. "First, I think there's something you girls might need even more than education."

CHAPTER SIX

Simon lay half asleep, slumped in a corner, when the knock finally came. He leapt to his feet, disoriented for a moment in the unfamiliar room before he remembered they were waiting for the all-clear signal. He glanced around and caught Aven watching him, one eyebrow raised, and forced himself to relax, leaning against the wall. He must be careful. Aven missed very little.

"Report." Aven's voice held a note of command as he addressed those on the other side of the door.

"All clear, sir." As the door opened, Simon matched the male voice to a tall, square-jawed man. "Everything is ready."

"Very good, Japheth." Aven turned to Simon and Loenne. "Come, we have much to accomplish."

As they exited the room, Loenne grabbed Simon's arm and leaned close. "Be careful with Aven. He has power." She continued past him to take her place one step behind Aven on his right.

Simon arranged his face in a neutral expression. All the pieces clicked in his mind. Aven must be an Overseer, one of the shadowy figures in command of the Organization. It only made sense, considering his air of authority and knowledge. Simon moved quickly to flank Aven on his left, opposite Loenne. Until Aven said different, he'd act as one of Aven's lieutenants. The powerful man turned his head slightly and smiled at Simon. It was an ambiguous smile but showed no overt malice. That was good.

Japheth set a brisk pace as they moved through the underground pathways. Simon saw more citizens than he'd expected. He noted they all scurried about with purpose, endowing the setting with the flavor of a military camp. He knew the Organization had many members, but how had so many had eluded capture? Perhaps this compound had more than just the flavor of a military camp.

They came at last to a large, well-lit room. An ornate table with six armchairs dominated the center of the room. Plasscreens and tech boards covered one wall, while technicians labored at corresponding workstations. Scattered throughout the room were other, more utilitarian chairs. These were occupied by various men and women. The room had been filled with chatter and activity that ceased when they appeared.

Three others were seated at the table, two women and one man. One of the women, an ancient crone, cackled and clapped her hands at their entrance. "I knew you'd evade them."

"Shut up, Salisa." The large man beside her narrowed his eyes at her comment. "You know playing favorites is forbidden."

"Perhaps now, Baanus." She showed no concern at his rebuttal. "But there was a time when it was expected."

"Welcome, Aven." The other woman rose, her tiny figure almost engulfed with a cloud of dark hair, and hurried around the table and gave him a formal kiss on the cheek. "Take your seat, there is a great deal to be decided."

"Thank you, Delaina." Aven seated himself at the table and motioned Simon and Loenne into chairs lining the wall.

Their formal use of names when addressing each other confirmed much of what Simon had already guessed. Here he was, in the council of Overseers. It took all his self-control to keep his expression neutral as he reviewed the events of the day in his mind.

This situation had catapulted him into the hierarchy of the Organization in a way that would normally have taken years to accomplish.

As Baanus called the meeting to order, Simon took stock of the other lieutenants in the room. He counted eleven, both men and women. They were seated in chairs near him and Loenne, but only the four had rank enough to sit at the table. Salisa presided over the gathering, calling for reports from various lieutenants scattered around the room. After all the information had been presented, she summarized the situation.

"We've lost three Overseers to the enemy and must replace them as rapidly as possible." She glanced at Aven. "We should have a timetable in place within the week. Don't you agree?"

"I do." Aven steepled his fingers and tapped his lips. "No time must be wasted. This opportunity can turn to calamity in a moment." He swiveled his chair to face her fully. "That's why they've already been chosen."

"Now see here." Baanus half rose from his chair. "I'm not at all certain that's the best way to proceed."

Aven turned toward Baanus, the almost cordial look on his face at odds with the sudden tension in the room. "You doubt my assessment?"

Baanus gulped, his large Adam's apple moving convulsively. His glance darted around the room. "I meant no disrespect, but this invasion came almost a month earlier than we'd been told." He swallowed again and settled back into his seat. "Shouldn't we be concerned about the information we're receiving?"

Aven sighed and shook his head, keeping his gaze on Baanus. "I'm afraid you're mistaken. The invasion aligned with my timetable exactly. Delaina?"

"I saw no discrepancies in the timeline." She matched Aven's sigh before looking at Baanus. Simon could read the pity in that glance from where he sat. Two of the lieutenants on the far side of the room shifted slightly in their seats, their eyes locked on Baanus. Simon would lay odds they belonged to his cadre. All the others looked wary but not overly concerned.

"My information specifically cited that Iscah would be at full and Iddo at half." Baanus looked at each of the three and his face grew white. "The moon Aldon is barely visible."

"Ah." Aven let the syllable hang for a moment. "That explains it. One of our messages to you must have gone astray."

Salisa nodded to Baanus, the skin at her neck keeping time with her movements. "I'm sure that's it, wouldn't you say?"

"Of course. I should have guessed as much." Baanus leaned back in his chair. "That must have been what happened." He turned slightly to Aven, his expression under control. "Are there any other, ah, developments I should be apprised of?"

Aven gave him a bland smile. "I'm certain you have all the information you require."

CHAPTER SEVEN

Bethany walked through the doorway outside, savoring each step. The brightness struck her first, with an almost physical blow, and she squinted her eyes to ease the transition between inside and out. The sun warmed her hair, while an errant breeze caressed her neck. The sulphur tang to the air didn't keep her from drinking in great lungs full of the stuff. It had been so long. She shaded her eyes with her hand and gazed at the clouds, searching for the bird she heard calling. Off to one side, Keturah gave a small gasp, but Bethany didn't turn.

"You may explore." Casiphia put a hand on her arm. "But please stay within sight of the compound."

That was all the encouragement Bethany needed as the urge to run, to dance even, filled her spirit. She tore through the dirt toward a small stand of aging Laisa trees. The dying trees rose above her, only twice her height, very few of the blue seedpods visible even though it was early fall. Slowing as she came within arm's length, she reached out a hand and plucked a broad leaf from the branch nearest her. Holding it to her nose, she fell to her knees as she drank in its pungent aroma.

Bethany had long since lost track of Keturah and settled against the trunk of a tree, studying the horizon. She could see a single field of green amid the barren wasteland and felt the pull of the past. From her father's notes, the location was in the correct area, but she'd worked so hard not to think about the what-ifs, she couldn't be certain. Besides, it was out of her hands. Her work now was to endure. The One had made it clear through her circumstances that she was no longer needed to ensure the survival of this world.

She shook her head. She mustn't allow the memories to surface. She couldn't wonder about how different her life might have been. She'd have a family by now, or at least a mate, someone to share her life's work. Her work. Did that field of green hold the fruit of her seeds?

Oh, well. What would it hurt? But as she let her thoughts chase through the memories, she realized she wasn't alone. Who was there? She lifted her head and shaded her eyes as she looked up at the towering stranger. The figure was obviously male, but his features were impossible to make out with the sun directly behind him. She got to her feet and stumbled, trying to brush dirt and leaves from the seat of her leggings. Even when she stood, he still towered above her. She bit her lip. Another of her captors…why couldn't they leave her alone for just a while?

He reached out, steadying her. "I didn't mean to disturb you. Casiphia said you'd come this way."

She recognized that voice. But how?

He motioned away from the compound. "Walk with me." It was part command, part request.

Bethany pulled out of his grasp and took a place at his side, as much to block the sun as to comply. "Do I know you?"

"I had my helmet on when we last met, and my armor." He smiled, and his golden eyes twinkled. "I am Josiah."

"Oh." Bethany's stomach turned over, and she looked away. Today, he wore charcoal gray trousers and shirt. His dark vest was similar in design to the uniforms of the Sintuen authorities. It had dozens of pockets, each probably the repository for some weapon or something. But in spite of the different attire, she knew it was him, the man who'd saved her from the mob on the express tram. She risked another quick glance at his face. Even without the armor, he was huge, taller than her by at least a foot. "I owe you thanks."

His arm brushed hers. "You don't owe me anything." He frowned slightly. "You were put in danger because of our ignorance. We weren't aware of how strongly your people felt toward Seekers. We didn't come to this world for harm."

"They…that is, Casiphia said you've come to restore our world?" She tried to keep pace with him, breaking into a half-jog every few steps.

He slowed when he noticed her difficulty. "I'm not sure how a race of destroyers can do that." He laughed, a hearty, contagious sound.

She had to work not to smile. "What is so amusing?"

"You, of course." He quit chuckling, but she could still see his lips twitch. "You're such a little one, but not afraid to speak your mind."

She stopped and glared up at him, her arms crossed. "I see. Is that your answer then?" Little one, indeed. Although she hadn't thought of it in years, as a child, her height had been a source of pride. She could do anything the boys in her section could. A trait her father encouraged.

The expression in his eyes as he gazed down at her was undecipherable. "What was your question?"

"I want to know how a race of destroyers can claim to restore?" Her question might anger him, but that didn't matter.

He looked out over the barren fields and sighed. "I think the race of destroyers you so easily speak of resides here." He pointed away from the sun, toward dusty hills sectioned by ribbons of brown. "I can see traces of waterways, now dry and parched. The fields which should be green are instead gray with dust." He turned as he spoke, searching the horizons. "We may already be too late to save your world." He stopped, and she followed his eyes to the same patch of green that had drawn her. "Then again, maybe not."

Bethany gulped. Of course it was too late, the One had made that plain. She shaded her eyes and gazed at the field. If that was the field, the answer was there. The vibrant green could be the combination of her father's research and her own outrageous ideas. The proof of their joint success could be blooming on the hill even now.

"Tell me what you see." His voice brought her back into the present.

"Excuse me?" She glanced up at him. "I'm not sure what you mean."

"You see that field, the green one with the healthy growth." His tone was different now, all commander. "What do you know about it?"

Bethany felt a tremor trace the length of her spine. She mustn't let him know. He was the enemy. She couldn't forget that. "I don't *know* anything." She refused to meet his eyes. It was true, she didn't know. Hope wasn't knowledge.

He turned her toward him, resting his hands on her shoulders with a light grip. "There's going to soon come a time when you'll discover you can trust me." He dropped his hands and sighed. "I know you have no reason to yet."

Bethany could feel the imprint of his hands where they had briefly touched her skin. Her thoughts and emotions whirled. She mustn't forget he was her captor…she couldn't think of him as a man. Only a fool would trust this stranger, a warrior from a race of conquerors. Yet he had shown her more kindness than anyone here on Sintue. She rubbed her forehead and longed for time to process the events of the last day.

He looked skyward. "I know you need time to sort out what has transpired. I'll see that you have it."

She stared, open-mouthed. Could he read her thoughts?

He laughed again. "Don't look so stricken. I'm no mind reader. Anyone in your place would need time to consider all that has happened." His eyes focused on some point in the distance. "I've seen many in similar circumstances."

"I suppose you've done this many times." She looked down. "Invaded a world, I mean."

"How can I explain? I've been on multiple worlds." He ran a hand through his black hair, leaving a strand out of place over one eye. "Yet I've never spent respite time with anyone other than my own kind."

"Oh."

He seemed to sense her confusion. "I'll leave you to your thoughts now. We'll talk later."

Josiah slapped his gloves against his thigh. He'd acted on impulse, like a raw recruit. What had he hoped to accomplish by visiting Bethany? Why couldn't he erase those steady blue eyes from his mind? She was a slave—from an inferior race. His lineage stretched back to the ancient homeland of the Master's. He stomped through the door of the compound, ignoring the startled glances turned his way.

As he jumped into his personal aircar, his com unit beeped. He settled into the seat and glanced at the screen. Bezek, of course. Who else would it have been. "What?"

"Commander, our presence has been requested by Elder Mahalah on the Admin ship."

Josiah slowly counted to ten.

"Commander? Do you copy?"

Josiah resisted the urge to sigh. "I'll be at headquarters within the hour. Have the shuttle prepped and ready."

"Yes, Sir."

Bezek was a good man to have at his back in a fight. Josiah grinned to himself as he lifted off. Bezek must have noticed his mood. Normally, his comments on their assignments took several minutes of airtime. As Josiah flew back to his compound, he pondered possible reasons for the summons.

CHAPTER EIGHT

Josiah piloted the shuttle into the hanger of the Admin ship orbiting Sintue. He managed the difficult docking maneuvers with only the slightest course corrections. He knew his companion, Bezek, brimmed with curiosity and concern over their summons. His red-headed lieutenant wasn't known for his patience. The request from Elder Mahalah was unusual but not completely unprecedented.

"Commander?" Bezek spoke as Josiah finished final shutdown of the shuttle engines. "Do you have any idea why we were summoned?"

"You know what I know." Josiah hid his smile as he unstrapped from the cushioned seat and made his way out of the cockpit. Bezek's curiosity had finally gotten the better of him. "Be calm, Lieutenant. It's not always bad news."

"I didn't say it was." Bezek hurried out behind him and grabbed Josiah's arm. "You and I both know we're not favorites of Mahalah."

Josiah turned, frowning. "His correct title is Elder Mahalah."

"I meant no disrespect." Bezek grimaced. "Okay, maybe I did."

"Your point?" Josiah looked down at his arm, still in Bezek's grasp.

Bezek released his arm as if it were an Adlakian worm. "You should be wary, sir. I have a bad feeling about this planet and this meeting."

Josiah tried to keep his expression from mirroring his surprise. Bezek was a big, burly, warrior—given to bluster and temper, not feelings and innuendos. "What concerns you, my friend?"

"I had a troubling dream last night." His light grey eyes, normally merry, showed only turmoil. "And the R'hobans were betrayed—by one of our own this time."

Josiah drew himself up to his full height, willing an iron control of his emotions. "You dare to imply I would ever allow such a betrayal again."

Bezek met his gaze. "You are not responsible for the past."

"Are you suggesting then, that I didn't learn from it?"

Bezek blew out a breath. "I'm suggesting, Commander, that you listen hard to what this particular Elder has to say."

"You would accuse one of the Elders of betrayal?"

"I make no accusation. Only speak caution as we go into an unknown situation." Bezek took a step back, shaking his head. "Nothing about this liberation has gone as it should. I meant no disrespect."

"Our Elders are chosen by the One to lead us." Josiah pitched his voice low. "To accuse them is to accuse God."

Bezek nodded. "I agree, in theory." He held up a hand. "I only counsel vigilance. My apologies."

This was the Bezek he knew—act first, repent later. "We'll speak of this no more." Josiah turned and exited the vessel, certain Bezek would follow.

As they rushed to the meeting, Josiah couldn't help but notice the men and women bustling through the spacious corridors of the Admin ship. Their jobs were necessary for the bureaucracy, he supposed, but he afforded them little consideration. He was, after all, a warrior of the One. They made way for him and Bezek as a matter of course, several pausing to bring fist to shoulder in the universal sign of respect.

Bezek and Josiah waited briefly in the anti-room of the assembly before a serious young man took their weapons and showed them into Elder Mahalah's chambers.

"Your Grace." Josiah dropped to one knee before the white-haired man seated on a padded, amethyst-tinted chair. His nose itched as it was hit with a spicy aroma, carrying undertones of floral. An odd thing to find such a strong scent in the Elder's chamber. Tradition held that those chosen as Elders eschewed the more luxurious trappings of life. This man was the exception to that rule. Josiah waited for Bezek to echo his greeting before he looked around, trying to pinpoint the odor.

"You may rise." Elder Mahalah's dark blue eyes held a steely expression, cold and uninviting. He waved a negligent hand toward the door where his servant still waited. "Leave us."

Josiah rose and stood comfortably, his hand automatically brushing the strap that usually held his accelerator pistol. He swallowed the flash of irritation that crossed his mind at the necessity of leaving it with the servant outside. One did not come armed into the chambers of an Elder. "You summoned us? How can we be of service?"

"I am concerned with this liberation of Sintue." The Elder shifted slightly in his chair, causing the iridescent fabric of his robe to flash, first silver then cobalt blue. "I believe it to have been sloppy and ill-timed."

At Bezek's low growl Josiah made a quick motion with his hand. "I'm aware that a small portion of the populace evaded our initial incursion, but I'm certain that will be quickly rectified."

"I do not share your assessment, Commander." The superior smile on the Elder's face grated along Josiah's spine. "I wish more concrete reassurances."

"What do you require?" Bezek moved to Josiah's side.

The Elder ignored him. "You were in command of the force tasked with locking down the capital, were you not?"

Josiah nodded. "I was."

"Can you explain your failure to detain all the citizenry?" Mahalah leaned forward, again setting off a swirl of colors in his robe.

There was something wrong here. No Elder had ever questioned his command in this manner. "I do not count it a failure, Your Grace." He forced a relaxed smile through gritted teeth, every muscle in his frame tense. "I see it only as a delay."

"And how long do you expect this…ah…delay to be?"

"As long as it takes." Josiah snapped out the answer, tired of mincing words. "You do realize at least some portion of the population knew we were coming." He heard Bezek draw in a breath and again gave the hand signal for silence.

"I suspected as much." Elder Mahalah leaned back, suddenly relaxed, as though Josiah had passed some kind of test. He motioned to a table set with bottles of Krenlic, a rare juice from one of the outer worlds. "Help yourself." He waited, declining Bezek's offer to pour one for him. As Bezek handed one of the two goblets to Josiah, the Elder continued. "I would appreciate your assessment, Commander. How did these people acquire this information?"

"I cannot imagine." Josiah took a slow sip and let the spicy liquid rest on his tongue before he swallowed. "I will find out, though."

"That is more like the Commander I expect in an invasion of this significance."

Josiah froze, avoiding the look he knew Bezek was giving him. "Excuse me, sir…invasion?"

"We speak freely here." The Elder's coal black ring glinted as he motioned around the room. "The citizens of the planets we *liberate* consider it an invasion, no matter how we choose to name it. Don't they?"

"They do." What game was the Elder playing? "But only until they begin to once again see the truth."

"Of course, of course." Elder Mahalah rose and crossed to a small, black cabinet. "That brings me to the reason for your visit today." He opened the doors and removed an order tube, much more ornate than the kind Josiah handed to his subordinates on a daily basis. He turned and gave it to Josiah. "These orders put you in command of the city. You are authorized to do whatever is necessary to find answers and get on with disseminating the truth."

"Your Grace?" Josiah set his unfinished glass on the table, a bubble of unease rising in his ribcage. The R'hobans never allowed expedience to drive their actions.

"You know what I mean." The Elder waved an unconcerned hand. "Within the laws dictated by our beliefs, of course." He returned to his chair and arranged his robe before sitting. "You have your orders, Commander." He narrowed his eyes. "See to it I'm not disappointed a second time."

Josiah knew a dismissal when he heard one. He dipped his head and strode from the room.

CHAPTER NINE

"I heard you visited Bethany today." Manaen cleared the remains of their evening meal, disposing of the organic waste and placing the dishes in the recycling unit.

Josiah watched her wipe off the food prep unit, seeing an echo of their mother in her economy of movements. "Who told you that?"

"Casiphia came by earlier and mentioned she'd seen you at the teaching compound." She stopped tidying the dining area and faced him. "Why the interest in this girl?"

"I have no interest." He sat up straighter. "What I have is an obligation—for her well-being."

"Ha." An unladylike snort followed Manaen's exclamation as she turned to stare at him.

Josiah rose. "I refuse to continue this conversation."

"Come now, brother." Manaen came up behind him and put a restraining hand on his shoulder. "None know you better than I."

Josiah blew out a deep breath and resumed his seat. "I tell you, it's just an obligation."

Manaen settled into a chair across the table from him. "I never thought I'd see the day when fear dictated your words."

He stared at her for a long moment. "I'll get no peace till we discuss this, will I?"

Crossing her arms, she looked at him. "Absolutely none."

"Very well." He shook his head. "I can't seem to get her out of my mind."

He could see that she tried to control her expression, but he caught the hint of a smile playing around her lips. "I knew this day would come."

"What day? What are you talking about?"

She leaned forward and reached for his hand. "I fear your heart has been beguiled."

"Foolishness." He jerked his hand away and got up, moving into the briefing area of their quarters. "My heart hasn't been beguiled. For the sake of the saints, she's just a slave. A Seeker, I grant you. But still just a slave."

"She may be a slave now, but her Creator is the same as ours." Manaen followed, her silk lounging robe rustling pleasantly around her ankles as she straightened cushions and opened the jars of Bryset herbs, sending the spicy aroma into every corner of the room.

His sister was a mass of contradictions, one moment a deadly warrior whose skills rivaled even his. Other times, he found her as domestic as their mother and just as beautiful. Were all women this perplexing?

"Josiah?" Manaen stared at him. "Are you considering a lifemate?"

"Absolutely not." He sat at the delicate desk that projected from the wall. "If I ever did, she would be one worthy of our ancestry."

"You sound just like one of those highbrow merchants on Vela Prime." She giggled as she curled up on the bench opposite him. "Where's all that humility we're supposed to practice as warriors of the One?"

Her remark stung him. "I meant her no disrespect. But, until she concludes the rite of immersion, I am forbidden to look at her in that way."

"Tell me about your meeting with Elder Mahalah." Her sudden change of subject should have bolstered his mood, but it did the exact opposite. He shot up from the desk, upsetting the chair. "I tell you, Manaen, I've never witnessed any Elder behave in this manner." Josiah righted the chair and then prowled through the briefing area of their quarters. "I just don't understand. He actually hinted at a betrayal." Elders, in his experience, didn't play games. They spent their time in study and meditation. The Elders were his people's conduit to the will of the One and as such, were beyond criticism. Their guidance made the R'hobans who they were. "If Elder Mahalah suspects a traitor in our midst, his behavior would be different."

His sister perched on the edge of the ornate bench, the dark jade hue of her robe making her green eyes even more brilliant. "I've never, before now, heard of a traitor from within our ranks. Yet, twice in as many days, the subject has come up. We don't know how an Elder would act in this circumstance."

Josiah continued to pace before coming to an abrupt halt in front of her. "His name." He put a hand to his forehead. "You're the student of origins. What does Elder Mahalah's name mean?" These men of God chose their own names after attaining the position of Elder. Why hadn't he considered this before? It was said that during the six-day elevation ceremony, the One whispered the essence of the Elder's purpose directly into soul and that was reflected in the name the Elder chose. History had shown each sobriquet always had meaning and relevance to the place and time of the Elder's ascension.

Manaen let out a deep breath. "Mahalah means disease." She held up a hand to forestall his response. "But whether he came to spread it or prevent it, is anyone's guess. Only the One and Elder Mahalah knows for certain."

"Don't be foolish, it's not a matter of guessing. He's an Elder." Josiah sank to the bench beside her and glared at her stubbornness. "It means the One sent him to prevent something deadly." He wrapped an arm around her shoulders and smiled down at her, comforted by his reasonable logic. "We must have faith."

She didn't return his smile and her troubled eyes seemed to look deep within his soul. "Faith is necessary, but faith not grounded in truth is a fruitless effort."

Josiah recoiled at her words. "Blasphemy." He rose and towered over her. "You may not defame an Elder of the One in my presence, even if you are my sister."

Manaen stood in response, her eyes almost on a level with his as she drew herself up to her full height, oblivious of her feminine garment. "Do not think to intimidate me." Her jaw worked as she gritted her teeth. "I am not a child to be bullied. My Lord's Spirit speaks to me as clearly as to you."

"Then why would you doubt those elevated by His Spirit?" He turned and rubbed his neck trying to forestall a headache. He could not understand her refusal to see the obvious.

"Because we're all mortal and fallible—even Elders." She moved to the darkened window and peered out. Night was full upon them and the moons had not yet risen. "Josiah, I fear you are too trusting,"

"And I fear you're becoming a cynic."

The door chimed. "Enter." Manaen moved to open it, graceful as a cat, as Josiah pulled his accelerator from its strap at his belt.

"Hello, my girl." Bezek strode into the room, enveloping Manaen in a rough embrace. "I see you're still keeping questionable company."

"What brings you out this evening, you brigand?" Josiah returned his weapon to his belt. In spite of his name calling, he moved quickly to exchange a handclasp with his lieutenant. It was obvious that Bezek hadn't had the opportunity yet to speak with Manean about his feelings.

Bezek studied them for a moment. "I gather your mood isn't any more pleasant tonight than it was earlier today."

Josiah resisted the urge to roll his eyes. This new, intuitive Bezek would take some getting used to. "What makes you say that?"

Manaen laughed and pointed at her brother. "If you could only see your face."

Josiah huffed and turned away, pretending to be preoccupied with an ornament on the side table. There was no talking to her in this mood.

Bezek settled himself in one of the ornate chairs. "Nice." He patted its gem-studded armrests. "Did he tell you of our audience with Elder Mahalah?"

"He did." Manaen resumed her seat on the padded bench, kicked off a slipper, and tucked her foot under her. "We were just discussing possible interpretations of that meeting."

Bezek's bark of laughter brought a frown to Josiah's face. "I bet you were." He readjusted his belt. "And have you convinced your brother there might be more than one interpretation to the events?"

Manaen arched a brow. "What do you think?"

"This is no joking matter." Josiah brought his fist down on the table with a loud crash.

Manaen was beside him in an instant, hand on his arm. "You're right. It's serious. Deadly serious."

"Then why insist on this foolishness?" He let her settle him into a massive wooden chair in the corner of the room. "Can you not see the repercussions?"

"I do see." She resumed her seat. "And I concede that your interpretation is the most logical. We have eons of history to back it up." She held up a hand when he started to speak. "But I'm trying to get you to open your mind to other possibilities."

Josiah looked at her without seeing, his mind's eye turned inward. To consider, even briefly, what she and Bezek had implied was unthinkable. Betrayal, by one or more Elder? He couldn't ignore the possibility any longer, even though it shook the very core of his belief. These men were chosen—set apart by the One. How could such a thing have happened? And even more troubling, what was he going to do about it?

CHAPTER TEN

Simon smiled as he surveyed his new quarters, complete with a palm-print lock. But he kept all excessive emotion from his voice as he dismissed the personal worker assigned him. "That will be all, Adela."

"Thank you, sir." The young woman dipped her head and darted toward the door, still not meeting his eyes.

He watched Adela until she closed the door, admiring the way her servant's robes moved around her supple form. Aven had officially admitted him into his personal entourage but, as yet, there had been no opportunity for private conversation with the Overseer. He'd have to take it slow, exceeding Aven's expectations without making assumptions.

He walked slowly around the main room and then into the sleeping alcove and bathing unit. Compact but nice—very nice. The forethought of the Organization in preparing quarters for this eventuality amazed him. The spare room came equipped with every necessity, even a small food prep unit. His current situation confirmed his decision to become a part of the Organization.

He glanced down at the chrono on his wrist. The unit had been upgraded with additional access and he would need to explore what exactly he now had access to. But later. Now, he just had time to splash water on his face before Aven required his presence.

Aven swiveled in his chair as Simon and several others scurried in, joining him in yet another meeting room within the underground complex. Simon took a seat midway down the table, a calculated move considering he still didn't know where he fit in Aven's cadre. He caught the Overseer's glance and dipped his head in respect. Aven's face remained impassive, but Simon thought he saw the leader's lips twitch in a prelude to a smile. Most of the rest settled themselves around the table, with two taking up positions on either side of the door. One of the guards at the door looked familiar, but Simon couldn't place him.

The Overseer steepled his fingers and rested his elbows on the black-topped table. "The time of preparation is over and the change has begun." He nodded to the man seated on his right "Invite our guest to join us."

A giant of a man with short gray hair and a beard entered the room.

A R'hoban? What business did he have here?

The massive man inclined his head to Aven, not as a sign of subservience, but respect. "I bring greetings, sir." He stood like a warrior—though he had no weapon—feet apart, hands loosely at his side, giving no hint of unease. "My Commander bids me to tender our offer of collaboration against a common enemy."

"We have the utmost respect for your leader and are anxious to hear his proposition." Aven rose and motioned the warrior to the vacated chair. "What does he propose?"

The stranger reached into a pocket on his thigh and pulled out a silver tube decorated with inlaid metalwork. He took a chair at the table and offered the tube to Aven. "This details his recommendations."

Aven accepted the tube and fed it into the reader in front of him. He returned to another seat and studied the personal plasscreen in front him. After a few moments, he looked up from the document and focused on the stranger. "Interesting." He arched an eyebrow. "But it seems the risk is all on our side."

The warrior pushed back his chair and stood, the look on his face scornful. "You are in no position to bargain."

Simon's gaze focused on Aven's face. How would the Overseer respond to this insolence?   Aven lounged back in his chair. "I wouldn't be so certain of that." A lazy smile curled his lip. "It seems we must have some value or you wouldn't have risked an alliance in the first place."

"It's little enough risk to talk to a ragtag band of outlaws on a no-count backwater world." He moved toward the door, but one of the guards blocked his way. Simon finally placed the guard at the door. He was the one who had led them out of the locked room.

"Japheth." Aven's tone held a hint of reproach. "Let our visitor pass. If he has no authority to negotiate, he's of no use to us."

The warrior swung around to face Aven. "When I return, we'll see who has authority."

He marched through the door, his boots echoing down the hallway.

"Sir?" Loenne spoke first. "Was he who I think he was?"

Simon barely managed to contain his expression of contempt. How on all that was holy had that female worked her way up to the rank of controller?

"Yes." Aven turned to Loenne. "He's a member of the race of warriors currently dominating of our planet. He's one of the R'hobans."

"Then how, if they're the ones in charge, can we negotiate with them?" Loenne's hysterical undertone was obvious to Simon. He wondered if any of the others caught it.

Aven sighed. "They may control the planet, but they don't control us." He sat forward in his chair. "Does anyone have a relevant comment or question?"

Loenne's face went red, but she kept silent.

"I assume there's a division with the ranks of our oppressors, correct?" Simon ventured his opinion.

"Ah, a man with a brain." Aven's eyes twinkled. "Very good. How does that division benefit us?"

Simon concentrated. This question was a test. He stared at his hands before choosing his words. "A force divided is always weak." He met Aven's eyes calmly though his heart hammered in his chest. "We can use that weakness against them."

"Yes." Aven shot to his feet and began to pace. "Exactly my thoughts." He beamed as if Simon were his prodigy instead of a newcomer. "We have aligned ourselves with those who believe every world should be free to decide their own fate."

Simon frowned. "They can't be in the majority or Sintue wouldn't have been invaded at all."

Aven brushed that aside with a wave of his hand. "True, but they are numerous enough—and powerful enough—to give us the chance we're looking for." He resumed his seat. "Our Prince will provide the strength and wisdom to capitalize on this opportunity."

"What do we need to do?" Simon had heard enough. The time for action had come.

"First," the Overseer held up a finger, "we must make sure our people are in key positions within the households of our ally's enemies." He looked at each of them in turn. "It's up to each of you to find out what slaves are in these positions. If they belong to the Organization, good, no contact at this point. If not, they must be vetted or replaced." He motioned once again to Japheth. "Pass out the information."

Japheth went to a cabinet set into the wall and withdrew a purple velvet bag. He pulled small silver message tubes from it and distributed them to each person seated at the table.

"Don't open them now." Aven nodded to Japheth as he returned the bag to the cabinet. "Study them and come up with a strategy to investigate your assigned contacts. We'll meet individually. I must personally approve your plan before you move to implement it." He paused, as if considering something. "These projects are just the foundation of my plan. As many of you know, I've had my eye on specific research for some time. Now, I think the time has come to incorporate this into my overall strategy."

"Are all the Overseers working on this?" Loenne asked. Simon wondered if she was brave or just plain stupid.

Aven glared at her, obviously displeased by the question. "The actions of the Overseers are none of your concern." He turned to include the rest of them in his look. "And should not be discussed among yourselves."

Simon doubted Loenne would be involved in future meetings.

Aven stood. "That will be all. You have your orders."

Simon managed to be one of the last to leave, and he heard Aven request Loenne to remain. Interesting—he would wager there was about to be a vacancy in Aven's personal cadre.

He continued out of the room and back to his quarters. Once inside, he locked the door and opened the tube. He felt the blood drain from his face as he read the first name on the list. *Bethany.* How had Aven known?

CHAPTER ELEVEN

Bethany leaned her head back and rotated her shoulders, trying to reconcile the things she'd been taught by her parents with the lessons the R'hobans shared. She glanced over at Keturah curled up in the window seat and caught her eye. "Are you having as much trouble with this lesson as me?"

Keturah nodded, and after a quick glance toward the food prep area, unfolded her long form and joined Bethany at the table. "I don't know if what I was taught growing up was wrong or just incomplete."

I agree." Bethany leaned forward, keeping her voice low. "Their view of the One seems to focus more on love and forgiveness than the list of dos and don'ts I memorized when I was young."

"It's not like their teaching completely disagrees with what I know." Keturah pursed her lips. "It definitely has the same foundation, but…"

"I remember my father telling me to test all I heard by what was written in the Book of Truth." Bethany said. "And so far, nothing they've taught contradicts them."

"But I can't help but think they're not sharing everything with us." Keturah glanced around again. "And it's what they're so careful not to say that worries me."

"It's almost like they're trying to lull us with kindness."

"True." Keturah smiled as she smoothed the soft tunic she wore. "But I have to admit I love their generosity."

"And I haven't spent this much time above ground in eons." Bethany rose and walked to the window, relishing the comfort of the supple ankle boots and leggings. "But I still haven't reconciled the difference between their teachings and ours."

Keturah joined her at the window. "It is troubling."

"I wish I knew what they wanted from us."

"Ungrateful wretches." Leah spoke from the doorway. "We've shown you nothing but kindness, and this talk is the way you repay us?"

Bethany's stomach clenched, but she drew herself up to her full height and turned to face Leah. "We meant no harm."

Leah strode across the room. "I don't know how you can dare to compare the instruction we're providing with the half-truths you grew up with."

"If we can't ask questions, we'll never be sure of the truth." Bethany refused to back down, even as Leah towered over her.

"That is exactly right." Casiphia joined them, hands on hips. "Leah, we have nothing to fear from their questioning."

"As if we'd ever fear anyone from this ignorant world." Leah snorted. "That notion is ridiculous in the extreme." She turned to meet Casiphia's hard gaze.

Keturah's hand found Bethany's as they stood close, watching the two exchange volumes with their eyes. Leah was the first to break eye contact as she turned and strode from the room once again.

Casiphia sighed. "I think you might be ready for a respite. Why don't you take a walk before evening comes?"

"I think we'd like that," Keturah said.

"We will discuss this further after you come back." Casiphia's smile was perfunctory and failed to animate her normally merry eyes. "I don't know what's gotten into Leah these days."

Bethany led the way out the back door and through the compound enclosure, waiting until they were well away before speaking. "What did you make of that?"

"It's the first full-blown disagreement we've witnessed." Keturah scanned the empty landscape. "But they have seemed to disagree on little things fairly often. I just wish I knew if the way they act is for real, or only a way to deceive us?"

"At this point, we haven't enough information to make that judgment." Bethany lifted her face to catch the sun's afternoon rays. "And I'm just glad to be outside again."

"You're incorrigible." Keturah threw up her hands and ambled off in the direction of a dried streambed. Even without water, it was a peaceful place to rest, with several trees interspersed along its banks. Their sparse foliage provided some protection from the noxious fumes of a nearby city.

Bethany trailed after her, grateful for the freedom afforded them within this strange situation. She and Keturah had been kept sequestered from other Sintuens since the initial invasion. But even though there was no doubt they were slaves, they'd been well cared for. To be completely honest, they'd been afforded more respect than the rest of her world's inhabitants gave Seekers.

She shook her head, forcing her thoughts away from the turning point. She wondered how others of her race fared. What about Simon—had he been captured as well? That thought brought her to a stop. Simon, during those last few months, had become a troubling enigma.

"Come on," Keturah called, turning and walking backward. "What are you doing?"

"I'll be there in a minute," Bethany said. "You go on ahead." Thinking about Simon left her with a knot in her stomach. She owed him a great deal. He had provided her with a way to survive when no one else would take the chance. But that last meeting hadn't been good. He must have been acting on orders. Simon's friendship had been hers since they were children. He'd always protected her. He would never hurt her. He was like the brother she'd never had. She bit her lip. At least he had been until the last few months when she'd worked for him.

She shrugged and hurried to catch up with Keturah. When she topped the rise, she was surprised to see her friend standing, as if frozen, instead of lounging beneath the trees. Bethany followed Keturah's line of sight and saw him. A Sintuen crouched beside the tree.

"Bethany? Is that really you?" The man rose and walked toward them, his movements somehow familiar.

"Simon?" Bethany couldn't help it. She was glad to see him, in spite of their last meeting. "You're here. You're safe."

Simon reached out and touched her face. "Of course I am. The question is—how are you?"

"I'm good. Really good." She smiled, then remembered Keturah, who still stood rooted in place. "This is my friend, Keturah."

"Hello." Keturah moved closer to Bethany and studied Simon. "You startled me. I didn't realize you two were friends."

"I've known him all my life." Bethany turned back to Simon. "How did you come to be here? What happened to you?"

"Let's sit in the shade while I explain." He motioned toward the trees. "I take it you were one of the thousands captured and enslaved?"

Bethany tilted her head, surprised to realize she didn't like someone else labeling her circumstances in that way. "I guess you could call it that." She studied her hands. "They brought me here." She looked up at his deep sigh. "They've treated us well. I don't really feel like a captive."

"That's the way they operate." Simon frowned. "This idyllic existence will end suddenly, and you'll find yourself a slave to one of these monsters."

"I'm not sure what to expect," Bethany said. "By their actions they appear to mean us no harm."

"I take it they haven't given you your assignment, yet?" He made the word sound ugly, endowing it with a meaning her imagination shied away from. "You know they're brainwashing you, using those Seeker beliefs to turn you against your own people."

"I have a few questions of my own, if you don't mind the interruption." Keturah seated herself a little apart, watching them. "Where have *you* been? Are you in a compound nearby?"

Simon turned his infectious grin on Keturah and thumped his chest. "I managed to escape capture." He looked around and lowered his voice. "There are a lot of us still free. I'm here to help you get free as well."

"Bethany? Keturah?" All three jumped to their feet at the sound of Casiphia's call coming to them over the hill. "Girls, where are you?"

Simon ducked behind the tree. "I can't risk being seen. I'll contact you later." As he disappeared, his voice floated to Bethany's ears. "Don't betray me."

"We're coming." Keturah hurried back over the rise, and Bethany followed after a cursory look for Simon.

As Bethany ran to catch up, she could see Casiphia's open and smiling face as she shooed them toward the compound. "Hurry now. You mustn't keep the Commander waiting. He's come with your new assignments."

CHAPTER TWELVE

Keturah and Bethany exchanged glances as they hurried past the official aircar and into the compound. Casiphia bustled around them, brushing stray leaves and grass from their clothing. Finally presentable to her standards, she ushered them into the main room.

Bethany's eyes widened as she saw the man in the uniform. It was Josiah.

His lips twitched, like he wanted to smile and was working not to. "Hello, ladies."

Bethany fought the urge to dip her head, raising her chin instead. "Hello."

"I have come with duty assignments for you both." His words were formal as he handed Bethany and Keturah each an order tube. "As Seekers, you now hold a unique and valuable place on your world. We acknowledge that and have entrusted you with positions of authority." He raised an eyebrow. "I expect you will prove yourselves worthy of this confidence."

"But you hardly know us." Keturah looked to Casiphia for an explanation.

Casiphia smiled, but it was Josiah who answered her concern. "We have watched you over the past weeks and been pleased with your progress." He shook his head. "Just the fact of your survival as Seekers recommends you to us."

Bethany opened the tube and let the papers slide into her hand. As she read, she could feel the heat on her face. She looked up to find Josiah watching her. "What exactly are the duties of Steward to the Commander? You are the Commander to which these orders refer, aren't you?"

"As Steward of my compound you'll be responsible for its smooth operation. You'll schedule visitors, oversee those who serve within its boundaries, and be in charge of daily operations." He frowned. "It's a position usually awarded only to R'hobans."

Casiphia came up beside her. "It's quite a mark of distinction to be chosen to serve in this manner."

Keturah waved the papers in her hand, smiling. "It seems we'll stay together. I'm to be your assistant."

"I'll leave you to discuss the transfer." Josiah inclined his head to them all, but his golden eyes held Bethany's for a long moment before he turned and left the room.

As Casiphia hurried out of the room after him, Bethany moved toward the bench and lowered herself down slowly, the papers still clutched in her hand. "This is so abrupt." She looked up at Keturah, who'd come to stand beside her. "It's almost like Casiphia wants rid of us before we can ask too many questions."

Keturah sat beside her. "That possibility occurred to me as well." She put her hand on Bethany's forearm. "So far, though, they've treated us fairly. We can't discount that."

Bethany shook off her hand. "Fairly? You call ordering us into slavery fair?"

"Shhh." Keturah looked around. "They'll hear you."

"So what?" Bethany got up and began pacing. "We don't really mean anything to them. For all we know, they are just using us—brainwashing us for their own purpose. We're just another world to be conquered, another race to be enslaved."

"Oh, child. How can you believe that?"

Bethany gasped and turned to face Casiphia who had just returned. "I meant no disrespect." Bethany squared her shoulders. "But what should I think? You've conquered our world and enslaved us all."

"I told you they were nothing but ingrates, just like the others." Leah stood in the kitchen doorway, arms crossed. "They've been happy enough to accept our hospitality, but now, when they're given responsibilities, ingratitude is their immediate response."

"Others?" Keturah rose to her feet. "What others?"

"Now, Leah, they've had a great shock over the past weeks. Let's all sit and have a cup of Roma tea." She motioned Leah back into the kitchen. "I'll put the water on to boil."

Leah stiffly lowered herself into a chair at the table and glared at Casiphia. "Fine."

Keturah settled onto the bench across from her, and Bethany slipped in beside Keturah. An oppressive silence invaded the room as Casiphia bustled back and forth from the cupboard to the cooking unit. She assembled the tea things and dropped the herbs into a kettle inlaid with blue veining. After the water heated, she added it and brought the tray to the table. A spicy aroma wafted around them.

"There, we'll all feel better for a restorative cup." Casiphia handed out stoneware mugs of the steaming beverage to each one of them before joining them. "Now." She looked first at Keturah, then Bethany. "I know this is all quite sudden, but you have studied the sacred texts enough to know all our lives have purpose." She held up a finger as Leah began to speak. "It's up to us, as the R'hobans, to help you find that purpose. This assignment is a starting point, not a dead end."

Bethany took a sip and let the sweet aroma fill her senses. "I want to believe you, but I still don't understand."

"How could you?" Leah sniffed. "You're nothing but a savage, from a race of savages." She glared, her icy gray eyes boring a hole through Bethany. "I don't know why we bother."

Casiphia shook her head, her lips in a tight line.

"Why do you bother?" Keturah played with the handle on her cup. "If we're so awful, why waste your time here?"

"It's our purpose." Casiphia took a quick sip of her tea. "The One has entrusted us with restoring His truth throughout the galaxy."

"But there are other worlds not as ignorant as yours." Leah's voice held a note of disdain. "I can't imagine what the Elders were thinking, dragging us here."

Bethany caught Casiphia's quick shake of her head, a quiet reprimand directed at Leah, before she turned to Bethany. "The position of Steward is a great mark of respect."

"And it's only accorded one of our own." Leah sniffed again.

"That is quite enough." Casiphia rose and pointed toward the back of the house. "Leah, you will use this afternoon to reacquaint yourself with the One's teaching on compassion and humility." Her voice held none of its usual warmth, and her eyes seemed to almost crackle with command. Although Bethany had known Casiphia was a woman of rank, she just now realized the depth of that authority as Leah bolted from the room.

Casiphia's air of command was gone as she turned back to the girls, her face grave. "I'm sorry you were subject to that. I wasn't aware of her true feelings, although I knew something wasn't quite right." She returned to her seat and took another sip. "Unfortunately, her attitude has gained a small following."

"I really don't understand," Bethany said.

"No one is beyond redemption." Casiphia seemed to be answering a different question. "No matter what anyone says, the scrolls are very clear on that issue."

Bethany and Keturah exchanged glances. "How many of us are left?" Keturah asked. "Seekers, I mean."

Casiphia looked out the window for a long moment before she answered. "Just over a thousand." She sighed and spoke so softly, Bethany had to strain to hear her. "Leah may be right about one thing. We might have come too late."

CHAPTER THIRTEEN

What wretched luck. Simon struck the tree with his fist. He'd almost had her. At least the informant had been correct about her location. He'd succeed next time. Carefully studying the surroundings, he waited a few minutes before dodging back across the open field and down into a gully. What appeared to be a pile of trash concealed the tunnel opening. When pushed aside, it moved in one piece, revealing the entrance. Once inside, he turned and pulled the camouflage into place, hiding it from prying eyes. How many years had the Organization been planning for this invasion?

"Well, did you find her?" Japheth carried a small hand light which he uncovered after Simon had hidden the opening.

"I found her."

"And?" The glow made a macabre mask of Japheth's countenance, the white of his face dissected by a dark slash of angry brows.

"I only got to talk to her briefly. Then some woman, one of the R'hobans, came looking for them." Despite the inky black, Simon darted back down the tunnel toward more habitable regions.

Japheth hurried after him. "Them? Who else was with her?"

"A girl." Simon snorted. "Another stupid Seeker, I think." He rubbed a finger across his chin. "She said her name was Keturah. We'll have to check her status as well."

"Were you seen by the enemy?" Japheth fell in step beside Simon. "Aven won't be pleased if you've given us away."

Won't be pleased? That was a euphemism if he ever heard one. He was almost certain Aven would order a slow and painful death for anyone who displeased him. "Of course not. Only the two girls knew I was there." He could see light ahead and fought the impulse to run toward it. "The R'hoban crone never even got close."

"Any chance the girls would betray us?"

"None." Simon spoke with a surety he didn't feel. "If I thought there'd been any risk of that, I would've taken steps."

"I'm glad to hear it." Aven stepped from the shadows. "I'd be disappointed to find my faith in you had been misplaced."

Simon gulped back an exclamation as he slid to a stop. "No, sir. I was careful."

Japheth saluted, hitting his left shoulder with his right fist. "None would do that, sir."

"We'll see." Aven led the way back into the corridors of their stronghold. He turned at a juncture and impaled Simon with his eyes. "Meet me in the briefing room as soon as possible."

Simon saluted and hustled toward his quarters, wrinkling his nose as the odors of chemicals and fear formed an almost palpable presence. What secrets did these tunnels conceal?

He gave a mental shrug, his thoughts returning to his upcoming meeting. At the very least, a change of clothes would be required before the he joined them. Aven, he had discovered, was fastidious to a fault.

He palmed open the lock on the door to his rooms and headed for his clothes chest.

"You're in quite a hurry, young man."

Simon dropped to a crouch even as he surveyed the room, tracing the voice to its source. Salisa sat perched on a chair in the corner. Her stillness and dark robes had rendered her almost invisible.

"Scared you, didn't I?" Her laugh cracked and sputtered, like a candle fighting to stay lit. "It's important to keep the new ones on their toes."

Simon straightened and gave a nod of respect. "How may I serve you, Overseer?"

"Have a seat." She pointed a long, bony finger at the other chair in the room. "We have a few things to discuss."

Simon perched on the edge of the chair, every sense at full alert, giving her the courtesy of allowing her to speak first.

"Cautious, aren't you? I like that about you." She folded her hands into her long sleeves, an ornate silver ring momentarily catching on a thread. "I know you have a meeting with Aven, so I won't make you tardy." She tilted her head. "I've tried for years to teach him patience, but so far, without success."

"How did you know about our gathering?"

Her mouth made a mockery of a smile. "I have my ways. But that's not why I'm here." Her lips thinned and the expression disappeared. "I need to know where your loyalty lies. Does Aven command your allegiance?"

This was dangerous territory. But he'd learned early on, timidity got him nowhere. "Does he yours?"

She cackled again. "If he didn't, I wouldn't be here."

"Yes, I'm loyal to Aven." Even as he said it, his thoughts raced to the possible implications of his commitment.

"Good." She leapt from the chair and crossed the room, scarcely giving him time to rise before she invaded his personal space. The top of her head barely reached his heart. "That was my belief, but I had to know from your own mouth." She cocked her head, fixing him with her coal-black eyes. "There are others in the

Organization who would like to see him fail. I plan to prevent that, if I can."

He nodded. "I understand."

"I doubt that." She swung on her heel and walked to the door, her movements quick and birdlike. "But you will soon." With that, she was gone.

He replayed the strange visit as he slid into clean trousers and a gray silk tunic. Had she come on her own or had Aven sent her? Hopefully, her allegiance really did rest with Aven. He grimaced. Well, he was committed now. He looked at the chronograph on the plasscreen and dashed from the room, almost running to make the meeting. He stopped a few turns before the room to collect himself. It wouldn't do to appear flustered.

He took a deep breath and walked the last meters to the door and knocked. Japheth opened the door. He stepped back to allow Simon to enter. Aven was already seated at the table, with Salisa beside him.

"Have a seat." Aven barely glanced up from the papers in front of him.

Simon settled himself and waited as Aven continued to study the report.

"Okay." Aven pushed the papers aside and focused on Simon. "Tell me about your rendezvous with the girl."

Simon leaned back, careful to make sure his body language conveyed ease and confidence. He summarized his meeting with Bethany, trying not to glance at Salisa as he spoke. "I believe she'll be easy to convince when I can spend more time with her."

"Unfortunately, that will be more difficult than we originally thought." Aven steepled his fingers on the table in front of him. "She's being assigned as Steward of the Commander. She will be much harder to approach once she reaches his compound."

"When does the assignment take affect?" Simon's thoughts raced. He couldn't let her escape.

Aven glanced at Japheth, who had also taken a seat at the table. "My source tells me she'll be moved later this evening."

"That position is key to our plans." Salisa leaned forward, drawing Simon's attention. "We must have her loyalty. Can you ensure that?"

"I will try." Simon was only willing to commit himself so far. "If I can't, I'll take care of that as well."

Salisa bobbed her head. "I told you this was the one we needed."

Aven raised an eyebrow. "We'll see. If you handle this successfully, then I guarantee you'll go far. If not…"

CHAPTER FOURTEEN

Josiah pushed back in his chair and tried to keep his voice low, although his hands were clenched. "I told you, I'm busy." Times like these, he regretted sharing a compound with his sister. "You pick them up and get them settled."

"We've all got things to do." Manaen stood in the doorway to his quarters, hands on hips. Her dark hair wafted around her head like a thundercloud, crackling with irritation. "If you go, you can brief them on the ride back and save us all some time." She narrowed her eyes. "I've never seen you so stubborn about so simple a task."

He didn't want to spend any more time with Bethany than was necessary. But more than that, he wanted to avoid Manaen's comments on his reluctance. "All right, I'll go." He got up from the worktable with a deep breath. "Anything to keep peace in the family." He stopped on the way out the door and gave her a quick kiss on the cheek. She was the only family he had left "I'm just worried about the occupation. Little things seem out of place."

Manaen followed him down the corridor to the main door. "What little things?"

"Seemingly unrelated things." He shook his head, stopping at the compound door to snap his accelerator pistol to his belt. "Maybe getting out will help clear my mind."

"Don't think we won't continue this conversation when you return."

He exited the building. "Oh, I'm sure we will," he murmured under his breath, hoping she was referring to the irritating details.

"I heard that."

Bethany stood in the middle of the keeping room with Keturah. Casiphia gave her a quick hug and pressed a soft pack containing her few belongings into her arms. "You'll be needing these."

"Thank you." Bethany's eyes filled with tears and her emotion surprised her.

Casiphia held her at arm's length. "You'll not get out of my care that easily."

Bethany smiled. "We'll keep in touch."

Casiphia turned to hug Keturah and handed her a similar pack. "I'll be watching out for you, too."

Josiah cleared his throat, but Bethany had known the second he entered the room.

"All right, girls." Casiphia nodded to Josiah. "We mustn't keep the Commander waiting." She turned toward the kitchen and raised her voice. "Leah, our guests are leaving us."

Leah appeared in the doorway, arms crossed and her expression unreadable. "May the One always keep you in His care."

From her position, Bethany could see the surprise on Josiah's face at Leah's behavior. She also caught the glance he and Casiphia exchanged before Casaphia hurried them out the door.

Casiphia pulled two palm-sized readers from her pocket. She handed one to Keturah and one to Bethany. "With these, the words of the One will always be close."

Bethany nodded, afraid the emotion in her throat would distort her voice. It had been so long since she'd held her own copy of the Book of Truth.

Josiah held the door to the aircar open while she and Keturah got in. He followed and buckled into the captain's chair. He turned to check they were also secure before he lifted off.

Bethany tried to concentrate on the view from the thick window as the aircar skirted across the sky, but her thoughts kept returning to the telling look between Casiphia and Josiah. Her thoughts tumbled and chased as the drone of the engines lulled her.

A flash of intense light, followed by an explosion, ripped the air outside her window. Bethany instinctively clutched at the straps holding her in the seat as the car jolted from side to side.

Keturah, in the seat across from her, squealed and lunged forward in her seat. "What's happening?"

"Commander One under attack." Josiah's calm voice cut through the panic in Bethany's mind. "Control Base relay information and respond." His earpiece kept Bethany from hearing the response. Before she could question him, another blast rocked the car.

"Commander One, emergency." His steady voice showed no fear, only irritation. "Mark my position and come get us. This dratted car won't be in the air much longer."

Bethany watched his sure, confident movements guide their bucking vehicle steeply toward a vacant spot in the middle of an apparently deserted industrial complex. As their descent sharpened, she watched his white-knuckled grip as he used both hands on the steering-stick, fighting the resistant craft. A deep boom and a cloud of black smoke coincided with a momentary feeling of weightlessness. Keturah leaned across the aisle and grabbed Bethany's hand as they crashed into the inner courtyard.

Smoke billowed up around the windows as Bethany tried to clear her head and process where they were and all that had happened. But the sudden silence was almost as loud as the explosions.

"Quickly." Josiah left his seat and was in the aisle between her and Keturah in the time it took her to draw a breath. "Unbuckle—we've got to take shelter. We're easy targets in here." He suited his actions to his words, almost ripping the straps that held her in place. He turned to help Keturah, but she was already free. He grabbed two utility vests and handed them to the women. "Put these on. They'll protect you."

He wrenched open the side door and leapt to the ground, pistol at the ready and his eyes searching. "In there." He gestured to an opening partially covered with a huge, rusty door. They sprinted the few meters to the door and ducked inside. Josiah put his weight against the protesting door, and it screeched closed in protest.

As Bethany's eyes adjusted to the gloom of the building Josiah prowled the interior, his voice echoing in the metal space. "We're in an abandoned manufacturing facility west of the teaching compound—in the building that looks like an old foundry."

When she started to answer him, he held up a hand and she realized he still wore the earpiece and his words had been directed to someone at the other end.

"I'm not certain where the attack originated. It came from the east, but I couldn't pinpoint the exact location." He grimaced. "We should have guessed they had ground to air capabilities." He patted his vest. "I have enough charges to keep us safe till you arrive, Bezek. Quit bellowing and get us out of here."

Keturah stood looking out a grimy window, looking across the inner courtyard. "I see some movement in the doorway on the far side of the aircar."

Josiah joined her at the window and pulled a farviewer from his belt and raised it to his eyes. "Whoever it was is gone." He snapped the viewer back in place and turned to grin at Bethany. "Perhaps they realized they've chosen the wrong target."

Bethany gnawed her lower lip and joined them at the window. "Now what?"

"We prepare in case they return. You there…" He pointed at Keturah.

"My name is Keturah."

"Yes, Keturah. You've sharp eyes, keep watch and report any movement." Josiah squatted on the dirty plascrete floor and pulled things from the pockets of his vest. He motioned to Bethany. "You can help me with the preparation. We should be fine. My team will be here soon."

Bethany knelt beside him, refusing to show her fear at the situation. "Just tell me what to do."

He nodded his approval and handed her another accelerator pistol. "Do you know how to use this?"

The weight of it felt familiar in her hands. "I've used small arms before, but never one quite like this." She held it up and sighted down the barrel. "It seems fairly simple."

"Good." Josiah outlined the basics of how to load and fire the weapon before moving on. "These are location chips." He handed a tiny black device to Keturah and another to Bethany. "You each need to wear one."

She examined the bug-like clip in the palm of her hand. "Wear one? Why?"

"In case we get separated. This will allow my men to track your location."

She and Keturah exchanged a glance and Keturah shrugged, clipping hers to the vest she wore outside her tunic. Before Bethany could follow suit, the wall to her right exploded in a mass of noise and shrapnel. Time stood still as she waited for the myriad of metal projectiles to pierce her body. Instead of the expected pain, she found herself pinned to the ground, protected by Josiah's body.

She heard the soft moan and was once again in real time. Her first thought was for her friend. "Keturah?" Bethany struggled to move, the acrid odor of explosives sharp in her nostrils. "Where are you?"

"Hush." Bethany could feel Josiah's voice as much as hear it since his body still covered her. "She's safe. Stay down." He rolled off her and moaned, bringing the realization that the first moan had also been his.

Keturah's gasp from nearby brought Bethany's head up, and she saw the red stain spreading across the right side of Josiah's vest.

Without conscious thought, Bethany ripped off her own vest as Keturah worked to expose the wound and inspect it. Their eyes met briefly, and in that moment, she knew they would do whatever necessary to keep him safe. His injury didn't appear deep but must involve an artery. They had to staunch the flow of blood if he was to survive.

He struggled against their ministrations. "Let me up, I'm fine." His breath whistled through his teeth as he tried to sit. "I have to make sure we're safe."

"Give me your pistol." Keturah wrenched it from his hand. She crawled back toward the hole in the wall. Unbelievably, the lower third remained somewhat intact. Keturah positioned herself to see the compound. "I don't see anyone approaching...yet."

Bethany was torn between worry for Keturah and relief that Josiah's heart beat was regular beneath her fingertips, even if his ragged breath gave away his pain. "Keep still." She bent lower, trying to make sure her voice stayed steady. "I have to stop the bleeding."

"Take my earpiece." He used his left arm to wrench it from his head and shove it in her direction. "My lieutenant's name is Bezek. He'll need an update when he gets closer."

The blast from Josiah's air pistol caught her unaware as Keturah fired out into the quad, and Bethany instinctively threw herself on top of him. The bandage slipped, and he sucked in his breath as she struggled to reposition it.

"Hey. Quit shooting, we're here to rescue you." A male voice drifted to them from somewhere on the other side of the compound. The familiar Sintuen accent made Bethany gasp. Even as her heart leapt at the possibility of escape, she knew abandoning Josiah in this condition would mean his death.

"Trying to blow us to bits is a strange way to go about it." Keturah's normally quiet voice carried easily. "I don't know you. Leave me alone. I'll find my own way home."

"Good girl." Josiah's voice barely reached Bethany's ears. "Don't give away how many of us there are."

"I told you." The shooter's voice was sharp and irritated. "I'm here to free you."

"What makes you think I need freeing?" Keturah called back. "I came to explore the crash site, and you attacked me. I claim salvage rights."

"Don't try that nonsense on me." Their attacker's voice was nearer now. "I know you and another woman were being transferred to a slave compound."

Bethany's unintentional gasp sounded loud, even to her own ears, and Keturah made a shushing motion with her hand.

"They hadn't told you where they were taking you, had they?" The voice had definitely moved closer to their building, and Bethany's own emotions continued to vacillate. She wanted to go, but she also wanted to stay.

Keturah fired across the quad again, and Bethany heard a crash and a curse. "Stop that, you diseased daughter of a leason."

Josiah's hand tugged at Bethany. She leaned over him to hear. "I wouldn't..." he began, then coughed. "I'd never allow you to be enslaved again. You'll always be safe with me."

Before she could process his statement, the roar of a large aircraft jerked her attention skyward. The voice outside cursed, even as it melted away.

The earpiece in her hand crackled, and she held it close to her ear to hear. "Commander, are you there? Report."

Josiah smiled at her as the voice drummed in her ear. "Don't worry, Bezek bellows like a bovine but is gentle as a hesit."

"Is this Bezek?" She stumbled over the strange name, uncertain of how to address him. "Is that you above us?"

"Who is this?" The voice rang in her ears, and she wished for a volume control as she jerked it away from her ear. "I'm Bethany. Your Commander has been wounded. He needs you."

His only answer was a string of foreign words delivered in a growl.

"Here they come," Keturah warned her as the aircraft landed and the courtyard filled with armored giants. At their appearance, Keturah stood and held out her hands in the universal gesture of peace.

Bethany wanted to rise, to meet these fearless beings as an equal, but she couldn't risk disturbing Josiah's bandage. Almost at once, a warrior was beside her, a helmet sailing across the room as she flung it from her head. The woman dropped to her knees and shouldered Bethany out of the way, somehow managing to keep the makeshift wrappings in place. "Brother, speak to me."

Bethany felt the shock course through her as she recognized this warrior as the woman with the amazing eyes.

"Calm yourself." Josiah's voice wasn't its usual stentorian tone, but the strength underneath stilled Bethany's thumping heart.

"Manaen, how is he?" Another warrior joined Josiah's sister, his helmet in his hands. He jerked around to face Bethany, his red hair snapping with his words. "Are you Bethany? The one on the radio?"

"Yes." She hated the quaver in her voice, but these soldiers still terrified her. How could any world grow beings this tall? "I stopped the bleeding as best I could." She lifted her chin, refusing to give in to the fear. "The wound doesn't appear to be life-threatening."

"Quit barking at her, you fool." Josiah tried to sit, but Manaen pushed him flat. "She and that other mite probably saved me."

"Then we owe you a debt of gratitude, little one." Bezek winked at her, his bluster gone as quickly as it had begun. "His hide is valuable to his sister, and she has a quite a temper."

Two other R'hobans, obviously medics, joined them. As they worked over Josiah, Manaen led Bethany to a quiet corner. Now that the crisis had subsided, Bethany didn't know what she felt. Relief and worry sparred in her mind, leaving only confusion to decide the match. Should she have tried to escape? Would they send her and Keturah to a slave camp? Her friend joined her, silent. They stood, shoulders touching, waiting.

CHAPTER FIFTEEN

Simon cursed as he followed Japheth back to their groundrover, a battle-ready version that had enabled them to bring down the aircar with ease. Even with the armaments it carried, they needed to be well away before the R'hobans began their search.

"That's twice." Japheth strapped himself into the driver's seat without looking up.

"Excuse me?" Simon stopped mid-buckle and stared at Japheth.

Japheth adjusted his goggles and nudged the rover in gear. "You'd best finish buckling in. We need to put some distance between us and them."

Simon only had an instant to comply before they were off at breakneck speed. As it was, he had to shut his eyes tight against the dust that filled the rover when they roared off. He situated his own goggles and reopened his eyes. He mentally shrugged. The effort of conversation wasn't worth it through this rough terrain. He was more likely to get a belly full of dirt instead of something useful with the taciturn Japheth sitting next to him.

The rapidly changing landscape brought a brief memory to mind. Simon knew this part of Sintue well. They weren't far from his home, only about fifteen klicks from where he'd grown up. These undulating hills used to be lush with the green grasses of open country. As a child, he'd spent summer days here with Bethany, exploring and playing. Now, the vegetation that remained was little more than matted clumps of gray and brown, thick with briars and thorny puffs of thindle.

"Do you know what you're going to say?" Japheth's shouted question brought him back to the present with a jolt.

"About what?"

"About your second failure to get the girl," Japheth said.

"It's not a failure."

Japheth startled him with a wide grin, his teeth gleaming bright through a dust-streaked face. "Yeah, go with that."

"Do you have a better idea?" Simon didn't know where this conversation was leading but wanted to give it a chance to play out.

Japheth downshifted and slowed slightly as he tackled an incline. "If it were me, I'd stick with only the facts. Reinforcements arrived before we could secure her release."

An interesting interpretation of what had happened, but Simon had a few questions of his own. "What will your report say?"

"Just that." They topped the ridge and began their final descent before entering the tunnels. "It's my reputation on the line as well."

"Good advice," Simon said.

They stopped under a stony outcropping, and Japheth toggled the communicator strapped to the roof of the vehicle. "Retriever One, reporting back."

"Pass code?" a static-riddled voice requested.

"Vista Open." Japheth let the rover idle as they waited for the two men who appeared to wrestle the roll-back covering out of the way.

They slowly drove through the short tunnel and into the vehicle bay. Japheth parked without further revelations. One of Aven's guards was waiting when he stepped out of the vehicle. "The Overseer requests your presence immediately." He gestured to Japheth, who was coming around the back of the rover, removing his gloves. "Yours as well."

"Of course," Simon agreed. Japheth nodded, slapping his driving gloves against his trousers to rid them of dust.

Aven's suite of offices were only two klicks below them, and they navigated the route in silence. Simon resisted the urge to glance back at Japheth, still unsure of his motives behind the sudden overture of helpfulness.

The guard left them at the outer office, resuming his place at the doorway.

"You wanted to see us?" Simon stopped at the open door of the inner office.

Aven looked up from the papers he was studying and motioned them in. The richly carved desk was a perfect foil for his almost military attire. The severely tailored black jacket echoed his air of command with dark braid around the cuffs and collar. Several emblems adorned the left side of his jacket, although Simon couldn't place where he'd seen them before.

"Very good." He looked up from the papers. "Your report, gentlemen?"

"Reinforcements arrived before we could secure the girl's release." Simon met Aven's dark gaze. "It will be necessary to contact her once she's in place."

"I see." Aven crossed his arms and leaned back in his chair, his expression unreadable. "Japheth, do you have anything to add?"

"I made certain we weren't followed," he said. "But other than that, the report stands."

"Excellent." Aven's face relaxed, and he waved them toward a small table. "Help yourselves to something refreshing. I can see you must be dry after swallowing all that dust. Unfortunately, your travels aren't over. We have things to discuss and plans to make." He stood. "But not here. We must make haste."

"Where do you think they're taking us?" Keturah leaned close to Bethany, although the roar of the airtransport's engines covered any conversation they might have wanted to keep private.

Bethany wrinkled her nose and strained to see outside. The only windows were in the front of the craft, and they showed nothing but blue sky. The hot smell of exploding ammunition had begun to dissipate, but she still couldn't understand how such a gorgeous day could hold so much violence. Bethany shook her head. "I have no idea what they'll do with us, and I wish I did."

Before liftoff, Manaen had made sure they were settled in the transport, introducing Bethany to the warriors on board as the Commander's Steward. The title got her instant respect but offered little comfort. Even though she was thorough, Bethany could tell Manaen's mind was with Josiah. Bethany felt an uncomfortable division within her own heart as she watched the medics load a loudly protesting Josiah into a red air vehicle. His sister and Lieutenant Bezek hopped in just before the craft sped away. No surprise there. But their disappearance left Bethany yearning for a familiar face, even if it belonged to one of her captors. She took a deep breath, exhaling slowly.

Keturah squeezed her hand. "I don't believe they're sending us to a slave camp."

Bethany turned to her and tried to smile. "I hope that's true. But we have no way of knowing where they're taking us." She shook her head. "And, really, no say in the matter."

"And no need." Keturah's words were so soft Bethany almost had to read her lips.

"You're right, of course." Bethany's chagrin became a lump in her throat. How often had she been protected by divine intervention, only to once again forget? "I know the One keeps us safe." She looked away, needing to be honest. "But at times, I get so tired of believing in what I cannot touch." She glanced up. "It's a failing I must seek to remedy."

"Casiphia would say it's something we all need to work on." Keturah's smile softened her brown eyes, making them seem even larger than usual. "But I don't believe *she's* had to work on it in a very long time."

Bethany raised an eyebrow. "You were in the compound longer than me…did you ever figure out Casaphia's age? She seemed so wise and yet, except for her silver hair, not all that old."

Keturah shrugged. "I'm certain Leah knew, but it was never mentioned."

"I wonder how long they live." Bethany glanced at the men seated in the front of the aircraft. "Of all the R'hobans I've seen, Casiphia's one of the oldest." She pursed her lips. "Although I haven't seen many of them."

"I know." Keturah sighed. "We spend years stuck below ground by our own people. Then, when we're rescued, we're held in a compound by a race of giants. I don't think we have much of a perspective."

Bethany twisted in her seat and glanced toward the windows again, hoping for a landmark or anything to mark their position. "So, what do we know?"

"First, our world was invaded—either for liberation or annihilation—depending on whom you talk to." Keturah grimaced. "Second, as Seekers, we were protected by the invaders and sequestered—either to be set free or enslaved. Finally, we've been re-educated on our beliefs—either to correct our inaccuracies or to brainwash us."

"So in other words, we don't know anything." Bethany tugged the straps across her chest to a more comfortable position. "We need information—reliable information."

"True." Keturah tapped her chin with a long finger. "But I do know one thing for certain. I've been well treated by the R'hobans and ill-treated by my own people."

"I can't argue that."

"Who exactly is Simon?" Keturah's abrupt change of subject caused Bethany to jerk slightly, but her friend appeared not to notice. "I know you told me he's someone from your childhood. But if he's not a Seeker, why did he continue to associate with you?"

"I wish I knew." Bethany's thoughts turned inward. Keturah's questions echoed ones she'd struggled with for months. For years, she'd thought of Simon as a friend. But of late, he'd seemed a stranger, and a dangerous one at that. Noticing her friend's patient stare, Bethany pulled herself back to the here and now. "I don't know. I just don't know."

"It seems strange he would seek you out and risk capture." Her expression of obvious disbelief made Bethany want to laugh, but the subject was anything but funny.

"I've wondered that, too." Bethany caught her lower lip between her teeth. "I can't figure out who to trust."

"Yes, you can." Keturah pointed her finger at Bethany. "The only person we've ever been able to trust—the One."

"I know that." Bethany looked down at her hands, trying to curb her impatience. "I mean from the people around us. Which of them are telling the truth and which aren't?" She once again craned her neck to see outside. "It seems that everyone has an agenda."

Keturah actually laughed. "It's strange isn't it? It wasn't all that long ago when nobody cared a flit about Seekers, and now, we're the center of attention."

Bethany's reply died a sudden death on her lips. The craft had dipped slightly, and she could see a small portion of the landscape in front of them. The familiarity captured her attention. It couldn't be. She had to be mistaken. Bethany felt her eyes fill with tears as her heart burned with hope and pain. They would never have brought her here. They couldn't have known.

"Bethany?" Keturah shook her arm. "What is it? What do you see?"

The tiny windows continued to give tantalizing glimpses into a world she thought forever lost. She ignored Keturah and drank it in. Reality or vision, she knew this place.

CHAPTER SIXTEEN

"I'm fine." Josiah jerked his uninjured arm away from the healer and turned toward his sister as the aircraft took flight. "You're the cause of this commotion."

"If you don't lie still, you'll fall off the litter." Manaen laid a hand on his chest, keeping him prone as the transport banked sharply. "Just let her determine what needs to be done." She raised an eyebrow. "The quicker she evaluates your wounds, the quicker you can get back to Bethany."

He chose not to think of the small Seeker who had so recently saved his life. He had to focus, and thoughts of her made that impossible. "We must infiltrate the attack origination site—right now." He used the noise of the aircraft's engines to provide him with an excuse to bellow. What he really wanted to do was hit something, hard. "Bezek, have you begun coordination of ground and air?"

"Already taken care of, sir." Bezek grabbed a ceiling strap and leaned over him, swaying with the craft's movement. "I began initial mobilization at your first alarm."

"I told you things were well in hand." Manaen kept her hand on his chest, her voice distorted in an effort to be heard. "We need to know exactly what happened. Some details would be helpful."

"This proves, beyond anyone's personal reservations, that we have a traitor in our midst." Josiah managed to rub his forehead and glare at the medic simultaneously. "Only our people and Casiphia's knew we were moving the Seekers."

"It doesn't tell us which group he's affiliated with." Bezek frowned as he continued to cling to the strap.

A slight smile tugged at the corners of Manaen's mouth. "Or if he's possibly a she."

Leave it to his sister to hit the heart of the matter. "There is that." Josiah grunted as the medic adjusted his bandage. "We have much to discuss. How long until we arrive back at my compound?"

Manaen exchanged a glance with Bezek. "You won't be returning to the compound. We're headed to the Chief Medical Officer's personal cruiser. They haven't yet broken orbit."

"Ridiculous." Josiah snorted and shoved at her hand, dislodging it from his chest. Ignoring the healer's squawk, he swung his feet over the edge of the medical berth. "Enough foolishness. I've been injured far worse in training exercises." He motioned Bezek into a nearby seat. "Your looming and swaying is giving me a headache."

"Don't be dense." Manaen rose, a futile but familiar attempt to dominate him. "You must have at least one full day under a healer's supervision. Kirstol insisted on seeing to your care personally."

Great. How many complications did one man need? Josiah pulled Manaen down beside him and leaned close, trying to communicate his sudden sense of urgency. "We don't have time." He took an experimental deep breath, feeling the phenomenal healing ability of his race begin the process of knitting tissue and bones. "Why would the insurgents have risked exposure to shoot down a single aircar? I carried nothing of value."

Manaen's brow furrowed at the question. "I can think of many reasons—propaganda and fear, to name two." She tilted her head.

"It was your aircar, Commander. What is your point? Why does their motivation matter?"

"Of course." Bezek slapped his thigh. "They wouldn't have dared, unless they were ready for a confrontation."

Josiah relaxed. He'd always known naming Bezek as his second was a wise decision. "Exactly. We must be prepared for an all-out offensive." He turned to Manaen. "I know it seems I've the brains of a yerman, but I'm certain I'm right."

He could see her processing the information. Then Manaen nodded slowly. "You probably are." She tugged at her ear. "Where do you think they'll attack?"

"The food processing stations, of course." He smiled grimly. "I'm sure they know it isn't possible to occupy a hostile world if you can't feed your forces."

"I sent our men back to your compound." Manaen's voice faltered. "With the two Seekers." Her green eyes darkened. "You would have to choose a dwelling in the middle of the granaries."

Before she had finished speaking, Bezek exploded from his seat and leapt to the front of the vehicle to speak into the captain's ear. Manaen reached for Josiah's hand. "I didn't think it through. I wouldn't have sent her into danger."

"Don't worry. We'll be there in plenty of time." His hand tightened on hers as the craft banked into another steep turn. He wanted to contact his men, warn them of a probable ambush — protect her. But it was all too likely their frequencies were monitored. He couldn't risk alerting the enemy of his plans. If they were able to quell this attack, they could regain control. He snorted, if they'd ever had it to begin with.

"Your thoughts?" Manaen had heard his snort. "Is there something else I should know?"

"Only that our enemy is far cleverer than your Commander." Josiah narrowed his eyes. "I've become complacent of late. I pray my lack of forethought won't cost us lives."

Bezek dropped into the seat beside him. "It's not complacency. It's the fact that we've never before battled an enemy within our own ranks." He rubbed his neck. "I know the scrolls warn of this very thing, but I hadn't seen a hint of it before this liberation."

"Neither did I." Manaen stared out the window, her expression grim. "I have been misled by an angel of darkness masquerading as an angel of light."

Strangely, her admission lifted some of the heaviness that had invaded his soul. Study and prayer were the foundations of his sister's life. If she could be deceived, anyone could. "This isn't your fault."

She turned to him with a wry smile twisting her mouth. "Isn't it? I'm the one who sent you on that fool's errand this morning." She motioned to the bandage covering a portion of his chest. "I'm responsible for your injury." She sighed and returned her gaze to the window.

Josiah knew he couldn't allow Manaen's thoughts continue on this path. Manaen took her duties as eldest daughter seriously—too seriously. Her remorse at their parents' death had almost put her in the grave. Josiah wouldn't risk losing her again, not even to cover his own feelings. "You were right, you know."

Josiah turned to Bezek with a slight motion of his head. His lieutenant took the hint and changed seats, choosing one toward the front of the craft.

"Right? How do you mean?" Manaen gave him her complete attention.

He stretched his legs to their full length. "I didn't want to go retrieve that Seeker." He held up a finger when she started to speak. "And I confess my reluctance had nothing to do with being busy."

Manaen's green eyes widened at his admission. "You do care for her."

CHAPTER SEVENTEEN

Bethany held herself stiff as the aircar's pilot cut the engines and glided to a stop above the courtyard of the compound. It dropped lightly to the landing grid, blowing dirt and sand in every direction. Still, she didn't move—her outer immobility a reaction to an inner turmoil too great to release. She dimly heard orders and shouts as the craft was secured. Then the door opened. She closed her eyes and took a trembling breath. It was the same…that pungent odor of grains and processing. Bethany had come home.

Ducking her head to exit the aircar, Bethany concentrated. It wasn't home, not any more. She must never refer to it that way ever—even in her mind. She knew she had to concentrate on that one thought, cling to it as a drowning woman clings to a life rope.

As she stood in the familiar courtyard, she looked down and noticed Keturah's grip on her hand. Bethany must have reached for her friend without realizing it. She met Keturah's eyes and willed her mouth to smile, but her lips only twitched in response to her mind's command.

"Madam?" One of the warriors towered over her, his tone oddly respectful. "Our orders are to see you settled before we rejoin the Commander."

Bethany still didn't trust herself to speak so she only nodded.

He led the way, past several others, into the small entry hall. It was at once familiar and strange. The etchings in the stone walls were echoes of her childhood, but the furnishings were unfamiliar.

The warrior stopped in front of a tall, silver-haired woman. "Gehazi, I present to you the Commander's Steward, Bethany of Sintue."

"Thank you, Jael." Gehazi turned and studied Bethany for a moment with steady violet eyes before extending her hand. "Welcome, Bethany. I'm pleased you're here with us." Her face lit up with her warm smile, and she cocked her head. "But this place is familiar to you, yes?"

Bethany's mouth went dry. Did the R'hobans have the ability to read thoughts? She'd been assured they did not, but this silver-haired woman had done just that.

Keturah moved to stand beside Bethany, placing her hand on Bethany's shoulder. "Thank you for your kindness."

Bethany cleared her throat. "Yes, thank you."

Gehazi moved aside and motioned them all into the great room. Bethany stepped into the memory, transported years back in time in a single instant. She turned slowly, taking in the changes and letting her spirit once again connect to rocks and wood.

Gehazi went immediately to the side table, filled goblets, and passed them around. By the time Bethany had her drink, a familiar peace had reasserted its healing presence.

"A toast." Gehazi raised her glass toward Bethany. "To Bethany, may she build a bridge between our two races."

"To Bethany." Jael lifted his beverage as well.

Bethany and Keturah exchanged looks. Their unexpected welcome had caught Keturah off guard as well. Bethany took a sip, letting the sweetness of the juice mingle with the uncertainty in her soul. She set her glass on a nearby table and turned again to survey the room.

"I know it's been an event-filled morning." Gehazi crossed the room in a quick, fluid movement and put a graceful hand on Bethany's arm. "I'll have you shown to your rooms." Her smile included Keturah. "You can settle in and freshen up before we have the evening meal. You must have many questions, but save them until then."

"I thank you for your kindness." Bethany found herself slipping into the warm formality that marked the members of this warrior race.

Gehazi turned and clapped her hands twice, a staccato sound that caused Bethany to jump. Almost immediately, a familiar figure entered from the food preparation area. Shocked, Bethany recognized the servant as the woman who'd kept her alive in the slave pens. But before she could do anything beyond suck in a breath, Elisheba lifted three fingers to her cheek, a stringent warning of imminent danger.

CHAPTER EIGHTEEN

Simon watched the roof of the underground parking area retract. What he had taken as rock smoothly divided and slid from view, leaving the vista of open sky. This was no last minute project.

The first aircar, containing Aven and three of his personal cadre, maneuvered into place and lifted off, trailing the warm odor of vaporized propulsion rock. He and Japheth had been assigned the fourth aircar. "Do you know where we're going?" Simon leaned close to Japheth so he didn't have to shout.

"Staging area." His clipped reply discouraged further questions.

When their turn to board came, Simon, Japheth, and two others buckled into the seats behind the pilot. When they were all secure, the aircar roared toward the sky.

The trip was uneventful except for the fact that it gave him much needed time to compose himself for the coming conversation with Aven. Simon allowed a smile, once again certain he could use the situation to his advantage.

The aircar landed and he followed Japheth to a domed shelter, mottled with colors that blended into the surrounding trees. Aven held court in opulent surroundings, with several of his cadre in attendance. Simon spotted Salisa, but Loenne was conspicuous by her absence.

"Come, sit." Aven waved him to a straight-backed chair before turning to Japheth. "Get our warrior a drink."

Japheth grimaced, but complied.

"My thanks." Simon was still uncertain of Japheth's exact duties.

"Now." Aven rubbed his hands together and leaned back. "I'd like to know exactly why you failed to return with this woman."

"The reinforcements came too quickly. There was no time to get her away." This wasn't time to attempt prevarication. Aven respected those who spoke directly. "But I believe this will work to our advantage."

"Of course you do." Salisa removed a hand from inside her bell-like sleeves and pointed a bony finger in his direction. "I'm sure you've figured a way to cover your part in this fiasco."

"Now, Salisa, let our patriot speak." Aven's voice was calm, but Simon could read the signs. Aven wasn't any happier with his performance than Salisa. "Enlighten us. Why do you think failure is good for our cause?"

"I don't think for a moment that failure is good for our cause." Simon snapped, refusing to rise to the bait. "But I do believe we can put the situation to work for us." He didn't restrain the smile that twisted his lips. "We should use her as a spy where she is."

"Ah." Aven steepled his fingers and nodded. "I see. Perhaps this is salvageable after all. Do you believe you'll be able to convince a Seeker to work with us?"

"Yes." Simon took a deep breath. "You know my history with this woman. She will listen to me."

Aven nodded and a slow smile spread across his lips. "Since you've chosen to speak openly, I'll do the same. I have it on good authority the Commander was wounded in your attack. This will work to our advantage." He held up a hand, forestalling interruption. "And she's been installed in his personal compound. Now, what conclusions can you draw?"

"With the Commander wounded, the troops will be slower to respond to the threat." Simon matched Aven's expression with a smile of his own.

Salisa sputtered and gasped, causing Simon to turn his attention to her. He made an effort to control his face as he realized the old woman was giggling.

Salisa covered her mouth and managed to control her audible contortions after a few moments. "So we haven't lost them after all, just postponed the inevitable."

Aven swiveled in his chair and exchanged a glance with Japheth. Japheth immediately left the shelter.

"Let's not be hasty." Aven got up to refresh his cup. "Perhaps, if you can sway her, this Seeker will be useful in the Commander's house. Especially when she sees our strength."

"Could be." Salisa's voice still carried an unpleasant rasp, like a file on a rusted bolt. "But can she be trusted?"

Aven pinned Simon with a glance. "I think that's a question better asked of the one who knows her best."

Simon hesitated only a moment. "I believe she can." He took a deep breath and forged ahead. "If she's fool enough to be a Seeker, she's obviously gullible."

Japheth slipped back through the door. "She's in place and ready for your orders, sir."

A broad smile limped across Aven's scarred face. "Good, good. All proceeds as it should."

Simon cut his eyes toward Salisa, but she was studying Aven intently.

"Sir?" It was as much of a question as Simon dared ask.

"No matter." Aven waved away his inquiry. "I want you on the ground, ready to infiltrate the compound when the troops engage the processing stations." He turned back to Japheth. "Make certain my orders are followed to the letter. I do not want that compound breached."

"But I thought we wanted to destroy the Commander." Simon struggled to understand their objective.

"That was the original goal." Aven adjusted the rare Corsanon ring on his right hand. "But now…how did you put it? We've found something that will work to our advantage."

Salisa leaned forward. "A wounded Commander, with a traitor by his side, is a gift from the gods."

"Gods?" Aven drew out the sibilant like a snake, his eyes narrowing. "We are our own gods, and we will soon rule this world and many more."

CHAPTER NINETEEN

Bethany looked away from Elisheba, trying to keep her expression neutral. She knew Keturah had noticed her intensity, but it appeared no one else in the room had.

Gehazi crossed the room to Elisheba. "I'd like you to accompany us to the steward's new quarters." She turned a questioning glance to Bethany and Keturah. "Do you all know each other? I would think with such a small population of Seekers, many of you would be acquainted."

Bethany's breath caught in her throat, but Elisheba answered smoothly. "No ma'am, we've not met."

"Oh, well. No matter." Gehazi motioned them out the door but took Bethany's arm as they left. "I've assigned you the suite of rooms against the western wall. I found the deep burgundy colors and view of the fields restful and hoped you would also."

Elisheba, a few steps in front of them, made a sound that could have been a cough.

Gehazi hurried to her side. "Elisheba, are you well?"

Keturah used the commotion to lean in close to Bethany. "She assigned us the mourning suite?" Her eyes darted toward Gehazi. "Is she unaware of its function?"

Bethany controlled her rocketing emotions with difficulty. "Not now." She kept her voice low and her eyes on Gehazi. "We'll discuss it later."

As Bethany followed Gehazi and Elisheba to the suite, the hallways were both familiar and foreign. She catalogued the changes, using them to reorient her perspective. It was difficult. There was a pleasant, lingering odor that reminded her of her mother's favorite scent. Bethany almost expected to hear her welcoming voice, but there was no hearty welcome. Instead, the stone corridors that once rang with laughter now echoed with the footsteps of the R'hobans. The lighting grates inset into the ceilings were darkened from what she could only assume was sporadic usage. For the first time, she allowed herself to wonder who had inhabited these premises in the intervening years after her family had been murdered.

Gehazi glanced over her shoulder. "How long since you've visited here?"

Grateful for the hallway's shadow, Bethany swallowed, trying to dispel the tightness in her throat. "It's been at least a tenspan of years." Relief flooded her as she managed to keep her voice level.

"Then you must be as disturbed as I with the disarray." Gehazi dropped back to walk with Bethany, shaking her head. "I admit I was dismayed with the Commander's choice of this compound."

Keturah made a slight sound behind them. "But it seems so lovely."

Bethany stifled a sigh. Lovely didn't begin to describe the home of her youth.

"Oh, I quite agree—now." Gehazi gestured back toward the main section of the home. "We've spent many hours returning it to its former beauty. We've managed to make most of the rooms habitable, but the corridors still need more work."

"Was there anyone living here when you arrived?" The question slipped through Bethany's control.

"No." Gehazi slowed her steps and studied Bethany. "Nor had there been for a long while."

Bethany waited to feel something, anything, but her emotions continued to simmer in a broth of confusion, no single one rising to the top.

"Here we are." Gehazi stopped at heavy double doors with inlaid metal filigree. She pushed them open with ease, revealing a spacious receiving room. After the dark hallway, the light streaming through the wide windows caused Bethany to blink.

"Ooh." The low exclamation came from Keturah as she moved to the center of the space and turned a slow circle.

"I couldn't agree with you more." Gehazi nodded, straightening a cushion and adjusting the angle of an ornate chair. "This suite has been outfitted for you." She smiled at Bethany as she pointed to the doorway on her right. "Both sleeping rooms open to this common area. We thought you'd be more comfortable sharing a suite." Her sudden frown caused two vertical lines to appear on her forehead. "But if we've misjudged, and you prefer an entire suite to yourself, that can also be arranged."

"Oh, no." Bethany smiled at Gehazi's thoughtfulness. "You've done just right."

"Very well." She returned Bethany's smile before turning to Keturah. "These shall be yours." She pointed to the doorway across from the one leading to Bethany's. "I believe you'll find them quite comfortable."

"I'm certain I will." Keturah crossed to peer inside her quarters.

"I'll leave you with Elisheba to get settled." Gehazi moved to the suite's entrance and paused. "May we expect you for the evening meal?"

"Yes," Bethany answered for them both. "We'll join you then."

Gehazi closed the doors with a soft thud.

Bethany stood, listening as the echo of Gehazi's footfalls grew softer. As the sound drifted away, she launched herself toward Elisheba. "You're here. You're safe."

Elisheba met her, her arms wide as she gathered Bethany into a motherly embrace. "I prayed that the One would see you safely by my side once again."

"As did I." Bethany pulled back out of her embrace so she could see the older woman's face. "How did you come to be here? Tell me what has happened."

CHAPTER TWENTY

Josiah gritted his teeth against the rough landing as he tried to brace himself while undoing the seat harness. Bezek had already pushed past him and was tugging open the transport door. Josiah exchanged a look with Manaen as Bezek leapt to the ground. Their uneventful landing in this compound confirmed the enemy's trap.

"Sir?" Jael's puzzled features appeared as the door opened. "I thought you'd been taken to the medical transport for treatment."

"I'm needed here." Josiah tried to hide his discomfort as he exited. Manaen steadied him from behind with an unobtrusive hand, and he was once again grateful for the bond they shared.

"Assemble the troops." Manaen dropped lightly beside him before reaching back into the craft for her battle helmet. "We're about to have visitors."

Jael's eyes widened for an instant before he sketched a salute and raced toward the honor barracks south of the main compound.

"Gehazi?" Bezek was only halfway to the compound's outer doors but his roar could be heard everywhere. "You're needed."

The compound door swung open and Gehazi stood, hands on hips. "There's no need to bellow. We've all got ears." Her eyes moved over the group and a pale eyebrow quirked. "Ah, perhaps this is a situation that calls for bellowing."

Bezek reached the wide, stone steps and bounded up, pausing at the top. "Greetings Ancient One."

Gehazi's smooth cheeks reddened as she glared at him. "You are treading a thin line."

Manaen joined her on the threshold. "It's a path he lives to walk."

Gehazi let out a sigh thick with implied martyrdom. "Be that as it may, it seems you don't come with good tidings."

"No." Josiah gestured to the door. "But the explaining will go easier with a drink."

Gehazi studied him for a long moment before she nodded and disappeared inside. The other three followed her into the main room, silence their only topic of conversation.

The forces traveling with Simon and the Overseers were eerily silent in the afternoon sun. That lack of noise, coupled with the dusty color of their uniforms, provided camouflage within the rows of golden stalks not far from harvest. Their stealth made Simon feel the need to constantly reassure himself that they were in fact in place.

"Your fidgeting is proving tiresome." Aven's eyes glittered.

Simon froze, mentally cursing his lack of control. "My apologies, sir."

Delaina's soft laugh lubricated the situation. "It's only natural that he should be nervous." She moved to stand beside Simon. "This is his first battle, and he's not been blooded."

Aven cocked his head and offered his arm to Delaina. "You always look for the best, my dear." He glanced at Simon. "I, on the other hand, expect my officers to perform without thought or fear."

Aven's gold uniform should have also helped him merge into the background. But rich details and glittering insignia prevented any such camouflage. Simon again wondered at his good fortune in meeting up with Aven, although he knew he'd have to pay attention to continue to perform at the peak Aven required from those close to him.

"As I require much, I also reward greatly." Aven's words penetrated Simon's thoughts a moment after they'd been uttered.

Simon saluted. "So I've noticed." The answer sounded flip, even to Simon's ears, but he knew not to hide behind too false a façade with Aven.

Aven laughed, a rich hearty sound, at odds with his spare frame. "I'm glad to hear the truth spoken boldly." He slapped Simon on the back. "I'm certain you'll be an asset in today's battle, have no fear."

Even though Simon knew Aven couldn't read his mind, Simon struggled to keep his private demons buried. It wouldn't do for Aven to get too close to his actual feelings.

CHAPTER TWENTY-ONE

Bethany felt the shockwave's rumble seconds before the sound explosion rocked the room and knocked her from the chair. Elisheba screamed as she flung herself to the floor, covering her face with her hands. Keturah was beside the old woman in an instant while Bethany struggled to move.

The concussion bombs had transported her to the past, to another attack in this same compound. Bethany shook her head, trying to re-establish here and now. She watched as dust motes, shaken loose from the ceiling joists, danced in the afternoon sun, a macabre contrast to the violence hammering her ears.

"Bethany." Keturah's shout pulled her into the present and made it possible to act.

Bethany struggled to get herself upright, then raced to the nearest wall. "I'm sure it's still here." Her fingers searched for a memory, a slight difference within the stonework.

Elisheba quieted, with only occasional sniffs, and Keturah joined Bethany. "What is it? What are you searching for?"

Running her fingers lightly over the inlaid stonework, Bethany searched for the one fire-polished rock set slightly deeper than the others. The different finish couldn't be detected by sight, but touch could discern it easily enough. "Ah." She glanced at Elisheba, then at Keturah, as the wall seemed to echo her exclamation and moved to reveal a hidden doorway. "We'll be safe here. Follow me."

Bethany darted inside the narrow, dark opening that had appeared in the stone, lifting her hand to the right, feeling for the glowtorch. As her hand closed around it, she let out a small prayer that it would still work. It took a moment longer than normal, but it apparently picked up the resonance from her skin and begin to emit a soft light. She moved a few paces down the corridor to allow her companions to scramble the rest of the way inside. When they were well in, Bethany reached for another firestone and the opening disappeared, leaving them in the glow of the torch.

"Where are we?" Keturah turned to study her surroundings, squinting in the dim light. "How did you know this was here?" Then Keturah grinned, and Bethany knew her friend had figured out her secret. "This is your home."

"We're doomed," whispered Elisheba.

Bethany could hear the barely contained panic and knew it had to be quelled. "We're not doomed." At Keturah's sharp look, she modified her tone. "This is—or was—my family's compound." She led them down the corridor. "We're between the walls, in an old tunnel. We'll be safe here."

Elisheba sniffed. "If it was so safe, how did the authorities get to your family?"

Shock coursed through her veins as Bethany absorbed her former mentor's jab.

Keturah lightly touched Bethany's shoulder. "There were several such corridors in my family's compound." Her voice was even, almost conversational. "I used one to escape with my younger brother. Leaving the safety of the tunnels was how we were caught."

"Where is he now?" Bethany followed Keturah's change of subject, filing away Elisheba's remark for later.

"We were separated during our escape." Keturah's low voice didn't quite mask the tremor underneath. Her redirection had cost her. "He's old enough to take care of himself, but I still pray I'll be reunited with him."

"Where does this lead?" Elisheba sniffed again. "How much further?"

"There's a chamber deep within the bedrock. No matter the weapons, we'll be safe there," Bethany said. Had Elisheba always been this way? Or in the desperation of finding herself in the slave pens, had she somehow missed it during the time they were together?

"Recirculation units?" Keturah had regained control of her voice. "The air in here isn't as stale as one would expect."

"Well hidden." Bethany shrugged. "I assume they're still viable."

Her assumption proved true as the musty air remained breathable. They traveled on, their shadows a flickering counterpart to their downward progress. Bethany found herself hard-pressed to keep a steady pace instead of breaking into a run. Her curiosity drew her deeper, hope warring with her almost manic certainty of disappointment. It couldn't still be intact, could it? Would any of her research remain?

"Where is she?" Josiah fought to be heard over the concussion bombs as Gehazi led him and his small band to Bethany's quarters. The missiles were more of a nuisance than anything, and he wondered why the insurgents were using them. Surely the terrorists weren't foolhardy enough to think his warriors could be thrown into confusion with a little sound show. But that small slave girl must be terrified. He didn't want to explore what made her terror eat at his heart. There would be time enough for that later, when she was once again safe.

"In here." Gehazi barely had a chance to move before he was pushing through the door.

"Little One?" His voice reverberated around the room. When his summons received no answer, he gestured for those with him to spread out and search the suite.

Gehazi stood quietly at his side. "There is nowhere they could have gone. They'll be found."

As his men reported back, he felt the knots in his stomach shift and tighten. He needed to know she was safe. "Cover the entire compound if you have to. I want them found."

Gehazi touched his arm. "We have only begun to discover the treasures the One has hidden within the walls of this compound."

He tried to concentrate on the meaning behind her words, but the incessant bombing coupled with the pain from his recent injury made that an impossible task. Then, as quickly as it had begun, the pounding ceased. He turned and raced for the door, the silence ringing in his ears. "The concussion rounds were just to soften us up and make the main attack that much easier." He caught sight of Gehazi's shocked look. "It's standard battle tactics. And we'll have to endure several more sessions before they move on to something stronger."

"Which should tell us they have something else in mind." Manaen blocked his way before he got two paces down the corridor.

He slid to a stop, ignoring the pain in his ribs. He didn't know which was worse, his injuries or his stupidity. There'd be opportunity later to consider his lack of forethought. Manaen's well-timed appearance had recalibrated his thought process, and he smiled. "I'd say it's past time to start anticipating their moves instead of reacting to them."

Manaen raised an eyebrow. "Finally feeling better, I see."

"Tell Bezek to assemble my personal guard in the main room. I'll brief them on our plans there." He inclined his head toward Gehazi. "I think you'll be able to add much to this discussion. Then we'll continue the search for our wayward Seekers."

CHAPTER TWENTY-TWO

Simon paced, unable to be still within the confines of his commander's large campaign tent. He could feel Aven's eyes following his movements, even as the commander reclined in his chair, sipping from a goblet so thin it appeared the weight of the wine would cause it to shatter. The table before him was littered with maps, notes, and message tubes.

"You really should let Japheth pour you a glass." Aven gestured toward the stoic man standing by table. "Siung wine calms the mind."

The thought of sitting calmly by, waiting for the next phase of the attack, made Simon's stomach roil. Still, it wasn't a good idea to continue broadcasting his unease. "You're right, of course." Simon adjusted his short jacket before sinking into a carved chair, close but not adjacent to Aven. He forced himself to relax against the cushioned back.

"I always appreciate a subordinate who understands the need to master his emotions." Aven nodded at Japheth, who slipped out of the tent. "I've asked the others to gather before we start the next phase."

Simon had suspected as much. "Are you ready to reveal the next phase?"

"I am."

He sat quietly, knowing Aven would speak in his own time.

Aven took his time before finally finishing his wine. He set the goblet on the table and steepled his fingers. "I'm impressed." He turned toward Simon. "Most would have badgered me past the point of irritation."

"Thank you."

"I requested your presence because I believe you will be able to provide additional information I need."

"Anything I have is yours."

"Of course it is." Aven got up and pulled a message tube from an ornate chest. He opened it and scanned its contents before settling back into his seat and studying the map. "I know you are familiar with this area."

"Yes." Every nerve in Simon's body twitched. He should have known Aven was well aware of his childhood allegiances.

"I didn't wish to call attention to your, shall we say, territorial expertise." Aven winked. "The others don't need to be burdened with the information."

"I'm not concerned about what anyone knows or doesn't know about where I spent my childhood." Simon let the anger he felt show briefly in his eyes before he turned them to the maps open on the table. "I have more than proved my worth to this cause."

"Of course." Aven's quick reply held no irritation. "But some are so easily sidetracked by irrelevant circumstances."

"True."

"I'm glad we understand one another." Again, Simon appeared to have passed a test. "Let's dispense with the banter." Aven handed the tube to Simon. "What can you tell me about this?"

Simon studied the tight script that composed the cryptic message.

Have confirmed the existence of subterranean passages connected to this compound. Unable to pinpoint exact location. Recommend more time for internal reconnaissance or outcome cannot be guaranteed.

This missive explained a lot of what Simon had suspected. Aven had spies everywhere. He looked up, frowning. "I seem to remember something…" He focused inward and tried to access memories he'd long buried. Afternoons running and playing, evenings spent at a child's game of seek and find. He snapped his fingers. "That's it."

Aven's smile froze as the tent flap was flung aside and the others began filing inside. He held up a warning finger and then rose to greet his guests.

Bethany stopped so suddenly Keturah bumped up into her.

"What is it?" Elisheba's continued monologue ended with a shriek, grating against Bethany's hard-fought control, shredding the remainder of her composure.

"Cease your screeching," Bethany stopped in front of closed door, holding the glowtorch high to brighten the area. She hesitated before placing her palm on the door-lock. Would her print still open the door? It did. The door slid open and they stood looking into the sanctuary of her childhood.

Their movement as they entered triggered the illumination grates inset in the ceiling, adding their hum to the familiar room. Bethany circled the main room, taking in the lack of change as well as the thin coat of dust. The center held a substantial table and six chairs, the last place her family had gathered. Her fingers traced the carving along the back of a chair. "This was my mother's accustomed seat."

Keturah also made a circuit of the room, pausing at the doorways dotting the wall. "Sleeping quarters, food prep area." She stopped at another door and turned back to Bethany, eyes wide. "Laboratory?"

"Where have you led us? This place is a mess." Elisheba leaned into the room, rubbing her hands on her apron. "Surely you don't expect us to stay here?" She looked back to the corridor. "Where does the tunnel lead from here?"

"It leads to an escape hatch in the side of a small hill not far from the compound." Bethany caught Keturah's eye and shook her head slightly before she turned toward Elisheba. "Would you rather return to the chaos above?" A rumble punctuated her point as dust sifted into the room, the motes dancing in the increasing light.

"What a stupid question." Elisheba scuttled into the room, craning her neck to peer at the ceiling. "Although it's likely we'll be trapped down here forever."

"That's not something we can control." Keturah said. "But we should check the condition of the sleeping room."

Good idea," Bethany said. "I'll inspect the food prep pod and take an inventory of our resources." She watched as Keturah motioned the other woman toward the sleeping quarters. She started to head for the food prep area before turning and striding to the area that had been her laboratory.

CHAPTER TWENTY-THREE

Josiah slammed the door inside a seemingly endless succession of rooms. "How can you have misplaced her this quickly?"

"I assure you—" Gehazi's answer was lost in another concussion blast.

"My apologies." Josiah softened his tone with an effort.

"I believe the blasts are coming with less frequency." Gehazi's violet eyes seemed to see past his defenses and into his soul. "She did not leave the compound. We will find her."

"Of course we will." Manaen strode into the room. "The troops are in place." She cocked her head and studied the bandage still wrapped around his chest. "But first, I need Gehazi to check your injury."

He bit back another sharp reply. Was there no end to the irritations of this day?

"Do not think you can argue and distract me, my brother." Manaen pointed a finger in his direction. "Your wound needs attention so you can finish the day in command. We still have a long way to go."

"This way, Commander." Gehazi brushed past him, and Josiah was almost certain he caught a glimpse of a smile as she led the way to her sitting room.

Gehazi directed him to a partially reclined bench. "So I can redress the wound."

He nodded and settled back.

Manaen leaned against the doorframe, her arms crossed. "Bezek has organized a few of the men to finish searching the compound."

"If anyone will find her, it will be Bezek." His breath hissed between his teeth as Gehazi tugged the bandage from the injury. "Must you be so rough?"

Her eyebrow arched, and she glanced toward Manaen. "I never thought to hear complaints from our normally even-tempered commander. The wonders of this day are truly a gift of the One."

Before he could frame an appropriate reply, a bellow echoed from the corridor.

"Commander?" Bezek repeated, as he appeared in the doorway behind Manaen. "You need to see this."

"Not until I'm finished." Gehazi fixed Josiah with a steely eye. "Only a moment more and then you'll be set to rights."

Josiah gritted his teeth but submitted to her ministrations.

"There." She gave the bandage one last tug and stepped back. "You may return to duty."

"My sincere thanks." He stood and bowed in her direction.

"It's this way, sir." Bezek darted down the corridor and disappeared into room assigned to Bethany.

Josiah strode after him, taking a deep breath. The pain had lessoned considerably. "What is it?"

Bezek was standing next to an inside wall, a grin peeking through his red beard. "The stonework is old, otherwise I'd never have seen it." He pointed to a perfect crack between the stones.

"That's too precise a seam to be natural." Josiah traced it lightly with his fingers.

"Is she here?" Manaen rushed into the room, and stopped. "Did you find her?" She gazed expectantly around the richly appointed room.

"I believe we have." Josiah pointed to the wall, knowing his face mirrored Bezek's grin. "But it might take a few minutes to reach her."

"I hope you have more planned than only noise." Salisa seated herself at the table. She turned and snapped her fingers at Japheth. He immediately brought her a cup filled to the brim with a dark, foamy liquid.

"Roma ale?" Delaina shuddered, taking a seat as far from Salisa as physically possible. "That's so second class."

"Not to mention pungent." Baanus rolled his eyes. "How you can get past the smell is quite beyond me."

Simon hadn't expected to see Baanus again, but the man must have decided not to challenge Aven for leadership. Was he a man who could bow to the inevitable or was he just biding his time?

"Our Salisa is obviously made of sterner stuff than you." Aven resumed his seat as Delaina giggled.

Salisa's rusty cackle joined in, and even Baanus allowed a slight smile to slip under the harsh line of his black mustache.

"Don't insult our colleague." Delaina managed to recover from her fit of giggles. "It's obvious he has a more refined palette."

Their bantering continued to swirl around him, laced with needle-sharp jabs and pricks. Simon did not join in. Although he was still learning to navigate this top-level hierarchy, he preferred the reputation of enigmatic to that of moron.

Delaina turned the full force of her turquoise eyes on Simon. "Does our teasing make you uncomfortable?"

"He just knows his place." Baanus snorted. "Wouldn't be right for such a youngling to poke fun at the rest of us."

"Ha," said Salisa. "That's a mouthful coming from you. Your grandsire was in soakers when I was in my prime."

Simon turned slowly, consciously willing his heart rate to remain normal. He'd categorized Salisa as ancient in his mind, but hadn't realized the accuracy of the term until now.

"And even your years pale in comparison to mine."

Bethany joined Keturah at the door to the laboratory.

"What is this place?" Keturah gestured into the once state-of-the-art room. "Who are you?"

Bethany knew at once what Keturah was asking. She wanted to know who Bethany was…before. Bethany hesitated, knowing once she crossed this line, she was committed. She'd be drawn back into a fight to save her world. A place populated with those who condemned everything she held dear—those who had facilitated the wanton murder of her precious family.

"She's no more special than you or me." Elisheba had peeked around Keturah. "How could someone this young have any idea what this was used for?"

Elisheba's jab gave Bethany the perfect way out, but her spirit rebelled. The lies had gone on long enough. It was time. "My father was Dr. Amariah Randolph." She paused, gathering her courage like a protective cloak. "And I was his assistant for the last six years."

Elisheba gasped, but Keturah turned slowly, facing Bethany full on. "So the planet-wide mystery of what happened to Dr. Randolph was nothing more than a cover-up. That explains much."

CHAPTER TWENTY-FOUR

Josiah paced as Bezek directed the dismantling of the wall. It was taking longer than he'd expected, the thickness of the stones not as much an obstacle as the unexpected layer of talarium behind it.

"Well, that certainly explains why we didn't know about the tunnels within this compound," said Manaen, a thoughtful expression in her green eyes.

Josiah just grunted. He knew it should concern him, but the only thing on his mind was Bethany. He'd sort through everything once he knew she was safe.

"We've broken in." Bezek stepped back as, with a sudden groan, a panel in the previously solid wall opened.

Josiah was there in an instant. "Grab a handlight and follow me." He didn't wait to see who obeyed, knowing Bezek would leave some of the force to guard the entrance while the rest followed him. The corridor ceiling was low but still allowed enough clearance for his seven-foot frame. He paused for a moment several lengths in, lifting his light to examine the interior walls. The concussive blasts were muffled here in the tunnel, although with each one, a fine sifting of debris rained down from the ceiling.

"This corridor is part of the original construction." Manaen joined him, adding her light to his. "It appears we're within the inner walls of the compound. They would have needed these tunnels in their recent history, but this compound is hundreds of years old. I wonder why they considered this secrecy necessary that far back."

"I suspect there's been strife on this world for much longer than we've been led to believe." Josiah resumed his pace, moving his light constantly to counter any possibility of ambush. "I think it's time for some answers, and I know where to begin to find them."

"Your orders, sir?" Bezek and several of his men halted a few paces behind him.

Josiah paused a moment, considering his options. "Keep silent. I don't expect any except the Seekers, but let's not be foolhardy. There's still much we don't know." He led the way, Manaen at his side. They continued on through the dark, circuitous corridor, its musty odor making it obvious it hadn't been used for a while...until today. Josiah pointed to the feathering in the dusty floor, knowing Manaen would understand what it meant. Someone had come this way recently.

As they rounded a bend, Josiah stopped and doused his light, motioning for the others to do the same. The faint glow ahead told him they'd reached their goal. When they crept forward, he could hear voices coming from a doorway but couldn't make out the words. He stifled a sudden smile when he recognized Bethany's tone.

He touched Manaen's arm. She'd know he wanted her to hang back with Bezek while he went forward alone.

He stood in the doorway several moments before anyone realized he was there.

Elisheba didn't make a sound, but the look on her face was enough. Bethany turned toward the entrance and saw Josiah planted there. She sighed and straightened her shoulders. It was too much, too soon, but she had no choice. The time had come to be honest.

"Care to join me in my study, Commander?" Bethany gestured to an office space opening off the main room and adjoining the laboratory. "I think there are some questions you need answered."

As they entered the compact room, the ceiling grates hummed on, illuminating the once vibrant office. Without hesitation, Bethany took the seat her father had always favored. The cushion had been worn away to fit her father's lanky frame and now cradled her with memories and strength. She swiveled the chair to touch a keypad that extended from the wall, smiling slightly as the plasscreen pinged in answer.

"It seems you may be the key to this whole mess." Josiah leaned against the doorframe and folded his arms.

"Have a seat, and I'll tell you what I know."

The chair he chose sighed softly as he settled, but it supported him with no further complaint. "Explain first about this compound and why you know it so well."

"This is my home. It's where I grew up." Her mouth tightened. "Until the cleansing came to us."

"How old were you when it began?"

"It had its roots before I was born." She closed her eyes. "But I remember when the worst of the cleansing started. The worst massacres were in the provinces, and we thought they'd lose strength as they came closer to the cities. We were wrong." She shook her head. "He was wrong."

"He?"

"My father." It was easier to talk about than she'd expected. "His belief was that the position he held with the Science League protected him…protected us."

"His work had to do with the trouble your world was experiencing?" His voice was low, non-threatening.

He made it sound so antiseptic and clinical, like Sintue had caught a childhood illness.

She grimaced. "We've known our planet's ecosystem was dying for some time. The Science League had been formed to find a solution. Top minds from every discipline were invited. Early on, cooperation reigned, but as time went by and no answer found, egos and ambitions began to worm their way inside." She focused on a point above his head. "Daddy thought the fact we were Seekers wouldn't matter, especially since his research held the most promise." Her eyes met his. "He was wrong. Dead wrong."

CHAPTER TWENTY-FIVE

"Are you bragging or looking for sympathy?" Delaina shifted her gaze back to Aven at his remark. "We all know you're the most senior among us."

"Now we do." Aven nodded toward Simon, then pointed a finger at himself. "Some were unaware of the magnitude of wisdom contained here."

"I suspected as much." Simon took a sip from his glass and swallowed hard. It was now or never. "Which leads me to ask why exactly I'm here as well."

"Something we've certainly been asking." Baanus's comment was low but audible.

"I'm not surprised you haven't arrived at the reason." Delaina moved to stand beside Aven.

"It's a worthy question…from Simon." Aven didn't glance in Baanus's direction. "And one of the reasons I've been including you."

Salisa harrumphed. "Get on with it, old man. Not even you will live forever."

"Oh, yes. Leave it to Salisa to hone in on the crux of the matter." Aven's eyes didn't match the warmth of the smile he aimed at Simon. "You've been chosen as one of the new Overseers."

Simon wet his dry lips with the tip of his tongue. "I'm speechless."

"Ha! I might have expected such wisdom from him," Baanus addressed Salisa, ignoring Simon.

"Our other new addition to the ranks of Overseer is Japheth," Aven added, almost as an afterthought.

"Wait just a minute...see here...what..." Baanus spluttered and let his words die.

"Really? Now who's speechless?" Aven quirked an eyebrow in Baanus's direction. "Did you have something you wanted to add?"

"Are you concerned about a servant being promoted?" Japheth poured himself a drink and joined them. "I've certainly more than proved my value, many times over."

Simon let the conversation bounce around him but knew they were just the surface of the communication. The undercurrents in the room were thick and murky. He'd have to learn what they meant soon or risk being carried away...forever.

"Commander!" Bezek skidded to a stop in the office doorway. "The concussion rounds have stopped. All's quiet now." He blew out air. "But I'd wager they're about to throw a lot more than just noise and lights in our direction."

Events were happening too fast to process. Bethany stared at Bezek, uncertain whether this was good news or bad.

"I'm certain you're correct." Josiah rose, glancing from Bethany to Bezek and back again. He held Bethany's gaze for a moment. "Stay put. You'll be safer below ground. I'll return as soon as I can."

Josiah went directly to Manaen. "I want you and the rest of the men to remain here until we know this is finished. I'll send more down and then we'll secure the door from above." Then he turned back to Bethany, frowning. "Do these tunnels extend to the outside? Could anyone get in that way?"

Get in? Who would want in? "I guess they could—if they were aware of the tunnel."

Manaen touched her arm. "Were there any beyond your family who knew of the tunnels?"

"I don't think there's anyone alive who knows. Very few who worked here were told they were here." The words caught in her throat, and she had to take a breath before she could continue. "All who did died with my family…in the cleansing."

"Still, be on your guard." He looked at Manaen, and they seemed to communicate something Bethany couldn't understand. "There's much at stake in these rooms."

She searched his face for a long moment, then nodded. "I'll see to their safety."

He gripped her arm, communicating his thanks for her unspoken support. "I'll return soon. We'll convene a meeting here and begin to plan our next move."

"Enough." That one word refocused the room toward Aven. "It's time to implement my next step." He nodded to Japheth, who rose and distributed message cylinders to everyone.

"Humph." Salisa looked up after reading hers. "I don't know whether to be irritated or flattered that you believe I'm capable of this."

"Do you really think—" A sharp glance from Aven cut the words from Baanus's lips.

"The reason you each have messages is because you're to work independently." His eyes continued to hold Baanus'. "If I wanted you to share, I'd have opened this up for discussion."

Simon's heart began to thud in his ears as he read his orders. This was it, his chance.

"I'll give you two squads." Aven's words pulled Simon's eyes in his direction. "That should be more than enough if you enter through the tunnels."

Was there anything this demon of a commander didn't know? "Yes, absolutely."

"I think you're all clear about the assignments you've received. I expect each to be carried out—to the letter." Aven looked at Japheth who nodded and left the tent. "By nightfall everything will be settled."

At this, they rose one by one to exit in silence until only he and Aven remained. "You've known who I was since the beginning." Simon didn't bother phrasing it as a question. "And you know my connection to the girl."

"Of course." Aven leaned back in his chair, dark eyes unreadable. "You truly don't think I'd have entrusted such an important part of my plan to someone I hadn't been grooming for years, do you?"

Snippets of memory played across Simon's mind. The ease with which he'd been admitted into the Organization, his quick rise to position of supervisor, even the knowledge of the hidden tunnels within the worker block he supervised.

A smile played around Aven's mouth. "You can go back farther if you'd like."

"But what...why...how did you know what I was thinking?" The words slipped out before Simon could censor them.

This time, Aven laughed out loud, a throaty sound that washed over Simon cold as ice. "I chose you long ago, making certain you had access to everyone and everything I'd need." He leaned forward. "And even now, you have no idea how far-reaching my plan truly is."

Simon could only stare as the truth of this man's manipulation shattered his world.

"You can see how this ensures my ultimate command of Sintue, yes?" Aven lifted an eyebrow.

"Absolutely."

"What you don't see yet is the control I will have throughout the galaxy."

"Sir?" Simon chose his words from the minefield of possibilities running through his mind. "I don't doubt your ability. I just don't get the connection."

"And why should you?" Aven stood and strode to the side table to pour a bit of wine from the decanter. "You know all you need to know. Bring me the girl, and we'll go from there."

CHAPTER TWENTY-SIX

Bethany could feel Keturah come up behind her even as Manean strode fully into the room followed by more than two dozen R'hobans. They filled the space, crowding out memories of the past with the urgency of the present.

"Take your positions." At Manaen's command, half the troops spread out and disappeared throughout the underground facility. She turned her full attention toward Bethany. "I need to know more about the tunnel system." She stopped and glanced around, her brow furrowed. "Weren't there three of you here? Where's the other one."

Bethany looked about her, Keturah was present, but where was Elisheba? "She may have gone to the sleeping quarters."

At Manaen's nod, one of the soldiers took off in the direction Bethany indicated.

Keturah leaned close. "I saw her scuttle back out the door and continue down he passageway." She nodded.

"Wait." Bethany reached a hand to stop Manaen. "Keturah saw her go that way."

Manaen's look was grim as she spoke into a com unit on her wrist. "Horus, secure the south passages." She pressed the earpiece with her fingers and cocked her head. "I see." She pursed her lips and blew three sharp, short notes. The whistle pierced the air on an almost subsonic level. Immediately, the soldiers began to return.

With certainty, Bethany knew where Elisheba had gone. But was her goal escape or something else? She put a hand to her head. Everywhere she turned, more questions appeared without answers. Perhaps she wasn't meant to know everything at this point. She jerked her head up. And maybe she wasn't supposed to just sit around and wait for things to happen anymore. The One had brought her home for a reason, and by His Hand, she'd find out what it was. It seemed like just enduring wasn't going to be her calling after all.

The time had come to make a choice and take action. "What do you need from me?"

CHAPTER TWENTY-SEVEN

Japheth was already with the captain of the elite group of fighters Aven had assigned them when Simon arrived. They were studying the three-dimensional grid map of the area, projected into the air from a portable viewer.

"Captain Stolis, Overseer Simon." Japheth introduced Simon.

The captain turned, gave a gesture of respect, and nodded. "It's an honor, sir."

The deep scar running from the man's left eye into the corner of his mouth gave his expression a permanent scowl. It took everything Simon had not to stare. The mark was emphasized by what could only be a wad of racca in his cheek. That substance explained the odor emanating from the man. He must smoke the obnoxious weed as well as chew it. Simon squared his shoulders and focused on studying the map. Orienting himself to the landscape was simple—after all, this was his home as much as hers. "You're in too close, widen the view."

Captain Stolis nodded, turned his head, and spit a stream of racca juice as he adjusted the map viewer. Simon took a step to his left to avoid the odor. "Much better, deep into that hill." He pointed to the spot of a rockfall. The tunnel access is hidden there."

The captain studied the spot Simon had indicated. "How far will we have to dig to open the entrance?"

"Not far. The rocks are camouflage, nothing more." Even as he said it, his words echoed from the past. From the last time he'd showed a force of armed men how to infiltrate this compound. He'd made sure Bethany hadn't been there then. With this foray, she was the focus of the raid. He shook his head. "Are your men absolutely certain of their orders?"

"Yes, sir. The girl's not to be harmed, but taken." Stolis grinned, and the scar pulled his mouth into a grotesque parody of a smile. "Although we'll also be leaving a present for those meddling giants. One they won't soon forget."

"Whatever." The man was a pig. Simon kept his face neutral as he turned to Japheth. "Let's move out. The sooner we've got her, the better for everyone."

Josiah stood with Bezek on the observation deck, alternately scanning the sky and the ground. Which way would the attack come? With his limited troops, he'd have to take a gamble unless the enemy gave themselves away. He didn't have enough men to cover all the possibilities. He'd gambled once before…and lost.

"Commander, we're going to have to make a choice soon." Bezek continued to gaze at the horizon. "If we don't, we'll be caught reacting instead of anticipating."

Those words froze his gut. Was his indecision obvious to all his troops or only the ones who closest to him?

Bezek turned to meet his eyes. "You already know what we need to do. Trust your instincts. Make the call. It won't be wrong."

"All right." He looked into his second's confident face for a long moment. "Station the bulk of the troops to the south. They've been raining concussion rounds from the north, so they think we'll expect them from there."

Bezek's grin peeked through his beard. "On it."

The setting sun dipped behind the hillside as four of the soldiers with Simon and Japheth slipped toward the pile of rocks where the entrance lay. They made quick work of exposing the opening and scooted inside. Simon moved closer to study the stonework that arched around the opening. This tunnel had to have been built centuries ago, but he wasn't familiar enough with the history of Sintue to guess at its origins.

"All clear." Two of the soldiers returned to the mouth of the entrance. Their movements were those of experts, efficient and concise. "No sign anything or anyone has been moving inside for a while."

"How far till we reach the compound?" Japheth turned toward Simon.

It had been years since he'd actually been down the tunnel, but he could still recall the seemingly endless trek to the underground portion of Bethany's family compound. "It's quite a ways—at least two klicks."

Captain Stolis peered into the deepening gloom of the sky before turning to spit. "We'd best be about it then. Don't want to be all night getting the lady to her new quarters." He grinned and directed them to precede him into the dark opening.

Even though they all carried handlights, it took Simon's eyes a few moments before they adjusted to the inky black. He pushed past several soldiers in the tight passageway before he settled behind the two lead scouts. He'd be held responsible for the success or failure of this mission, and that meant he needed to be where he could affect the outcome.

He heard the footfalls approaching them just as the two scouts flattened against the walls, blending into the stonework. Whoever it was coming toward them made no attempt at silence.

The old woman's scream as she caught sight of Simon was cut off as one of the scouts grabbed her from behind. He lifted her off the ground as she squirmed to get away.

"Shut up, you fool." Simon put his face inches from hers as she froze, still dangling above the rocky floor of the tunnel. "You know who we are, right?"

She nodded.

Simon moved back and studied her. "You're Elisheba. I didn't realize you'd been reassigned here." He gestured for the soldier to release her. "Make your report and do it quietly."

"I just left her in the underground laboratories." Elisheba mopped her face with her sleeve. "They expect your attack, but from above. They only have a small force down here."

"Excellent." Simon pointed ahead. "Let's get on with this before they realize their mistake."

The trek through the tunnel took just under an hour before the darkness began to lessen. Before he could remark on the change, the soldiers in front had halted. They were close.

Now that they were still, he could hear the murmur of voices. He motioned to the men to stay put and crept ahead, hugging the rough wall. The tunnel sloped downward and turned to the right. As he inched along, the voices began to sort themselves out into individuals. The inflections were those of the R'hobans, and they *did* expect an attack after all.

Retracing his steps, Simon concocted and discarded several possible plans before coming up with one he believed would work. Captain Stolis had moved the men further down the way they'd come and was waiting when Simon returned. He explained how he wanted the captain to direct the soldiers as they rejoined the group.

"Seems pretty straightforward, if you ask me. But I agree, it gives us the highest chance of success." The captain directed a stream of racca juice just to the right of Simon's booted foot. "Assuming the girl is even down here."

She'd better be. Stolis and his men were obviously some of the best, otherwise Aven would never have sent them. But even the best would be no match for an entire company of R'hobans. Those monsters were just too big. Their best option was surprise. If they didn't catch them off guard, they'd not be able to succeed.

"Agreed." Japheth flashed a look at Simon. "We'll give you room to work, then come in for the girl."

CHAPTER TWENTY-EIGHT

Bethany could hear the battle long before it reached them. It hadn't occurred to her that the R'hobans would have trouble defeating the rebels. She'd been wrong. And she could feel the anguish in the tall woman beside her as one after another of the giants were cut down. The Sintuen fighters were well armed and much better trained than a ragtag group of rebels should be. Something wasn't right about their discipline and drive.

"Horus, report." Manean kept her head cocked, one ear obviously listening to battle reports. She caught Bethany's eye and waved her over. "This is more than just a random attack. Do you know what their goal could be?"

Bethany's heart pounded in her ears. The rebels must be aware of the lab, but the other? "There's no way they could know."

"Know? Know what?" Manean turned her full attention to Bethany. "This compound is critical because of the food production, but is there something else? Something you haven't told us?"

"They can't. But they must." Bethany looked around and grabbed Keturah by the hand. "There is truly only one thing of value down here, and we have to get it out of here. It mustn't fall into their hands."

"Hold on." Manaen's lips tightened, and she held up a hand as she once again listened to reports on her headset. "Whatever you need, we've got to get it and get out of here. We'll sort it out when we have you safely away."

Years of memories washed over Bethany, a tidal wave of images and corresponding emotions. A half-forgotten image of her father swam into view. She could hear an echo of his voice. *"If anything happens, it's all in the wall. If you can save the books, you'll have all you need. Remember, you have the key."* Why hadn't she trusted the R'hobans sooner?

"You have less than a minute to gather anything important. If it's this critical, we must not let it fall into their hands." Manaen once more reached for the com unit. "Fall back. Regroup in the underground tunnel. I'm gonna rig the door to blow. We cannot allow access to this facility."

"The notebooks." Bethany ran to her father's workroom. "I must have his notebooks."

Keturah and Manaen followed, stopping in the doorway as she quickly counted the stones from top to bottom on the nearest wall. "Over here." She dropped to her knees and began to work at a large stone at the base of the wall. "Do you have a knife? Or something I can pry this loose with?"

Without hesitation, Manaen handed her the knife from her belt. Bethany slid the blade between the stones, working it back and forth to loosen the stone. "It's coming." She let the knife fall and used both hands to work the stone completely out. Manaen pushed it aside as Bethany reached into the hollow it left. She withdrew six dusty notebooks and cradled them to her chest. A brief glance at the cover of the top one confirmed her father's handwriting.

"I hope this is all you need." Manaen half-pulled Bethany to her feet. "We're out of time."

He'd done it. Thank the One for guidance from above, he'd done it. Adrenalin coursed through Josiah's body as he watched his troops below routing the rag-tag group of rebels. He wanted to be there with his men, letting the release of battle relieve the tension in his body, instead of observing from here on the battlements.

Bezek grabbed his arm, almost dancing with excitement. "We've got them on the run now. I can give the order, and we'll follow them and finish them off."

He knew Bezek wanted this finished as much as he did, but he couldn't risk it. "We don't know how many more they have out of sight." He clapped his second on the back. "Be patient. We'll get them. The favor of the One is upon us."

Bethany looked around as Manaen pulled her out into the main room. Soldiers had attached large silver discs with blinking blue lights to the doorway into the tunnels. "You're only blowing the door, right? It won't destroy the lab will it? Just cut off access?"

"It shouldn't cause any damage that can't be repaired. Although it could take a while to get back inside." Manaen settled her helmet on her head, faceplate up, fastening it securely to her suit. "I sent someone for reinforcements. But we have to be prepared for any eventuality." She ushered them into the tunnel where one other soldier was waiting.

The sounds of battle reverberated through the dark tunnel, and the acrid odor of arms fire made Bethany's eyes water. They must be just out of sight, but it was difficult to tell as the twists and turns of the underground passageway distorted her perception. She clutched the notebooks to her chest. Perhaps she should have left them in place. But if they'd been discovered, the cost would have been too great.

An explosion rocked the tunnel, and Bethany stumbled and fell. It had to have been the door to the lab, unless the attackers had explosives. Immediately, the two R'hobans arranged themselves in front of Bethany and Keturah.

Manaen pushed her back down when she started to rise. "Stay quiet. I don't want them to know you're here."

Why would it matter if they knew she was here? Before she could form the question out loud, a blast erupted nearby and a shower of debris rained down on her head. She and Keturah ducked low as she heard Manaen and her comrade return fire.

The passageway, seconds before almost empty, now teemed with noise and combatants, and Bethany automatically extended her hands as Manaen swayed and went down on one knee. Bethany heard the warriors's exclamation of pain. Josiah's sister had been hit.

Without concern for her own safety, Bethany rushed to her, partially blocking the giant from further injury with her body.

"No!" Manaen grabbed Bethany's arm. "Go. Find Josiah. I'll keep the rebels from following you. You must be kept safe."

"Hush." Were all these giants so blind to their own mortality? She once again found herself exchanging looks with Keturah over another injured R'hoban.

"Cease fire!"

That had been Simon's voice, she was sure of it. But why would he be here? She stood, searching the now quiet tunnel for his familiar face. He was there, striding through the rebels.

He reached her and put an arm protectively around her shoulders. "Thank the One you're safe."

She jerked away from him. What game was he playing now? "Why are you here?"

"You don't need to be afraid." He moved closer, pinning her between his body and the fallen R'hoban on the ground. Keturah hovered protectively over Manaen. "I'm going to get you out.

Elisheba told me you were here." He glanced at the notebooks in her arms. "Are these your father's notes?" His eyes almost glittered with avarice.

What had she been thinking? As more of his troops came toward them, she put a hand out. It was too late to hide the notebooks, but perhaps she could salvage something from this. "Wait. If I come with you, will you leave?"

"Of course. You're the reason we came."

The reason? They came for her?

"I'll go with you if you promise she won't be harmed further." She pointed at Manaen. "And Keturah can stay with her."

She watched Simon exchange a look with another man, who nodded assent. "If that's what you want…" He sighed. "I'd have thought you'd be ready to be rid of these marauders permanently."

She couldn't allow herself to be drawn into a long conversation. If there were reinforcements coming, she had no way of knowing if they'd fare any better against this team. "Okay, but tell your men to move back. You and I can follow."

Simon once again put an arm around her, and it took everything she had not to pull away. "Of course. Stay close, and I'll see you safely out." The other man barked an order, and the rebels melted back into the tunnel.

"Commander, quickly. They've accessed the tunnels." One of the men he'd left with Manaen burst onto the observation deck.

Josiah didn't hesitate. "Bezek, send two squads after us." And then he was off at a dead run. He wasted no time confirming that his second had obeyed. He had to reach Manaen and Bethany. He couldn't separate his emotions about them so he lumped them together, repeating the words in his head. She would be fine…she would be fine…the cadence of the words echoed his footfalls as he sped downward, toward the tunnels and—and what? No, he wouldn't think about it. She would be fine.

He was through the entrance to the tunnel and reached up to snap on the light attached to his helmet and discovered he'd left it behind. He paused for only an instant to grab the handlight from his belt. His men behind him raced behind him, their boots ringing on the stones. Below, only an eerie quiet. He slowed to a fast walk, but still the cadence of hope rang in his heart. She would be fine.

He navigated the tunnel with ease, rounding the last corner in time to catch only a glimpse of Bethany escaping with the rebels. His mind balked as he processed the scene before him. Manaen lay on the floor of the tunnel with Keturah bent over her. Bethany, leaving by choice with another Sintuen. His heart ripped as he made his choice.

He dropped to his knees beside his sister. "Manaen, speak to me."

"She's hanging on." Keturah put a hand on his arm when he made as if to lift her. "Get the healer before you move her. She's gravely wounded, and I fear more injury if she's lifted without being checked first."

He rose as Bezek ran into view. "Gehazi's close behind me." He slid to a stop. "Is she…"

"No." His answer came with more force than he intended, but what did it matter? "She lives. Take a squad and secure the tunnel from here. They're just ahead of us."

"The Seeker?" Bezek's voice was neutral.

"She left Manaen here to die and made her escape with the rebels." He nailed Bezek with a stare. "Bring her to me."

"But…you don't know—" Keturah drew a sharp breath at the look he turned on her.

"Silence." He looked back at his second. "Do it. Now."

He heard rather than saw Bezek's gesture of salute because his attention was once again on Manaen. Her helmet still covered her head, but the faceplate was open. Except for a thin trickle of blood darkening one corner of her mouth, she could have been asleep. He leaned close to her face. "Stay with me. Our time here is not yet done. You have much to do as we finish what the One has commanded."

He was still crooning softly to her when Gehazi sunk to the stones beside him. "Move, Commander. There is still work to be done, and this is mine."

PART TWO—CAPTIVITY

CHAPTER TWENTY-NINE

They emerged from the tunnel into a dark landscape, but Bethany knew in an instant where they were. The scents had a different twist. The odor of green things growing no longer dominated but played a subtler melody. Instead, the night smells were overlaid by a cacophony of dust and dying vegetation. Even that called to her as home.

In spite of the familiarity, her jumbled thoughts raced as fast as her heart. Would Josiah get to Manaen in time? She drew a deep breath, trying to steady her rocking world. Most importantly, where was Simon taking her, and how could she protect her father's work? Why hadn't she remembered that Simon knew about the tunnels? There was something more going on here than she could grasp, and she had been flung into its center.

"We'll split up now." A scar-faced man spit a stream of racca juice, barely missing her booted foot as he spoke to Simon. "I'll send three groups in separate directions. You stick with me and cut back to camp when we're sure they're no longer following."

"Be quick about it, Stolis." Even in the dim light, she could see Simon's frown. Most details eluded her in the intermittent moonlight as it played a game of tag with the gathering clouds. "I saw the Commander round the corner as we ducked out of sight. They'll be close on our heels."

Josiah had seen them? Would he come for her? A trickle of ice spread through her veins. What must he think? Surely Manaen could make him understand her decision to go with Simon…if she lived.

"Bethany." Simon touched her arm. He'd obviously tried to get her attention earlier. "Can I carry some of those for you?"

"No." She pulled them closer to her chest as he reached for the notebooks. "I've got them…uh…they're not heavy."

He raised an eyebrow but made no further move to take them.

"Let's head out." Stolis returned and motioned them forward as groups of men melted into the night.

Gehazi stepped back from the still unconscious Manaen and turned to the men ready with the medical lift. "Raise her carefully."

Josiah had taken a position where he could watch but not interfere as Gehazi and Keturah worked on his sister. At least one of the Seekers had proved trustworthy. Another piece of his heart turned to ice, but he willed himself to focus on duty.

The men loaded Manaen's motionless body on the lift, and Gehazi activated the air-cushion and lightly touched the controls used to guide it. He followed it through the dark passageway, the odors of battle and blood clinging to the walls and to him.

Gehazi looked at the Seeker beside her. "Accompany me to the infirmary. Your assistance has proved invaluable."

Keturah looked over her shoulder at him, and Josiah knew she wanted an opportunity to speak. Not yet. He could bear no more lies. The image of his sister laying in a puddle of her own blood would be forever linked with betrayal. A still-life illustrating the consequences of following his heart.

Simon positioned himself between Bethany and Stolis. He didn't like the way the man eyed her slender frame. He couldn't blame him. During the weeks she'd been with the R'hobans, her auburn hair had begun to grow out, and her cheeks had lost the gaunt thinness that characterized those who labored in the worker blocks below ground. The knowledge that Aven would soon have access to her remained as troublesome to his mind as a rock in his boot.

"Where are we going?" It was the first time Bethany had spoken except in response to a question. Her tone had a different flavor from the one he'd become accustomed to as her supervisor.

But before Simon could answer, Japheth insinuated himself between them. "We're returning to the staging area." He shot Simon a look before inclining his head slightly to Bethany. "I'm Japheth."

Bethany frowned. "Staging area?"

Japheth leaned toward her. "Our resistance is much more organized than you realize."

Simon dodged to Bethany's free side and cleared his throat. Japheth would need to know Bethany belonged to him, but now wasn't the time. "It was important to get you out of there before things progress any further."

"Is that concern for me or because of what I have access to?" Her frown was gone, replaced by an expression he couldn't quite identify. Regret, perhaps?

"A lady of your credentials would always be a welcome ally," Japheth said.

What was going on with Japheth? Simon had never seen him make the least effort to ingratiate himself with anyone. Now, he practically oozed goodwill toward Bethany.

"I know you may not have thought you came with us on your own accord." Japheth grabbed her elbow as her boot toe caught on a rocky outcropping, invisible in the unreliable moonlight. "But we both know the ways of the One aren't always easily discernable."

Simon had to give him credit. Bringing in Bethany's beliefs would be the fastest way to win her cooperation. Why hadn't he thought of it?

"Stop. Make plain your purpose." The barrel of a laser rifle, glinting in the moon's intermittent glow, led Bethany's eyes to the sentry who had issued the challenge. She didn't recognize his dark uniform, what little she could make out. And the combination of hood and helmet he wore on his head made his camouflage a success.

Japheth let go of her elbow and walked forward. He only nodded once at the guard, who seemed to recognize him instantly.

The sentry hit his chest in a gesture of respect and inclined his head at both Japheth and Simon. "I'm to take you directly to the Overseer's tent on your arrival."

An Overseer? Bethany knew the term, what Seeker didn't? Her knees went rubbery, but she forced herself to continue at the pace her captors set. Had the One truly abandoned her to this den of darkness?

The ornate tent, surrounded by guards outfitted in the same dark uniforms, announced their arrival at the Overseer's tent. She could almost smell the evil carried on the aroma of spicy incense when the tent flap opened. How could these Sintuens not see the danger in their midst?

Ushering her inside, Simon kept his hand at her back. For once, it didn't make her skin crawl.

"We're glad you could join us." The speaker sat in an ornate chair, his dark eyes cold in spite of the smile that decorated his lips.

This had to be the Overseer. "And you've brought the information I sought." He nodded at her and the bundle in her arms.

Fear raced from her gut to the back of her throat where it congealed into a mass she couldn't swallow. Why hadn't she left the notebooks hidden? Now, it would be up to her to keep their contents safe…somehow. No wait, what had Casaphia taught her? In the One, she had weapons, with armor to match. In the Book of Truth, the trainer had showed them where the One warned of spiritual battles. The Book promised He never abandoned those who were His.

Small comfort now.

If the One had chosen her for this battle He'd better show up soon.

CHAPTER THIRTY

Josiah paced outside the quarters that held his sister. Although he could hear the muffled sounds of conversation, it gave him no clue to her condition.

"Is everything secure?" He stopped pacing as Bezek appeared.

"Yes, Sir." Bezek's eyes locked on the closed door. "Any word?"

"Nothing." Josiah sank into a cushioned chair. He wanted to add words of comfort to this man who also loved Manaen and be the Commander, but here he was, reduced to a worried brother with no encouragement to spare. The best thing for them both was to get their minds back on the work at hand. "Give me the details you have now."

Bezek sighed and slumped into a nearby chair. "From what I've been able to surmise so far, the main attack had a two-fold purpose. First, they wanted to test our defenses, and second, it was cover for the covert attack."

"As I thought." Josiah ran a hand through his hair. "And I fell for it."

"Truthfully, I don't see how you could have foreseen this." Bezek pulled at his beard and squinted. "We hadn't had the opportunity to explore the extent of the tunnels before the attack began."

"We'd have had the time...if she had given us the information we needed." Josiah refused to speak the little traitor's name out loud. He rose and started pacing again. "And now we know why she didn't."

"I'll admit it looks bad." Bezek shook his head.

"Looks bad?" Josiah stopped, hammering his second with a stare. "Don't you dare attempt to defend her to me."

Bezek held up a hand. "All I'm saying is that if she hadn't led us to the tunnels we'd probably be overrun by rebels even now."

Josiah snorted. "She didn't *lead* us there. We followed her and discovered the laboratory. And she did a pretty fine job of getting us back out long enough to take off permanently." His muscles vibrated as he fought for control. All he wanted was to grind all Sintuens into submission. He drew a shaky breath. He still had a job to do. It wasn't his place to condemn an entire race. Only the One had that authority. "Speaking of the lab, is it still intact?"

"Yes. No more than minor damage to the interior, although the entrance had to be cleared." He paused. "Inside, we found something suspicious."

"What?"

"In the office there were several stones laying on the floor, leaving an empty cavity in the wall."

Josiah groaned. "Are you certain they weren't knocked loose by the explosion?"

"Nothing else in the room had been damaged. Or even moved. All the items on the desk were undisturbed." He glanced at the still closed door of the sickroom. "But I can't say for sure."

"And we won't know until we can speak with Manaen." He buried his face in his hands. If they ever would be able to talk to her again.

"Take a seat, my dear." Aven indicated another, less ornate chair not far from his own. Bethany didn't want to come close enough to sit, but the adrenalin in her system had long worn off. Beyond that, she needed to rest, and the other chairs were filled. She compromised and perched on the edge of the proffered seat, even as the soft cushions tempted her to relax into its comfortable recesses.

"We want to give you a chance to get to know us." He gestured around the room with an open hand and nodded at the woman across from him.

Even though his words had been nothing but courteous and welcoming, she found herself glad Simon had taken a position behind her, standing almost close enough to put his hands on her shoulders. What a strange turn of events.

"Absolutely." The woman bobbed her head, causing the mass of dark curls to shift and catch the light of the fire. They gleamed almost red in spots. "I'm Delaina, of course." She pointed to the older man to her left. "And this is Baanus."

"Humph," came the only reply. He reminded Bethany of a stubborn hesit, all stiff-necked and spikey.

Delaina gave a musical giggle. "Don't mind him, he's the grump of the group."

"And if he's the grump, how would you categorize me?" An ancient crone to the right of Delaina cocked her head.

"Hmm." Delaina put a well-cared-for finger to her chin. "I always think of you as the voice of reason."

Bethany gaped at the old woman as she began gasping and croaking. Was she choking? No, her thin lips had parted and tilted, proving the rasping cackle erupting from her dark-robed form was one of amusement. Bethany glanced about the room. No one else had reacted to the sound, so perhaps it was normal?

"I'm Salisa." The old woman's eyes shifted toward Aven. "And I'm the ancient one of the group."

There were polite chuckles from those in the room, but Bethany didn't see the joke. She rubbed her temple where an ache had begun. It was too much to take in and decipher.

"You've met Japheth, of course." Delaina waved a perfect hand in his direction. "And you and Simon are old friends."

The cozy tone Delaina had taken belied the dark undercurrents that swirled around the tent, leaving Bethany's mind whirling in a jumble of thoughts that refused to coalesce into clarity. She shifted the books in her arms before realizing it. Aven's eyes were on her in an instant.

"I know you must be exhausted. We will see to your comfort." Again, his concerned tone failed to match the menace in his eyes.

"No, I'm fine. Really." She straightened her back to ease the ache.

"Of course you are. Anyone who could survive the clutches of those monsters is much more than fine." He turned and nodded at Japheth. "But you're among friends now. We only want to help you recover from your ordeal."

Japheth reached down to take the books from her arms.

"No!" She clutched them tighter. "I'd like to keep these with me."

Aven pointed a finger at her. "That would not be best for you."

"Let me." Japheth gently pried them from her grasp.

The tears blinded her eyes, but she didn't have the strength to fight as the last precious part of her father left her grasp.

"They'll be safe with me."

She swiped at her eyes and focused on Japheth but he gave no indication he'd spoken the words or even heard them. No one else seemed to notice either. Had they been audible or only in her mind?

Delaina rose and and touched her shoulder. "I know you're beyond exhausted. Let me show you where we'll be staying."

We'll be staying? Bethany gave a mental sigh as she rose to follow Delaina out. Would she forever be under the supervision of another?

CHAPTER THIRTY-ONE

Simon watched as Delaina led Bethany from their meeting tent. He tried to analyze the mix of emotions running through his veins. Why wasn't he more thrilled with the outcome of the night's work? Turning, he caught sight of Aven watching him, hands steepled, fingers resting on his chin. That was the foundation of his distress. *He* didn't have her—Aven did.

"We have much to discuss," Aven told them, clapping his hands together. "Simon, since you're up, why don't you pass around some refreshment."

Being cast in the role of servant suited him fine. It gave him time to compose his thoughts. He poured the rare and expensive Siung wine and handed the delicate goblets to each one left in the tent. First to Aven, then to the others, wondering as he did where Aven obtained an almost endless supply.

Salisa wrinkled her nose at the offering. "I suppose this will do if you don't have anything better to offer."

Aven just chucked at her comments while Baanus shook his head. "Only you could complain about a delicacy so prized throughout the galaxy."

Simon let their familiar banter drift around him as he poured himself a glass and took a seat.

"Have you completed your task as well as Simon?" Aven directed his question to Salisa.

She raised her head and fixed him with rheumy eyes. "Is there any doubt?"

"Oh, come off it." Baanus glared at her. "You're no more infallible than the rest of us."

"Does that mean *your* assignment isn't finished?" Aven turned his attention to Baanus, whose face reddened.

"It's not." He looked away from Aven. "But it will be. Soon."

"I see." Aven let the silence stretch before he turned his attention back to Salisa. "Let's begin with your report then."

Following the tiny woman, Bethany stepped into the warm night air and took a moment to gaze at the stars. How she'd taken those for granted while growing up. Well, never again. She looked around, searching for landmarks, but the camp was completely dark, no fires or anything that would give away their position visually. But how did they hide from sophisticated scanners? Definitely a well-planned and well-equipped force. What did this mean for the R'hobans?

"This way, my dear." Delaina motioned for Bethany to follow. Two guards trailed behind at a respectful distance. "We're pleased Simon was able to get you out." Delaina broke the silence as they continued through the camp.

What was she supposed to say to that? Thank you? Bethany didn't feel thankful. She felt…what? Trapped, stalked, cornered? Any of those would do.

"I know a lot has happened, but we want you to know we're so happy you're with us."

Bethany only half-heard Delaina's comments. The camp was too fascinating. As they walked to the quarters they'd share, the odd shapes resolved into tents, and snatches of low conversations floated around her. She smelled the smoke from fires but didn't see a single telltale glow "How do you do it?" At Delaina's puzzled look, she continued. "Keep the tents so dark. And I smell fires, but I don't see them."

"The outside of every tent is lined with a composite sheet of talarium. It prevents any light from escaping and has the added benefit of protecting us from sensors."

"I see." It explained several things but left many more questions.

Delaina stopped and turned to face Bethany square on. "You must understand. Ours isn't a thrown-together force or a ragtag band of patriots fighting a last stand. This has been planned down to the tiniest detail. We've had help from many different places to put this into action."

"Help?" Bethany could only grasp the edges of the idea Delaina presented. "From who?"

"Many beyond our world." Delaina waved a hand at the sky. "But our goal has united us. To see the R'hobans stopped. Here. On Sintue."

Bethany's mind raced, but she only gave a quick nod.

"Here we go." Delaina halted outside a large tent with two sentries posted at the entrance. "It's primitive, but we must make sacrifices during war time."

Bethany followed her in and tried not to gasp at the opulence before her. The glow of a single lamp in the corner should have given the space a calming ambiance. Instead, it threw looming shadows on the tent walls draped in striped silk. That the tent belonged to a woman couldn't be argued. The furnishings were soft and frilled, decorated with ribbons and braid. The palette of muted colors, gold, mauve, and pale blue were everywhere. It was a direct representation of the woman called Delaina. Even her scent lingered here. Sweet with undertones of musk.

Delaina walked to a large trunk near one of the cots—hard to call it a cot as it was piled high with soft blankets and inviting pillows. "Here are some night things." She laid a froth of white fabric on the bed. "This is my extra trunk. You're welcome to anything you need." Delaina laughed and pointed to herself. "Anything that will fit that is."

Bethany smiled. She did get a sense of what the R'hobans must feel around those of her race. She stood a full head taller than Delaina. "Thank you. I'll be fine, I'm sure."

"All right, I know you're so ready to rest. I'll leave you for a bit." Delaina grimaced. "More meetings, you understand. I won't disturb you when I return."

"Commander? Commander, wake up."

A gentle touch on Josiah's shoulder brought him awake in an instant, although it took a moment longer to place his location. He'd fallen asleep in the sitting area beyond his sister's sick room. He bolted to his feet, glaring around the room until his eyes met Gehazi's gentle smile. "Manaen?"

"She appears to have turned the corner toward wellness. But time will give us a better picture of what's to come." Gehazi cocked her head at him and then nodded at the softly snoring Bezek who still occupied the other chair. "Wellness is something you'll both lose if you don't get some sleep."

"But—"

"No arguments." She shook her head. "I'll not have the two of you for patients if I can help it." She turned back toward her patient's quarters. "I better not find you here when I return again."

As the door closed softly behind her, he strode across the room and shook his second. "Up man. We've been given orders for bed."

"Huh...what?" Bezek focused on Josiah and jumped to his feet, catching his belt on the chair arm and almost upsetting the chair in the process. "Manaen? How is she?"

Josiah laughed at his predicament. "Gehazi assures me she's turned the corner toward wellness."

"Why can't that woman talk straight?"

"It's the best we'll get tonight, I'm afraid." Josiah motioned to the doorway with his head. "We're under orders to seek our beds and sleep before we're allowed back."

Bezek finally freed himself from the chair and stood, glancing at the window. "Doesn't look like we'll have much time. Morning's gaining on us."

Josiah followed his gaze. "True. But I think we're going to need this bit of sleep before seeing what the day brings. Something tells me there'll be very little good news for either of us."

"You were right, of course." Salisa gave a nod of respect to Aven. "Our allies have an agenda outside the one they agreed to."

Simon fought the urge to lean forward in his chair. Finally, some information about what they were doing here.

"It seems their ultimate goal is one of revision and redefinition for their own people." Salisa narrowed her eyes. "And total annihilation for us."

"That was not part of the bargain!" Baanus jumped to his feet and began pacing. When he reached Salisa's chair, he turned on her. "How do you come by your information? I demand to know its credence."

Salisa put a boney finger on his chest and pushed him away with little visible effort. Where did she get the strength to do that? "Be careful who you threaten, young man." Her voice rasped into almost inaudible tones as her eyes seemed to flash sparks. "Do you dare to question me?"

Simon darted a quick glance at Aven. The man sat back, a slight smile on his face, as if he were enjoying the exchange.

"I meant no disrespect." Baanus resumed his seat, his face still not happy.

"I should think not." Salisa continued to glare at him before returning to her report. "As I was saying, their goal is our population's total annihilation."

"You say population." Simon spoke before he thought, and felt the flush creep up his neck. At Aven's nod he continued. "What are their plans for our planet?"

"Very good." Aven's smiled widened, and even Salisa gave a toothy grin.

She turned to Aven. "You were right, this one has a quick mind that sees straight to the heart of the matter."

Baanus snorted, and Aven moved his attention to Baanus. "Did you have something you wanted to add?"

"No." Baanus folded his arms.

"To answer your question," Salisa continued, nodding in Simon's direction. "They intend it for their own use. Without any Sintuens to contaminate their bloodline."

"Who is worried about their bloodline being contaminated?" Delaina stepped into the tent and walked over to pour herself a glass of wine.

Aven allowed her time to take a seat. "Is our guest settled comfortably?"

"She should be." Delaina gave a little huff. "I offered her free run of one of my trunks."

"Very generous of you. We want her to feel right at home." Aven motioned to Salisa. "We were just receiving the report on what some of our allies have planned for us."

"And their plans are?" Delaina tucked one foot underneath her.

"We're to be completely eliminated, it seems." Baanus lumbered to his feet and over to the table to pour more wine into his goblet. "It appears the authority of this statement is unassailable."

Although the man grated on every nerve in Simon's body, he had a point. Where had Salisa gotten her information?

"Oh, Salisa. Quit teasing the poor man." Delaina glanced at Simon. "I imagine Simon is just as in the dark as Baanus about how you get your intel."

Salisa actually giggled at this, a horrid squeaking sound that bubbled up from somewhere deep inside the woman. "Very well. I'll let them in on my secret."

"Yes, my dear, enlighten them." Aven's tone remained cordial, but an undercurrent of something Simon couldn't identify caused Salisa to look at him, eyes wide. "No, I insist. It's time we were all on the same page."

"What do you mean I can't talk to her?" Josiah worked to keep his voice low as he paced in front of his sister's sickroom. The antiseptic smells leaking into the sitting room reinforced the urgency racing through his veins. His last glimpse of Manaen had haunted a morning filled with the daunting task of examining where he'd gone wrong.

"I only mean what I say, Commander." Gehazi took a seat on the bench, and patted the spot beside her. "She needs time to allow her body to heal. She was gravely wounded. Even with our extraordinary healing capacity, it's better for her to have complete rest." She held up a hand when he would have interrupted. "And to that end, I've kept her in a deep sleep. She couldn't talk to you even if I let you in."

"I know she needs time to heal. But I have to ascertain how those rebels were able to defeat her squad." He blew out a breath.

"You know how important this information is for my report to the council of Elders—why I must have it sooner rather than later." This tirade about needing his sister's input was nothing more than a cover for the real reason he wanted to see her. He knew it and so did Gehazi. He needed to assure himself she was still here.

"We each have our priorities Commander." She rose and patted him on the shoulder, a familiarity few would attempt. "The answers you seek are available elsewhere. Of that, I'm certain." She shook her head at his glower. "Make your appointment with the council of Elders. You've nothing to report that should shame you."

He began to pace again. "Perhaps not, but there is much to consider in the way this liberation has gone."

"True, but the fault does not lie with you." Cocking an eyebrow, she watched him. "Neither with this liberation or the one that came before." With that, she rose and glided past him to disappear once again into Manaen's room.

Did everyone know his history of failure? Had there been a message tube sent out with a catalogue of the mistakes that even now haunted him with doubts and hesitation?

"Commander, you're needed. The reinforcements are arriving." The young warrior skidded to a stop inside the room, and backed away a step. "I...uh...didn't mean to interrupt."

"Don't be a fool. Does it look like I'm doing anything?" For a moment, Josiah let the full force of his emotions target the man. Then he held up a hand. "Never mind. You've done nothing wrong. I'll be down shortly."

The warrior saluted and turned to leave.

"Wait." Josiah stopped him. "I'll walk with you. Remind me of your name."

"I'm Calamus, Commander." He stood tall and straight in spite of his boyish face topped by blond curls so bright they were almost white. "I was assigned by your second, Bezek, less than a week past."

That explained his unfamiliarity with the warrior's name, but not why his face was familiar. The warriors he led got younger with each passing year.

Josiah gestured the man to precede him into the corridor. "How long have you been away from Majesty?"

"Less than one cycle, sir." The boy blushed like a girl but continued. Who had approved this youngling for the special guard? "My father is…was…Kanah," Calamus answered without being asked.

Now Josiah understood. He missed the wisdom Kanah shared. He'd had an almost eerie sense of what a man was thinking. His estimation of Calamus inched upward. "Your sire was a great warrior. I miss him much, even now."

Calamus stopped and turned full on toward him. "I've proved myself, sir. And while I take pride in my line, this position is my own."

Josiah clapped the man on the shoulder. "Well spoken. I meant no disrespect. All in this unit get here on their own merit, not that of others." As they continued down, Josiah found his anger had dissipated, leaving in its wake a sense of peace. He would not fail his warriors, and they would not fail him. Together, they'd complete the daunting task set before them.

CHAPTER THIRTY-TWO

Simon picked up the tray of food for Bethany from Aven's personal chef. The aromas of freshly baked bread, perfectly browned sausage, and fruit made his mouth water. He'd insisted there be enough for two. He hoped Delaina had already left the tent so he could enjoy the meal with Bethany. If not, it would at least be a goodwill offering for Delaina.

The sentry outside the womens' tent saluted then pulled open the flap to allow entry.

"Breakfast for two charming ladies." Simon set the tray on a low table in front of Bethany and Delaina. He'd obviously interrupted a conversation, and Bethany didn't look pleased.

"Aren't you a dear." Delaina clapped her hands. "I can tell it's from Aven's cook, too." She frowned and rose. "But I have a meeting, and I'm already late."

"I hate you can't stay." He did his best to appear disappointed.

"I just bet you do." Delaina looked at him through lidded eyes. "But you will keep sweet Bethany company, won't you?"

"Of course." He turned to walk Delaina to the entrance of the tent and tried to hide his smile. He'd caught Bethany's grimace at Delaina's comment.

"So you're to be my guard for the morning?" Bethany sat on the low bench with her arms folded.

"No. I'm not your guard." He busied himself with removing lids from the tray of food and handed her a bundle of silverware. It was going to take some time to break through her defenses. But he would. He hadn't failed yet at anything he put his mind to. "Eat. The food is excellent." He smiled as he began serving himself a plate of food.

Josiah strode into the command center. Stopping just in the doorway, he surveyed the activity inside as they continued to analyze the events of yesterday. His elite team of fighters also contained those with multiple disciplines. Beyond their master warrior status, some were leading experts in ecobiology, cryptology, and digital technology. He caught Bezek's eye and motioned him into the inner office.

"Do we know anything new?" Josiah asked as he took a seat behind his desk.

"Not really." Bezek shook his head and pulled up a chair to the other side of the desk. "But I'm noticing some mighty big holes in the preliminary reports we were sent."

Trust Bezek to hit at the heart of the matter. All the issues he'd had with this liberation could be traced back to missing information. Not tiny details, but huge, gaping holes. "So it would seem." He tapped the flashing message light on his plasscreen and squinted at its contents. "And it seems we've been summoned to a council of Elders."

Bezek sighed. "It's not like we didn't know that was coming."

"True. But what do we actually have to report?" He leaned back in his chair. "Except failure."

"I'm not thinking the Elders will see it that way." Bezek pulled at his beard. "I'm almost certain our enemies may have overplayed their hand. There's just too much here that can't be explained except by a faulty or altered preliminary report."

Could it be true? He began to tick off the events of this liberation in his mind. The tunnels, the almost complete annihilation of the Seekers before they arrived, the condition of the planet's ecosystem, the organized resistance. He looked up to find Bezek watching him intently. "You're right. It all adds up."

"What I'm curious about is how the Council will react."

"Yes, that will be interesting." Josiah smiled. "But the thing that will be even more intriguing will be watching how *certain* members of the Council respond to our report."

Bezek returned his smile with a grin. "So you've come to believe Manaen was right? About the traitor among our people? You see that there has to be at least one Elder involved."

At the mention of his sister, his own smile drained away, washed out of existence by tears he would never shed. She was even now fighting for her life because of a traitorous faction. If only he'd been willing to look at what she had seen so clearly. He could hear the echo of her voice in his mind. *There are many things you don't understand, big brother. And I fear the One is about to make them known.*

"You know she's going to be good as new." Bezek had obviously read at least the direction of Josiah's thoughts from the expression on his face.

"Of course she is." He managed a hint of a smile. "Gehazi would have it no other way."

Bezek gave him a sharp look then continued on in a different vein. "What I want to know now is your plan. Do we lead off with the knowledge of traitors in our midst?"

"No." Josiah folded his arms, gathering his thoughts. "No, we go in soft. Present the report and watch the reactions."

"Any particular members we're concentrating on?" Bezek's mild tone didn't fool anyone.

"Oh, yes." This time, the wolf-like grin came easy. "I'll be focused Elder Mahalah."

Bethany sat back from her plate. The food had been extraordinary. But then again, Aven hadn't struck her as one who skimped when it came to pleasing himself. What a change the past few weeks had made. She could almost forget the nearly constant hunger pains that punctuated her days and tormented her sleep.

"Did you get enough?" Simon picked up the carafe of juice and motioned toward her goblet.

She covered the goblet with her hand. "Yes, thank you." This third reincarnation of Simon puzzled her. Where did the real man lie? Was he a mix of all three, or were there yet others to come? Might as well begin to find out. "What exactly is planned for me here?"

Simon took his time answering. Surprising, because he'd always seemed to have a ready answer in every situation. "First, I wanted you away from those monsters. I couldn't bear to think of what they were doing to you."

He appeared sincere, but she'd long ago learned not to trust appearances. "They weren't *doing* anything to me. We've misjudged them. They're here to help our poor planet." She looked him full in the face. "And they believe as I do."

"You've been brainwashed." He shot to his feet and began to pace. "Their one goal is to destroy us all and take the planet for their own."

Bethany thought back to the way she and Keturah had been treated. The respect and care was genuine, of that she had no doubt. No, these people might be termed monsters by those who didn't know them. To her, they were the answer to an unvoiced prayer. "Simon, it doesn't matter how much you carry on, the truth is still the truth."

Simon turned and smiled, a ghostly reminder from the childhood summers they'd spent together. "I remember you telling me that years ago." He motioned outside. "Not far from this very place."

She returned his with a sad smile of her own. "And it's still true."

Japheth entered the tent, brushing dust from his jacket. "What's this?"

"Nothing important," Simon said. "Is it time?"

"For what?" Bethany could feel her stomach tighten and began to wonder if a large breakfast had been such a good idea.

Japheth glanced at Simon. "You didn't tell her?"

Simon shook his head. "We got sidetracked."

"Is there something I need to know?" She rose and joined them. They probably wouldn't tell her, but she was tired of letting others dictate what happened.

"We're taking you back to our headquarters. There's a lab set up, ready for you to begin working," Japheth said.

A knife-like pain stabbed her heart, and she turned to Simon. "You…you knew this? My purpose for being here is because of my father, isn't it?"

"It's not the only reason." His face was back to an unreadable mask. "I just hadn't had a chance to tell you yet."

She turned away, about to gather her things, when she realized that once again, she had nothing to call her own.

"You'll not be harmed." Simon was behind her and put his hand on her shoulder.

She resisted the urge to jerk away and instead, faced him. "I've already been harmed."

Japheth cleared his throat. "Did you find nothing of our lovely Delaina's you liked?"

Glad to focus on something else, she gestured toward the trunk Delaina had offered. "I greatly appreciated her generosity, but as you can see, I'm not so dainty as she." Bethany pointed to the soft tunic, leggings and short boots she wore. "I'm quite comfortable in these."

"You look lovely." Japheth smiled and motioned for her to precede him out of the tent. "And I'm sure we'll have things more suited to your stature once we reach headquarters."

She looked at him sharply. The word carried several meanings, and his tone had left his meaning unclear.

CHAPTER THIRTY-THREE

Josiah once again piloted his personal shuttle into the hanger of the admin ship, this time not at the summons of one Elder, but to make his report to the Council of Elders. He was fairly certain it wouldn't be the entire Council of twenty-five, but only a quorum. That could tip things either way, depending on who was present.

He negotiated the delicate process of docking by rote, and soon, they were out of the shuttle and striding to the Council Chamber. "Are you ready?" he asked Bezek under his breath.

"No doubt." Bezek's normally jolly face held an expression of determination until he winked. "I'm wearing several types of armor this day."

"Me as well." Good to know his second's outlook mirrored his own. The confidence of being in the middle of the One's plans suffused his entire attitude.

"Commander." The sentry, a young man they'd both known during training, stood at the door of the Council chambers and saluted as they approached. "They're waiting for you."

"How many, Phichol?" Bezek pulled at the collar of his dress uniform.

"Twenty-one, sir." Phichol lowered his voice. "Been a long time since we've seen a gathering of this magnitude. If you ask me, something's got them stirred up."

"And no one asked you." A Council assistant stepped through the doors and glared at the sentry, who reddened. "Gentlemen, you may follow me and leave your firearms in the anti-room."

When the assistant turned, Josiah saw Bezek give the sentry a slow wink and smiled to himself. Bezek was indeed a good man to have at his back.

Once inside, Josiah handed his accelerator pistol to another attendant, bothered by the thought he should have a backup weapon hidden somewhere. Where had that sacrilege come from? These men were chosen by the One and spoke with His voice here. To consider of violence in their presence was unthinkable. But then again, so was the fact that one of them had to be a traitor.

Josiah strode into the Council chamber, grateful for the sentry's warning. It had been years since he'd seen so many Elders in one place. This gathering could also be dangerous. This planet had offered more questions than answers, and that alone made it a less than secure place for a meeting like this. He felt the hair rise on the back of his neck. It would be the perfect opportunity for a coup or even something worse. All this rushed through his mind as he took a knee before the honored assembly.

"Rise Commander." It was Elder Reuel who had spoken. As he rose, Josiah glanced around the circle of seated Elders, each behind a small desk fitted with a plasscreen. Yes, Elder Reuel was the senior most Elder present and as such, would act as the Presiding Elder. He found himself assessing the individuals as men. Friend or foe? Reuel nodded to two ornate chairs set facing the Council. "Be seated gentlemen. We have much to discuss."

Another surprise. "My thanks, your grace." Those reporting to the council were rarely provided seats. This would prove to be a long day.

"We've all seen the preliminary report you sent today." He glanced down at the plasscreen in front of him. "It appears to raise more questions than answers. We'd prefer to hear the assessment from you directly."

Let me feel Your Strength. Give me the clarity I need for this battle. His unvoiced prayer to the One slowed his heart rate, and he rose. The Elders would have all studied what he sent before they landed on the planet. The intelligence briefs were a key factor in the timing of any liberation. So he only touched on the contents of those, to make certain they'd actually had what he'd been sent.

He enumerated the events as they'd occurred, not deviating from the timeline or minimizing the things he thought of as his own failures. He shared the citizenry response to the initial wave of liberators. That had been the one normal thing in this entire mess. The small pockets of resistance had been quickly thrown together and overcome in minutes. Although the R'hobans learned of the existence of the tunnels during the first few hours, the second liberation wave was where the true battles began. As he spoke, he tried to gauge the reactions of those seated before him. He noted those who took detailed notes and which ones just watched, fingers steepled.

After more than two hours, he finished and returned to his seat. For a few minutes, silence reigned, and he resisted the urge to exchange glances with Bezek. An assistant brought them each a goblet of Krenlic, the spicy bite of the juice a perfect answer for his dry mouth. He needed this respite before the questions and clarification process began. By his reckoning, they had at least two more hours to go. It was all he could do not to sigh.

Finally, Elder Reuel rose and faced them. "This has been very enlightening. Let me extend the gratitude of the Council for how you've managed this difficult situation." He motioned to include the Elders arrayed behind him. "We have much to discuss, and I know you too must have pressing matters. So we'll keep you no longer. I do expect we will have need of your clarifications once we've finished our deliberations, but we'll send word."

That was it? No questions, no discussions. Peculiar didn't begin to cover the actions of these Elders. Josiah rose, bowed to the room, and they left. As they entered the anti-room, Bezek opened his mouth to speak, and Josiah silenced him with a look. They retrieved their weapons, nodded to the sentry outside the door, and rounded the corner before Josiah broke the silence. "We will discuss this." He held up a hand to forestall Bezek's reaction. "When we reach the shuttle."

"Aye, Commander."

The long ride in the groundrover gave Bethany a chance to see more of her planet's devastation. She thought back to the brave warrior she'd left laying in a pool of blood. Had help arrived in time for Manaen? If she did recover, would she understand the sacrifice Bethany had made, or condemn her? Would Josiah? *Please, please…* Her prayers were without words. She had to trust that the One would protect Manean.

The lump in her throat threatened to push the tears from her eyes, and she swallowed hard. She would not give her captors the satisfaction of seeing her in pain. She struggled to focus on the scenery surrounding her. So much of the vegetation had died in the few years she'd been underground. She fought against the urge to insist they stop so she could gather soil samples. From the look, even the microbes were dying. She grabbed again at the safety harness, trying to keep from being thrown against Simon. The sturdy vehicle had been outfitted for battle but lacked much in comfort. Even with the protective gear they wore over their faces, the thick dust raised by their passing filtered into her lungs and made her eyes water. Unless she could apply her father's research, and soon, the planet would truly be beyond help.

Bethany looked up as the groundrover slowed, but all she saw was another rocky hillside. She'd been about to lean back when the largest boulder withdrew into the rock face above it. Several armed men, in uniforms like those at the camp, motioned them through the entrance. It took a few moments to adjust to the indoor lighting, but when they did, she looked around a huge cavern filled with all types of vehicles, from groundrovers to battle-ready monsters she couldn't name.

Japheth inserted their vehicle into a space while Simon helped her extricate herself from the harness. She pulled the headgear off, and a shower of dust sifted over her clothes. She brushed at her tunic then gave up. Only a bath would remove the grime. Sand coated every pore.

"This way." Simon pointed in the direction of several doorways. "I'll take you to your quarters, and you can get cleaned up before you see your lab."

Bethany moved to follow him, then paused when Japheth didn't follow.

He grinned at her, teeth white in a mask of grime. "I'll meet you for the midday meal."

Simon guided her into a tunnel. "We're still a little ways from the living section. Are you okay?"

"I'm fine." Long walks and hard work were no strangers to her. Simon should know that. They passed quite a few others who nodded and hurried on their way. "How many Sintuens escaped?" This huge complex must house hundreds.

"Thousands." Simon smiled down at her. "We were prepared for this."

"We?"

"The Organization, of course." He nodded to a group that swept past them in some type of electric cart. "I haven't lied to you."

"Really? I seem to remember that being one of your hobbies while we were growing up." She shouldn't push him, but was too tired to mind her words.

He chuckled but didn't rise to her bait. "Aven sent someone yesterday to prepare your quarters. They should be ready for you, complete with clothes and anything else you need."

"I see your master has thought of everything." She wondered at her own audacity as she pushed for a reaction from him.

"That's the old Bethany. I knew she was in there somewhere."

Bethany gave him a small smile, but it didn't thaw the ice surrounding her heart. His attempts to return to their easy childhood friendship lacked sincerity. Simon was not a friend, but what was he? Captor, ally, protector? None of those fit. She'd just have to wait and see.

They continued on in silence as Bethany tried to keep track of where she'd come from. But the maze of underground corridors made that impossible. The corridor they were on widened into a circular common area, with small doorways set into the walls equidistance apart.

"This will be the pod where your quarters are," Simon said as a woman at a desk in the center of the room motioned them forward.

"Name?" She barely glanced at them, concentrating on the small plasscreen in front of her.

Simon cleared his throat, and the attendant looked up, frowning. Recognizing his face, her entire countenance changed. "Forgive me, sir."

"Are her quarters ready or not?"

"Of course." She managed to give the impression of bowing, even though she stayed seated. She turned toward Bethany. "I've made certain it contains everything you need. If anything's lacking, please let me know and I'll see to it immediately."

"Excellent." Simon nodded. "Do you have her map-cuff or is it in her room?"

"It's here, sir." The woman reached down and picked up a wide silver band, inset with a tiny light and keypad, and handed it to Simon. "Type in where you want to go, and the light will flash faster the closer you get to your destination."

"Handy." Bethany made no move to extend her wrist. "I'm sure it also has a beacon on it to keep track of my whereabouts."

The woman gasped and presented her own arm, complete with cuff, for Bethany's inspection. "We all wear them. It's for our protection."

"See, nothing to worry about." Simon's tone was nonchalant, but something in his eyes warned her to not make a scene. Whether it was for his benefit or hers, she couldn't decide. She extended her wrist without any more argument. If nothing else, she'd like to be able to approach the woman at the desk in the future as a possible ally instead of someone to be mistrusted. He snapped the cuff closed around her wrist, and she pulled it close to examine it. There was no visible seam where the two edges had joined. Difficult to remove then. Probably required some sort of device to release the catch. Handy…for them.

"Type in *personal quarters*," Simon said. "And I'll make sure you know how it works."

Bethany did so, and the amber light began to blink in a slow regular rhythm. "Which entrance?" She didn't want to wander around the room more than necessary.

"You're down corridor 7C." He gestured to the designations above a doorway to her right. "The number represents the pod and the letter is the hallway within that pod."

He trailed behind as Bethany watched the unit on her wrist. Sure enough, the flashing rhythm increased and then glowed continuously as she reached a door halfway down the hallway. The palm print panel and keypad on the wall beside the door also gave off a soft light that matched her cuff.

Simon placed his hand in the recessed print of the panel, and the door whooshed open. He held her back when she'd have entered. "Let's get your palm registered before we go in." He typed in a code on the keypad. "Now, press your hand on the glowing area."

She fit her hand where Simon's had been and a green light flashed. "Does that mean I'm registered?"

"It does." He ushered her into what would be her quarters.

As they entered, soft ambient lighting poured from the overhead grates. The minimal furnishings offered a utilitarian comfort. She wandered into the sleeping alcove which held a single bed, inviting with warm blankets and several pillows. A trunk rested at the end of the bed and probably held the promised necessities. Obviously a woman's touch here. She glanced into the standard bathing alcove and returned to the main room where Simon perched on a low couch.

"Do you have everything you need?" He patted the seat beside him.

"I think so." She continued to stand. All she wanted now was for him to go so she could get clean.

He rose, smiling. "I can take a hint. I'm sure you'd like a bath as much as I would." He stopped at the door and looked back at her. "Either myself or Japheth will call for you in about an hour and we'll eat." His gaze held hers, trying to convey something she couldn't decipher. "Don't leave with anyone you don't know."

CHAPTER THIRTY-FOUR

Josiah strapped in and maneuvered the shuttle from the hanger of the admin ship before he turned toward his second. "All right. Let's hear your assessment."

"Where do I begin?" The words fairly exploded from Bezek, and his face matched the color of his beard. "No questions? Have you ever even heard of such a thing?"

Josiah just shook his head, managing the thrusters for a soft takeoff. Once back on a planetward trajectory, he faced Bezek. "No. I have not. Beyond that, I've never encountered one in all my studies." He rotated his neck, trying to forestall the ache in his head.

"But Manaen's the expert, not us." Bezek glanced over at Josiah. "No disrespect meant, Commander. We need her input…now more than ever."

"Buck up, man." Josiah reached across to grab his shoulder. "We've been in tough spots before. Together, we'll figure this out." He grinned. "After all, we have the One on our side." He pulled the portable tablet out of the pocket beside his seat. "And we'll begin by listing the reactions of the Elders present."

In the short ride between the admin ship and docking berth within his compound, they began a comprehensive list. Josiah stowed the tablet and adjusted the thrusters to allow for a vertical landing. He set the craft lightly on the pad and shut down the engines. He saw one of his men running toward the shuttle and toggled the door lock, opening it from inside to allow the man to board. "Now what?"

"Huh?" Bezek looked up from his task and blew out a sigh. "It just never ends."

"Commander?" Josiah recognized Calamus's voice.

"Enter," he bellowed back.

A slightly breathless Calamus appeared in the doorway. "I'm to finish shutdown for you. Gehazi has requested your presence the moment you arrived."

Josiah could feel his heart stutter in his chest, and his ears rang with nothingness. He glanced at Bezek and saw the man looked as white as he felt. The both leapt from their seats, nearly mowing down Calamus in their haste, and ran full-bore toward the sick room.

Bethany judged they were eating lunch later than most as she looked over the nearly vacant catering section. She went through the line between Japheth and Simon, accepting what was offered. The workers noticeably straightened when they caught sight of the three of them and whispers echoed through the open space. Those in charge must not dine here regularly. Thinking back to the breakfast she'd been served—had it only been this morning?—she doubted Aven ever ate in this place. No reason for him to, with a chef that talented.

They found a table against a wall and sat. The food was good but not outstanding. Funny how she'd already developed a finicky palate in the short months that she'd been above ground.

"I know it's not spectacular." Japheth gestured with his fork to the food on her plate. "But it's tolerable."

"No, it's fine." She smiled at him. "I'm just a little tired."

"Perhaps you'll feel better after you've eaten." Japheth gestured to her plate with his fork. "We still have to at least visit your lab this afternoon before calling it a day."

She noticed the look that passed between them but couldn't decipher it. She took a deep breath, hoping for a casual tone in her voice. "Will my father's books be there?"

Simon looked away. "They'll be delivered to the lab before you get there tomorrow morning."

"Can I move them to my rooms?"

Japheth sighed. "That won't be possible. For their protection—and yours—they need to stay in the lab." As tears began well in her eyes he continued. "But you won't be restricted on the time you spend in the lab."

"Your quarters aren't secure enough. In the lab, there's a coded safe." Simon held up a hand to forestall her next question. "And yes, you'll have the code. But so will several others, including myself, Japheth, and of course, Aven."

She nodded and they ended the meal in silence, although she only toyed with food on her plate.

"Are you finished with that?" Japheth reached to take her plate with a grin. "Or did you want to play with it some more?"

Although she appreciated his effort, she couldn't work up an answering smile.

"All right, then, it's off to the lab." Japheth led the way from the catering center.

"I do think you'll be pleased with what's in store." Simon motioned her to follow Japheth, and he brought up the rear since the narrow exit had only enough room for one person at a time. Once back in yet another corridor, Japheth continued on without a backward glance, but Simon lengthened his stride to catch up with them and walk beside her.

Bethany adjusted the cuff on her wrist. The thing irritated her, and she wanted nothing more than to fling it away and disappear.

"You'll get used to it." Simon nodded at it.

"How do I use it to find the lab?" she asked.

"I showed you how to use the cuff to find anywhere you needed to go." He cocked his head and frowned. "Don't you remember?"

"I do." She nodded. "I meant what is the designation for the lab. Surely there's more than one laboratory in this underground city."

"Oh that." He smiled. "We made it easy. It's known as Bethany's lab. You can just enter *my lab* on your keypad."

He'd managed to answer her question without sharing any information. Now, she wanted to know how many labs there were here. What kind of testing did Aven do? Obviously, a great deal with talarium. How much about what went on was Simon privilege to?

Josiah surveyed the sitting area outside Manaen's sick room, Bezek close behind him. The smell of strong antiseptic was now augmented by that of the healing herbs which were Gehazi's foundation for all her treatments.

A smiling Gehazi waited for them at the open door. "There's someone awake and asking to see you two."

The weight of dread slipped from Josiah's heart. He inched his way around Gehazi and beheld a conscious, although wan, Manaen. He eased into the chair near her head. Bezek took the one on the other side. Even with the tube down her throat it was the condition of her face that caused him to catch his breath. The right cheek had some cuts and already yellowing bruises, but the left was wrapped in layers of white gauze. A light sheet covered her sick gown to mid-chest, but from what he could see, bandages still swathed a good portion of her body.

"How are you?" Josiah reached out and took her hand. Stupid question, she couldn't talk around the tube. "No don't try to speak. I'm just glad to see you."

In spite of his warning she began trying to tell him something.

"No." He put his fingers against her lips. "There's nothing you need to say. We have things well in hand."

She made a writing motion, and he smiled. She was a stubborn one, that sister of his. "No. Your job now is to make a full recovery. We're getting the information we need." He nodded to Bezek on her other side. "I think there's someone else who'd like to say hello."

She twisted her head toward Bezek, and her mouth relaxed into a small smile. "Hello, my girl." Bezek laid his hand on her free one. "I'm glad to see you."

Again, she tried to make herself heard.

"No." Bezek shook his head. "You follow your brother's orders. We've plenty of time to talk when they get that wretched tube out."

She nodded, the most vigorous movement Josiah had seen since they entered.

"I know it's frustrating." Bezek squeezed her hand. "But follow what the healers say, and you'll soon be ordering us all about again." His nose turned red, and he looked away.

"All right you too. She's still got a lot of healing to do before that happens." Gehazi appeared in the doorway. "And it won't happen if you tire her out."

Josiah rose. He knew better than to argue with Gehazi. "When can I return?"

She smiled at his obedience. "Later this evening would be a good time."

"I'll be staying right here." That look on Bezek's face was one he'd seen before. Josiah leaned against the doorframe. This battle of wills should prove interesting.

"Not if you want to be allowed back again, you won't." Gehazi crossed her arms.

"I'll keep so quiet and still you won't even know I'm here." Bezek squirmed in his seat.

"Absolutely not." She glanced at Manaen whose good eye had begun to flicker with the effort to stay open. "You're already interfering with her rest."

Bezek followed her look and gave a deep sigh. "Have it your way. I'll go, but I'll be back."

She sighed and moved aside to let him pass through the doorway. "Of that I'm certain."

Josiah followed him out in the hallway, chuckling. "Nice fight you put up in there."

Bezek growled underneath his breath. "Not sure why I even bothered."

"Yeah, me either." Josiah shook his head. "You know better than to argue with her, especially over a patient."

"I'm not sure what came over me." Bezek scratched his beard.

"Oh, I know exactly what came over you." Josiah poked him in the chest with his finger. "You, my friend, are a man in love."

Bezek's face reddened and he started to say something, then shut his mouth.

The smile left Josiah's face. "You still haven't told her?"

"No." Bezek shook his head. "I hadn't found the right time. And then…"

"Well, I suggest you do it while she still has that tube down her throat." Josiah clapped him on the shoulder, and they began retracing their frantic steps back to headquarters.

Upon entering headquarters, all movement and sound ceased, and questioning eyes turned their direction. Sometimes, Josiah forgot how much Manaen meant to his entire unit. He answered their unvoiced question with a wide grin. "She's awake, and she's going to be okay."

A spontaneous cheer met his words, and he and Bezek returned to his office through the many exclamations of relief and well wishes. Everyone needed to hear something good for a change.

He closed the door to his inner office. Now to decide what to do with all the bad news. "I think we were about to analyze the Council meeting when we were interrupted."

CHAPTER THIRTY-FIVE

Bethany's eyes widened as she stood at the doorway of her new lab. From the equipment it contained down to the arrangement and colors of the chairs, it was identical to the one she'd grown up sharing with her father. If she hadn't been inside her father's lab just yesterday—had it truly only been one day?—she'd have thought it a trick of her mind. "How did you do it?" she whispered as she stepped inside.

"It wasn't our doing." Simon ushered her into the suite of rooms after registering her palm print on the pad by the door. "Aven has been planning this for a very long time. He's even provided you with familiar staff."

Before she could register what she was seeing, a squealing Elisheba embraced her. "Isn't it perfect?"

"What are you doing here?" Although Bethany could remember glimpses of Elisheba throughout the night of her capture.

"I was rescued too. Same time as you." Elisheba guided her to an elderly man off to one side. "Do you remember Dr. Stanos?"

"You've grown into quite a lovely young woman." He offered her a hand and led her to a couple of chairs. "I'm sure this is all a little overwhelming."

A little? But Dr. Stanos had been known for his understatements. This man mentored her father and seemed old when she was only a child. Now, he appeared not to have changed at all, from the sparse white hair on his head to the blue eyes that missed little. It had been years since he'd spent weeks at their home, closeted in the laboratory with her father for days on end. It had been during that time she'd taken to spending hours in the lab, wanting to be with her father. "Of course I remember you. But what happened? When you disappeared, we assumed the worst." She remembered watching her father fret for days, making inquiries and calling in favors. But no one had been able to tell him anything.

"It's a long story, and we'll have plenty of time to share it soon." He nodded at Simon and Japheth who stood a little distance away. "But for now, I think you should see the rest of your lab."

"One more surprise and then you can look around all you want." Japheth beckoned her to an open doorway that, at home, would have led to the office.

As she joined him there, she discovered this room was as uncanny as everything else in the lab. Where had they gotten their information? "It's identical," was all she could say.

Simon stood by the wall that had contained her sire's books. Here, the hollowed out section of stonework near the floor had been replaced with a safe, now open and empty. "This is where we'll deliver your father's books. We need to add your retinal scan to the locking mechanism so you can retrieve them any time you wish." Simon closed the door and typed in several codes on the keypad on the front of the thick door, then motioned her forward. "Bend down, and let it read your eye."

She stood where indicated, trying not to flinch as the bright beam scanned her left eye. There was no pain or really any sensation at all, and it only took moments. When the light stopped, she looked up. "Is that it?"

"Now for the code," he told her. "It's easy to remember. The real security lies in the retinal scan. Just type in THE PRINCE."

Simon and Japheth left Bethany at her quarters, but before Simon could turn to his own quarters, Japheth stopped him. "Walk with me."

"Sure. What's up?" This was unusual, but not out of the bounds of reasonable.

Japheth glanced up at the ceiling, to a section where Simon knew the hidden cameras were located. "I just thought it might be a good time to check on troop morale."

Definitely unusual and obvious Japheth didn't want what he had to say recorded, visually or otherwise. "That makes sense." Simon nodded. "I should have thought of that."

They snaked through several corridors, taking a route Simon was unfamiliar with. They ended up at a small exit to the outside. Only one sentry stood guard. "May I help you?" He saluted as they approached.

"No." Japheth winked at the soldier. "We're doing a little checking on the guards around the perimeter and prefer not announce our presence."

The sentry's lips twitched without breaking into an actual smile. "Of course, sir. Always a good idea to keep the forces on their toes."

This wasn't Japheth's reason for inviting him outside, and Simon knew it. But it was a clever way to disguise whatever it was he hoped to accomplish.

The doorway led to a short tunnel and around to the backside of the hill that helped cloak their underground hideout.

This was Japheth's rendezvous. Simon would let him take the lead. He'd long ago learned that silence led to the most interesting revelations.

They took a dusty trail up the hill and stopped near a rocky outcropping. The heat of the day continued to radiate from the rocks as they cooled in the night air.

Japheth pointed up at the stars and the emerging moons. Iddo, the smaller moon was almost at full, while Iscah was just a sliver of silver. "Do you ever think about our lives in relation to the galaxy? How we're nothing more than the lantern flies that used to flit in the fields of Sintue during the summer. Busy going to and fro, shining a light that seems big to us but isn't even measurable to others."

Simon looked at him sharply, but the rocks blocked the moonlight and left Japheth's features indistinct in the nighttime shadows. "Noooo. I can't say that I have."

"Well perhaps you should…before it's too late."

The hair on the back of Simon's neck prickled. "I don't know where you're going with this, but I think it's better if you get to the point."

"That is the point." Japheth's face twisted into a barely discernable ghost of smile. "Do you really believe this life is all we have?"

"I hesitate to even say this out loud, but that sounds like the things Seekers have said." Surely not though. This man was Aven's right hand. He couldn't be a Seeker.

"That's exactly what I'm saying." His emphatic nod was obvious. "And I'm trusting you with my secret because I need help." He looked around. "We have to get Bethany, and her father's books, out of here before it's too late."

"But I thought there were only two choices here—Aven's plan to save the planet or the monsters' plan to destroy us. Is there something else?"

"The plan of our leader doesn't end only with saving our planet. He believes the research Bethany carries can be mutated to not just bring life back to Sintue, but destroy it on other planets." Japheth moved closer and lowered his voice. "If he isn't stopped here and now, he'll take over the galaxy and we'll be responsible for unleashing a plague of unimaginable consequences across the known and unknown universe." He gripped Simon's arm. "Do you really want that on your conscience?"

"Wait a second." Simon backed away. "You're going a little fast for me. Slow down and fill in the details." But even as he demanded an explanation, he felt things click into place in his mind. He held up a hand. "Scratch that. Tell me one thing first. Who is Aven really?"

Japheth dropped both hands to his sides. "He's The Prince, of course. And we either choose him and die or serve the One and live."

Bethany punched the pillow again, willing sleep to come. Truthfully, her problems came from an overactive mind, not the poor pillow. She surrendered and padded barefoot into the main room, stopping at the food prep unit to put water on to boil. Perhaps some Roma tea would quiet her spirit. Or at least soothe her thoughts enough so she could make sense of the past two days.

She curled up on the padded couch, her feet tucked beneath her, staring at the wall. How she longed for the windows that graced her room at the teaching compound. Even at night, she could stare out, counting stars, watching Iscah and Iddo play chase across the sky.

Had she begun taking her circumstances for granted? Was that why the One had chosen to throw her into the hands of the enemies? He'd not only tossed her to them, but done so in a way that she'd never be able to return. Or was the One punishing Sintue, and she'd just been caught in the crossfire?

The kettle began to whistle, and she crossed the room to assemble her tea. The act of making the tea reminded her of those days—and nights—in her father's lab. The small food prep unit there had served to keep him fed while he worked all night. It was also where she'd prepared tea for them both as they discussed his experiments and theories, although in later years, they'd added her own thoughts and suggestions to the discussions. He'd encouraged her exploration of possible applications for the compounds she'd discovered with the Yuofosh bush. But he'd sent her away to school before they'd been able to test those ideas.

Now, she realized he'd insisted she leave for safety's sake. Somehow, he must have known they were coming for him. He'd left a message the night before he'd been killed, telling her he'd discovered the key right where she'd thought it was. No details, just a promise to follow up with a visit in person. A visit that had never happened.

It had all been so long ago, and she'd had so many ideas she couldn't pinpoint which exact theory he'd referenced. She sighed. Just thinking about that dark time made her want to hide in the bed, covers over her head. She drained the last of her tea and set the cup on the counter. She'd think more about it in the morning. Exhaustion had finally won out. Whatever tomorrow would bring, she needed rest to face it.

CHAPTER THIRTY-SIX

Josiah checked the chrono on his arm. Bezek had left thirty minutes earlier. He'd offered to wait, but Josiah cited pressing matters and told him to go ahead. Truthfully, he wanted to give Bezek and his sister some time. Smiling, he rose and settled his accelerator pistol on his belt. He'd never imagined himself as matchmaker to anyone, much less his independent sister.

He entered the sitting area beyond her room, pleased to see no sign of Gehazi. Her hovering—or rather, the lack thereof—indicated the wellness of her patient. Through the open sickroom door, he heard voices. A surprise because he assumed she'd still have the tube. He stopped in full view of the couple so they wouldn't think he'd tried to eavesdrop. They didn't see him. They were so engrossed they didn't look up.

"I wish you could have been there instead of me." Bezek held Manaen's hand. "You would have been able to read the council much better."

"Perhaps." She stroked his cheek with her free hand. "But the One allowed this for a purpose, and we must rest in that." Her low voice still held a horse rasp.

Bezek looked down and rubbed her hand with his thumb. "I cannot believe you could love me."

"I've loved you for a long time." Even swathed in bandages, her smile was the same. "I was just waiting for you to realize you loved me."

Bezek let out a belly laugh. "Then the joke's on you. I've known I loved you since you were too young to care."

This had gone on long enough. Josiah cleared his throat. They both started and turned. He noticed Bezek didn't release his hold on her, though. "Is everything settled between you two?" Bezek's red face betrayed his answer.

"Yes, brother of mine." Manaen tilted her head at him. "Is that why you came, or did you have other matters you wished to discuss?"

He pulled up a chair close to Bezek's so she could see them both without turning. "I do indeed come with a purpose." He glanced at Bezek. "Although I'm certain you've already got a grasp of the basics."

"I have." Her fingers intertwined with Bezek's. "I see that your eyes are wide open. Tell me what you want from me."

"A list of the traitors would help." Josiah sighed. "But barring that, I need any insight you can bring."

She nodded. "What were your impressions at the council meeting?"

Josiah looked away, taking time to remember the undercurrents he had sensed as well as all that had transpired. "My first thought was that all the Elders were concerned about something, and my report was just a small part of it. Watching them as I spoke, I got the impression my information caught many by surprise."

"It was almost as if they'd been kept in the dark by Elder Mahalah." Bezek pulled on his beard. "And he didn't appear happy about the meeting. Could another source have called them to this conclave?"

"Yes." Josiah snapped his fingers and leaned back. "That's it exactly."

Manaen closed her good eye, as if trying to picture the scene. "Tell me who else appeared unhappy or uneasy at the gathering." She looked at them. "Not concerned, but deeper than that."

Josiah got up and began to pace. Moving always helped him concentrate. "Of those who were present, the most troubled were Elders Phichol, Koz, Eli, Bidkar, and Bukkiah." He turned to Bezek. "Any you'd add?"

"I think Hanoch and Vajezatha belong on that list." Bezek ticked them off on his hand as he listed them. "That gives us seven we find suspicious, not counting Mahalah."

"Excellent way to categorize them." Josiah returned to his seat. "It's important not to make judgments too early."

"Too early hasn't been a problem of yours in this particular instance." Manaen's lopsided smile softened her words. "I think the time for caution has fled, and the moment for action is at hand."

Josiah met her eyes. He knew only too well his own shortcomings in this circumstance. "I'd say I've learned a valuable lesson here. Faith in the wrong things can be just as deadly as no faith at all."

"Excellently said." Manaen gave him a long look followed by a smile.

"So." He cleared his throat to dispel the mood. "What exactly do you recommend?" He'd already assembled a list in his own mind and begun prioritizing the steps.

"The first thing needed is to rescue Bethany."

The breath left his body as if he'd received a physical blow. His jaw worked as he fought to keep his voice low. "I forbid mention of that traitor's name in my presence again."

Manaen struggled to sit upright, wincing at the pain the movement brought. "I will speak of her. And you will hear my words—whether you wish to or not."

Bezek helped her sit up, refusing to meet his eyes.

Josiah got up to resume pacing. "I don't see how you can say that. She left you for dead and took off with the enemy. I know. I saw it with my own eyes." He stopped and stared down at her and spoke past the lump that threatened to clog his heart. "Nothing you say can change her actions that night."

"Sit down and quit pacing like a caged feline." She pointed to the chair. "I can imagine what you saw. The important part happened before you arrived."

He folded his arms and sat. "Go ahead."

"After I was wounded, I tried to get Bethany and Keturah to run, but they wouldn't leave me." She frowned at the memory. "As the enemy continued to approach, I could hear them call out her name. She was why they were there. They'd come for her."

"I'd assumed that was why they came. You're not telling me anything I didn't already know or suspect."

"I'm not finished." She pointed a finger at him. "She bargained for my life. She promised to come with them if they'd spare me and let Keturah remain to care for me." Manaen looked down at her hands. "It's my fault she's gone. If I'd forced her to leave sooner, she'd still be here."

"But you'd be dead." Bezek took her hand, glaring at Josiah. "And none of us would have chosen that."

Josiah didn't answer. Instead, he leaned back and stared out the window. Could it be true? What if she hadn't left on her own? That meant she'd sacrificed herself for his sister. The lump in his heart began to loosen. But he had to be certain. He heard a small sob escape his sister and refocused his attention on her. "It's not your fault. You did everything you could." He reached down to push the hair away from her face. "You acted well, for her and for our warriors. And you're right, the first thing we need to do is plan how to retrieve her." He drew himself up and nodded at Bezek. "Go get that other Seeker. Keturah, I think her name is."

Manaen exchanged a glance with Bezek, but refused to loose his hand when he tried to rise. "Why do you want Keturah?" she asked.

"I'm not going to hurt her." Josiah blew out a breath. "I know what you think you saw and heard, but you were badly injured. You may have interpreted the situation incorrectly. I need more." He wanted to believe her. Wanted it with every fiber of his soul. But that was the very reason he needed more proof. This time, he would not allow his feelings to override the evidence.

Manaen looked at him for a long moment then nodded at Bezek. "She should be with Gehazi."

Somehow, Simon had half expected the summons from Aven today. What he hadn't anticipated was the timing. He'd hoped for more time to process the information Japheth had given him and try to verify it. A private breakfast invitation with his leader would at least give him a chance to ask some discreet questions. He frowned as he gave his clothes a final inspection in the small mirror. He had come to one decision. He wouldn't betray Japheth. If he was a traitor, Aven would ferret it out soon, of that he had no doubt. If he wasn't...well, that left him with a completely different set of decisions to face.

He strode down the corridors toward Aven's block of quarters. The only one who could appear late for a summons was Salisa, and even she didn't push Aven too often. The sentries outside the main entrance saluted when he arrived. All of Aven's guard knew him by sight and by rank. He nodded as one opened the door for him.

Inside, another sentry requested Simon leave his weapons with him. He hadn't meant to add the sidearm this morning, but the ingrained habit had made that impossible. He unstrapped the accelerator pistol and handed it to the man, who motioned him toward the inner door. Opening it, odors of a perfectly prepared meal assaulted his senses. No one ever turned down breakfast—or any meal—with Aven.

"Excellent, I see you're punctual, as always." Aven already sat at the opulent table, sipping qua. He set his cup in its saucer and motioned him to the seat opposite. "Please sit. As you can see, my Jakan has just served out our meal."

"He is an amazing chef." Simon took his seat and dropped his napkin into his lap. "Where ever did you find him?"

"You might say I made him."

In light of last night's discussion, that cryptic comment left Simon with more questions than answers.

They exchanged occasional pleasantries as they ate. Simon let Aven set the direction of the conversation, waiting for the right opportunity to slip in his own inquiries.

Aven dabbed at his mouth and pushed back his chair. "Let's move to a more comfortable place to talk while the table is cleared." At those words, two servants entered and began silently stacking plates and carrying off the remains.

They took opposite chairs on either side of a fireplace. Simon knew it had to be only a projection. This far down, venting would be a nightmare. But it radiated real heat, and Simon could swear he smelled the smoky odor of burning logs.

Aven stretched out his legs. "I've decided it's time to let you in on phase two of my plans."

A second phase? That implied still more unrevealed. "It's an honor to be included, sir."

"You have proven yourself trustworthy." His lips twitched, hinting at a smile. "And such devotion deserves recognition. You will find even greater reward when we've not just pushed these monsters from Sintue, but gone on to destroy them completely."

Simon dipped his head in thanks but also to hide the smile he couldn't stop. There was the confirmation he'd hoped for.

"And your usefulness extends beyond being trustworthy. You're useful to me." Aven waved away a servant's offer of additional qua. "You must be my eyes and ears in the lab. It's up to you to convince the girl you're her ally, no matter what you have to do. Do you understand?" He pinned Simon with a glance.

Did Aven realize the power he'd just handed him? "I will do whatever you wish. But I assumed the lab had the surveillance equipment necessary to give you that information."

"It does have state of the art equipment. But the things I seek go beyond mere facts. I want your impressions." He studied the black ring on his finger. "And there are things said outside my hearing. That is the information I expect from you."

Simon kept his face still. Did Aven know about his meeting with Japheth last night? They'd gone on and inspected the troops, catching several unaware. He made a quick decision. "You know my goal is to have Bethany for my own. This falls perfectly in line with that." He gulped. "I hope you know I'd do it anyway."

"See!" Aven pointed at him. "That's what I like about you. You take risks, but you also lay it all on the line."

"Thank you, sir."

Aven's mouth relaxed into a full smile. "And of course I know you want her. She is yours. No one will take her from you. That is my gift to you." He held up a finger. "But she has tasks to perform for me as well, and she won't be as willing a servant."

"Tasks?" Simon cocked his head.

"Yes, her job is twofold. First, I need her to decipher her father's books." He sighed. "I suppose you know they're in code."

"No. I didn't." Code? That wasn't much a surprise if he thought about it. Dr. Randolph would have known the end was coming. "I have never had the chance to look at them."

"Well they are." Aven frowned. "A momentary roadblock. I'm sure the girl wants to read what's in them as much as the rest of us. The second thing she has to do may be tougher."

"What is it?"

"Part of her father's theories stem from her own suggestions and input. Through that, Dr. Randolph found a gene which can be manipulated to restore the entire ecosystem on a planet. I want her to further manipulate it to take that life away."

CHAPTER THIRTY-SEVEN

Bethany awoke early, in spite of a restless night. They'd promised her father's books would be in the lab by the time she arrived today. Her morning reverence consisted of one single plea. *Please, please let them be there and intact.*

She didn't even take pause for a cup of qua but rushed out. Although she hadn't paid attention yesterday, if it truly was a replica of her father's, there'd be a small food prep unit where she could get some tea. The cuff she wore proved useful as she wove through the maze of corridors. Standing outside the lab door, she took a deep breath. She pressed her palm print in the pad and the lock clicked, inviting her to enter.

The lighting grates in the ceiling immediately shimmered to life as she entered. That meant there'd been no one inside for hours. Did it mean the notebooks weren't there either? Only one way to find out. She crossed the main room to the office. The closed door of the safe didn't offer any clue to its contents. She couldn't remember if they'd left it open or shut.

She bent down and punched in the code, then let the scanner read her left eye. She heard the click of the mechanism and stared at it for a moment. *Please, please…* And she pulled the door open. She blew out a breath she hadn't realized she'd been holding. They looked as undisturbed as when she'd retrieved them from home two days ago. She gathered them up, rose, and walked the few feet to the desk. She spread them out, not certain if there was a particular order to the information they contained. She chose one at random and sat to begin the process of catching up with her father's work.

The pages in front of her made no sense. They were covered in gibberish. These couldn't be notes he'd left for her. Her stomach contracted as she studied the confusion. She rubbed her temples. No, this was his handwriting. But the words, the equations, the scribbles, were just bits and pieces that didn't belong together. Nothing made sense. Biting her lip, she tried to concentrate, to think back on their last few conversations. At one point, he'd told her something. She could hear his voice telling her it didn't matter what happened to him, the work was safe, and she'd have the means to unlock it. No, not quite. *Only* she would have the key to open it. At the time, she assumed he'd been talking about the location and combination of the safe. Now, she knew there had been much more to his statement. But how did that help her now? He hadn't told her what she needed. They hadn't ever talked about a code. How could she hold the key if he hadn't given it to her?

She opened the rest of the notebooks, flipping through pages without rhyme or reason. They were all covered in the same confusing formulas and words. Something about it seemed familiar. Was that because of his well-loved handwriting or that something else she couldn't bring to mind? Bethany pushed her hair back from her face—this would take time, if she could even figure it out.

Before she tackled it, she'd need some qua. She rose and walked to the area that had held the small food prep unit at home. Sure enough, there it was, tucked between the cold cabinet and the counter. She opened the storage unit above and found it stocked with cups, qua, and other things appropriate to help a busy staff stay fueled and focused.

While Bethany prepared her tea, the outer door opened. She turned to see Elisheba and Dr. Stanos enter.

"Good morning." Dr. Stanos joined her and gestured to the teapot. "Is there enough for two there?"

Bethany smiled. "Certainly."

"What about me?" Elisheba inserted herself beside Bethany. "I could use a cup as well."

"I have plenty for all of us." Bethany reached up and removed two more cups from the cabinet. She also knew what Elisheba liked in hers, so she grabbed the sweetener and dropped the requisite amount into the cup. Then she turned to Dr. Stanos. "How do you take your qua?"

"Just plain for me," he said. "Do you think we three might have a meeting before we begin the day?"

Bethany nodded. "That sounds like a good idea."

Bethany poured the tea, and they took their cups to the large worktable in the center of the room.

"What did you want to discuss?" Bethany turned to Dr. Stanos. He'd asked for the meeting so she'd let him begin.

He cleared his throat and looked directly at Bethany. He seemed as uncomfortable at Elisheba's presence as she was. "This is your lab. But I thought we could all benefit from defining our roles and the overall goal that has brought us together."

Elisheba folded her arms and glared at them both. "Well, I know my role. It's to keep the two of you in line."

Simon whistled as he strode down the corridor to Bethany's lab. He should be able to convince her to come to lunch with him. After all, she had to eat. He'd made sure the lab hadn't been stocked with anything substantial enough to replace a meal.

He stopped in front of the door and pressed his palm print into the pad. The door opened, and Elisheba came to greet him. "I'm glad you're here." He hid a frown. She'd been much less irritating when she'd been pretending to be a slave in the worker's block. "They have been closeted in that office for hours and won't allow me in."

Nevertheless, as a spy for the organization, she held a certain amount of power. He needed to tread carefully. As a spy, she'd done well, and Aven might be using her to do more than watch Bethany. She could be watching him as well. "Did they say why?"

She waved a hand. "They said they needed quiet and privacy to work." She folded her arms and huffed. "Like I don't know how to be keep my mouth shut."

What a truly irritating little woman. "I'm certain their only concern is moving forward with the project." He stepped around her toward the office door.

"Did you know her father's notebooks are worse than useless to us?"

"What? How so?" He stopped and turned back. She had his full attention now.

"They're in code. No use to anybody if they can't crack it."

"We already knew that." Simon shook his head. "That's the reason Aven brought her here. One of the reasons, at least."

She narrowed her eyes at him. "And why wasn't I told?"

It was time to put her in her place. "Because you didn't need the information." He kept his voice even. She swallowed several times as he stared her down.

She looked away first. "Of course. I'm only here to serve."

"It's well you don't forget that."

"Bethany, Dr. Stanos?" He knocked at the door. "Will you please join me?"

The door opened, and they came out. "How can we help you?" Dr. Stanos asked.

"I don't need anything urgent." Simon smiled. They both looked anxious. "I just wanted to see if I could convince Bethany to come to share lunch with me. We have some things to discuss."

She and Dr. Stanos exchanged looks. "I'm pretty busy here…" She let the sentence hang.

"But you still must eat." Dr. Stanos patted her on the shoulder. "Take a break. You're way too thin."

"You're right." She gave Dr. Stanos a quick smile. "We can both use some time away." She turned to Simon. "I'm ready when you are."

CHAPTER THIRTY-EIGHT

Bethany rose from the desk chair and arched her back. All day spent studying her father's notes and still no closer to finding the key to making sense of them. She returned to her seat and began going through the pages of her own notes. These were proof she'd tried any and everything that came to her mind. Shaking her head, she studied them. There had to be a more efficient way to find the answer. She glanced at the closed office door and sighed. Elisheba and Dr. Stanos had offered their help, but she'd turned them both down. She flat-out didn't trust Elisheba, and still felt wary about Dr. Stanos.

The thing was, while she wanted to break the code, she did *not* want her father's formulas and research to fall into Aven's hands. Nothing good could come of that. The cuff on her wrist blinked several times in rapid succession, and she twisted it so the light didn't show. It seemed to pulse at odd moments and without a discernable reason.

A knock startled her, and she looked up. "Who is it?" Elisheba was not setting foot in here if Bethany could keep her out.

"It's Japheth. May I come in?"

She jumped up to let him enter. "How can I help you?"

He nudged the door shut with the toe of his boot and grabbed both her arms.

"Wait! Stop!" The attack came out of nowhere, and she fought him with all the strength she had.

He let go with one of his hands, using it to cover her mouth. With her now free arm, she swung at him, but he didn't even acknowledge the blow. His large hand covered her the lower part of her face and a portion of her nose. She had trouble pulling in air and began to see dots dancing in front of her eyes.

He bent her back over her desk and brought his mouth down where his fingers covered her lips. She struggled but couldn't free herself. When he was close enough for her to feel his breath on her face, he stopped. "Don't be frightened. We're being watched, and everything we say is recorded."

She froze. Surely she hadn't heard him correctly. He'd spoken so low it could barely be called a whisper.

"This was the only way I could get a message to you without suspicion falling on us both." He loosened the grip on her mouth, and she gulped in air. "I need you to meet me at the Pod six, south exit tonight, just after Iddo's moonrise. I have some information you must have. He glanced at the door as a commotion began just outside it. "Nod if you understand."

The swift attack followed by a plea for a meeting made her head swim. Thank the One he hadn't asked her to answer him with words. She nodded.

He grinned at her nod. "Okay, hang on. It's about to get noisy, and don't forget our rendezvous." He pulled his hand completely away from her mouth, although he kept her bent over the desk. "Here they come."

She finally found her voice. "But what—"

Josiah paced outside Manaen's sick room, pausing to gaze out the window. What was taking that woman so long? Gehazi had insisted on changing his sister's bandages before they met. He'd wasted enough time before going after Bethany. Plans needed to be in place before nightfall.

"All right." Gehazi opened the door and stepped back for them to pass. "But remember, she's still healing. Do not over-tire her."

Bezek bounded into the room before him, giving Manaen a small kiss on the cheek and settling into the chair closest to her bed. She sat propped up in bed today, and the bandages had mostly been removed from her face. The wounds, though ugly, appeared to be healing. But the sight of a dark blue swath of cloth over her left eye caused his stomach to roil. The only reason for a patch was to cover a non-functioning eye. Without a word, he turned and followed the healer back into the outer room. "A minute of your time, if you please."

"Yes?"

"Her eye. Is it…will it…."

The sorrow he saw mirrored in Gehazi's eyes gave him his answer, but he waited for the words.

"It was beyond my skill to save, Commander." She looked down at her hands. "I had to choose between the time needed to save it or that needed to save her life."

He knew how much she loved his sister and what the choice must have cost her. He swallowed his own feelings and put his hand on her shoulder. "You chose well. And it wasn't your skill that was lacking, it was the facilities."

When he walked back into the room, Manaen and Bezek looked up from a whispered conversation. "Did she tell you about my eye?" Manaen had never been one to shy away from a difficult subject.

"She did." He took the other seat in the room. "And I swear it will not affect your position in my corps." Josiah nodded toward injury. "Others might have trouble compensating for the lack, but I know you won't." He grinned at her. "Besides, the patch seems to fit your personality."

"Oh, thank you, brother dear." She clasped her hands together in such a show of irony they all laughed.

Despite the release, he sobered as he thought of the small Seeker. There was nothing to laugh about until Bethany was safe. "We have plans to make, though."

Manaen looked from one to the other. "Do you have any idea where they'd have her?"

Bezek pulled a rolled up map from under his vest and pinned it to the wall of Manaen's quarters. "We thought we'd bring a little of the briefing room to you." He glanced at the door. "Not enough to irritate anyone, but enough to get your insight."

Josiah resisted the urge to grin at Bezek's wariness. "My thought is they're holding her deep within their main camp." Josiah sighed. "And no, we haven't devised a way to penetrate the talarium shielding well enough to get any kind of detailed info."

Bezek pointed to several lines radiating out north from their current location, back toward the city. "These represent the places we've sent the scouting parties."

"We could pinpoint this section as the origin of the attacks." Josiah joined him and pointed to a large area north of where they were. "All but two scouts are back. We're expecting word from them soon."

Manaen leaned forward. "What were their orders?"

"I told them to go as far as possible into the enemy's camps and stay as long as needed to gather intel." Josiah shook his head. "I'm concerned about the two who haven't contacted us."

"So their absence means one of two things." Manaen continued to study the map. "Either they're still gathering information or they've been killed or captured."

"I thought I just said that." Sometimes, his sister's fondness for the obvious could irritate a statue.

"If you'll just let me finish." Manaen glared up at him. "I think it might be a good idea to send a larger party in the same direction. No matter what's happened to them, the key to the enemy appears to lie there."

Simon burst through the door, Elisheba and Dr. Stanos right behind him. He'd heard Bethany's screams and didn't wait for an invitation. "What do you think you're doing?" In two steps, he was at Japheth's back, jerking him away from Bethany with such force Japheth landed hard on the couch against the wall.

Out of the corner of his eye, he saw Dr. Stanos and Elisheba go to Bethany's aid so he concentrated on Japheth. Even as the blood pounded through his veins from the sight of his attack on Bethany, a voice of caution whispered in his ear.

Japheth made no move to rise so Simon satisfied himself with standing over him. "Let's hear it. What were you thinking?" At a sound from Bethany, he turned and nodded at Dr. Stanos and Elisheba. "Why don't you two escort her to her quarters? She's had enough excitement for the day. I don't require any assistance to deal with this…this…infraction."

"No." Bethany backed away from their ministrations. "I need to put things in order, first."

Simon stared at her for a moment. "Okay, new plan. Everyone out. Bethany, get things settled, then let them take you to your quarters. Will that work?"

"Yes, thank you." She reached with a trembling hand to gather the papers spread over her desk. "I just need to get these things back in the safe."

"Would you like some help?" Dr. Stanos seemed reluctant to leave her.

Elisheba jumped into that opening with relish. "Absolutely. We'll help you get them back in order in no time."

"No. Stop." Bethany blocked Elisheba's path toward the desk and threw an almost desperate look at Dr. Stanos. "I'm fine. Just let me wind things up in peace."

Dr. Stanos took Elisheba by the arm and began leading her out of the room. "She'll get it done much faster without our interference." There was nothing slow about him. He'd read Bethany's unspoken plea as easily as Simon. Her father had trusted him. Perhaps she could as well.

Simon nodded at Bethany before turning back to Japheth. "Now it's your turn. We have some things to get straight, but this obviously isn't the place for it."

Japheth rose and grinned down at Simon as he walked to the door. Simon gulped. How *had* he managed to throw a man of Japheth's size across the room like that? Something was off about this entire situation.

He took a second to turn back to Bethany. "Are you sure you're okay?"

She nodded as she sorted the papers. "Yes. I'm just glad you came in when you did."

He left the office, closing the door behind him. Japheth waited for him by the lab's exit. Simon nodded once to Dr. Stanos, ignored Elisheba, and followed Japheth into the corridor.

Josiah knew he could handle the battle, but the thing that concerned him most was the governing council. What was going on with the Elders? He should have heard back from them. It was past time when they would normally have asked him to return for clarification on his report. Had they all believed everything Mahalah had to say? Were they even now being ambushed since so many were together? He needed answers, but everywhere he turned, he found only more questions.

The com unit beeped on his desk. He reached across the jumble of papers and swiveled his plasscreen so he could see who called. The screen showed an open channel on the securest of connections. He'd only seen this configuration a couple of times, and it took him a moment to place the origination code. Then it hit—the council. This code was reserved for nothing except the most urgent council business.

He rushed around his desk and settled into his seat before opening the com line. He could see by the icon in the corner of the screen his own video was working well, at least planetside. One could never guarantee what was seen from space. Moments passed, then the video on the other end appeared. As Elder Reuel's image filled the screen, Josiah had to fight the urge to jump to his feet in respect. Custom dictated both parties on a vidcall remained seated, no matter the disparity of rank.

"Commander." Elder Reuel inclined his head. "Thank you for taking my call. We have had many things to discuss, and I'm only now able to bring you up to date on the happenings in this council."

Josiah nodded. "My thanks for getting back with me so quickly. I can imagine there were plenty of things to keep you busy for upwards of a year."

The Elder signed. "That is too true. But I felt this information would give you the strength you need to continue on. Unfinished business drags at one's soul, I've found."

"What have you discovered?" Maybe that was a trifle blunt, but Josiah was at his wit's end with people who didn't get to the point and let him get on with his job.

"I seem to remember you're a man of action and few words, Commander." Elder Reuel smiled. "I'll see if I can summarize so as to allow you to get back to your valuable duties." There was no sarcasm in the Elder's tone, and Josiah breathed a sigh of relief at his leniency. "As you may have suspected, we have found evidence of malpractice, if you will."

"Excuse me?" He'd heard of the term used in medical references, but not in this connotation. An interesting choice of words.

"I'm certain it won't surprise you to find that Elder Mahalah was the brains behind this scheme, although he did have plenty of help. We've done a thorough vetting of all our ranks and removed the Elders who had any part in this tragedy." He sighed. "Even though we never expected to face an ordeal like this, our ancestors had all eventualities covered and there were specific strategies in place should such a situation arise."

It would have been nice to know about the precedents before he began losing sleep about everything that had been going on.

"Although we have, in essence, cut the head off the snake, you'll still need to do the mopping up job." He smiled. "But I thought you'd want to know the accusations concerning you have been entirely disproven. We all have the highest regard for your abilities, spiritual as well as mental. We couldn't be in better hands."

"Thank you, sir." High praise indeed coming from an Elder.

"So set your mind at rest, and do what the One has prepared you for. You have our full and complete blessings."

Elder Reuel signed off, leaving Josiah staring at a dark plasscreen. He'd been told approximately nothing about the inside attempt at subterfuge. Josiah leaned back in his chair to consider what had just transpired. Truthfully, he'd learned a great deal. First, all the traitors had been or were being dealt with. Second, the remaining Elders had faith in his abilities and had just empowered him to finish this freedom operation strong. Not a bad night, all things considered.

Simon stepped into the corridor close on Japheth's heels. "Bethany is mine, and anyone who touches her answers to me." He hadn't intended to be that blunt, but he meant every word. Everything clicked in his mind and he knew if Japheth didn't come up with a good explanation, he'd use the accelerator pistol sitting comfortably at his waist on the man. He'd waited too long, no one, not even Japheth, would get in his way of winning her.

Japheth stared down at him a moment, his expression unreadable. But before he could answer, two attendants hurried by. "Perhaps we'd better discuss this somewhere a bit more private."

"Where do you have in mind?" It didn't matter if Japheth took the lead—as long as they found a place less crowded.

Japheth nodded in the direction of their last clandestine conversation. "Troop inspection again?"

"That's probably as good a place as any." Simon blew out a breath and followed Japheth through the passages to the small side door. It would be better for everyone if this conversation weren't recorded. If it didn't go just right, he did not want any witnesses.

This time, the sentry smiled as they approached. "Going to teach them another lesson in staying alert?"

"Something like that." Japheth winked and motioned to the door. "We'll see how well they learned from the last time."

They retraced their previous path and didn't speak until they arrived at the rocky outcropping. "I'm not after Bethany," Japheth faced him squarely. "I never was."

"Then what have you been doing?" Simon folded his arms. "Nothing you do adds up."

"Actually, it does." Japheth began to pace, then stopped and turned to face him head on. "But you're not listening."

"Oh, I'm hearing what you're saying." The heat rose on Simon's neck. "But your words don't line up with your actions. From where I'm standing, nothing makes sense."

"Okay. Let me try it again." He glanced at the darkening sky. "But we don't have much time."

"Time for what?" Simon worked hard to keep his voice low. It wouldn't do for them to be interrupted. Japheth hadn't given him any reason not to use his weapon.

"We have got to get Bethany and the notebooks as far away from Aven as possible."

Simon blinked. "From Aven?"

"She's in terrible danger." He threw up his hands. "We all are."

"Slow down. What are you talking about?" Simon had never seen Japheth this close to losing control. "In case you hadn't noticed, we're on the winning side here."

Japheth just shook his head. "You couldn't be farther from the truth. We're not on the winning side." He cocked an eyebrow at Simon. "And you're about to lose everything if you don't figure this out."

"What do I need to figure out?" The words exploded from Simon's mouth and hung for a moment in the silent night air. They exchanged quick glances and scrambled further up the hill, separating to do a short reconnaissance.

They returned to the rocky outcropping, and Japheth motioned him close. "I don't have time to argue, so I'm going to lay it all out." He signed. "When you've decided, then I'll make my decision."

Was he armed as well? Simon stared hard at Japheth, but the other's face was unreadable in the shadows of twilight, and first moonrise was still at least an hour away. "Then get on with it."

"Foundational to all of this, that you need to understand that everything you've heard about the One from Bethany is true." He ran a hand through his hair. "We've done our best to wipe out truth from this planet, but the One won't be denied. That's why the

R'hobans are here." He held up a hand when Simon would have interrupted. "Second, Aven is pure evil. His goal isn't to free Sintue and the galaxy. He plans to enslave everyone—and if he can get his hands on Bethany's research, he'll be close to meeting that goal."

Simon stood still, feeling the words burn deep inside his mind. He'd always believed Seekers were nothing but superstitious idiots, but what if they'd been right all along? His thoughts raced as he catalogued the recent events. Odd pieces clicked into place, and a picture began to emerge. He squatted on the ground as his world reeled around him. "Could they have known the truth after all?"

"Yes, they could." Japheth bent down beside him. "You see it, don't you? The way everything fits?"

Simon could only nod. He saw the possibility—not the certainty, but definitely the possibility.

"This is what's going to happen next. I'm leaving for a few hours. I need you to cover for me, and be prepared when I return to get Bethany out." He pulled Simon to his feet. "Can you do that? Will you do that?"

"I will, but I still have a lot to consider."

Japheth looked at him a long moment. "That's good enough."

CHAPTER THIRTY-NINE

Josiah made the rounds at from sentry to sentry, working his way upward until he stood on the observation deck overlooking the compound and the brown fields surrounding them. The sun had already set, and Iscah had just appeared. Iddo's appearance was still several hours away. The twilight glow seemed to hold the moment suspended, almost like the silent upbeat of a conductor's baton.

"Commander!" Sure enough, right on cue, Calamus's shout heralded the crashing chords of a warrior's symphony.

"Over here." He guided Calamus with his voice.

"Sir, it's Bezek. He sent me to find you." Calamus grinned as he drew a deep breath.

"Easy man." Josiah's gut tightened in spite of Calamus's smile. "Slow down, and give me the message."

"They've captured one of the rebels. And he says he'll only speak with you."

Josiah's pulse leapt. Perhaps this was what he'd been waiting for. He motioned Calamus toward the exit. "Where are they now?"

"Bezek has him in your holding rooms."

Bethany sank onto a chair in her quarters, still shaken by the encounter with Japheth in the lab. It had all happened so fast. Why had she agreed to meet him? She rubbed her temples. Life was getting muddier by the moment. The time had come to slow down and separate fact from supposition. Leaning back, she closed her eyes to collect her thoughts.

Aven was evil personified, that much she didn't doubt. And he wanted to use her father's research for his own purpose. But did that mean all who worked for him were also bad? Even though she couldn't verify it, she thought some might be working on the side of good.

That led her to thoughts of Simon, and she sighed. He truly was an enigma. Once, one of her closest childhood friends, then a resource that kept her alive by providing her a means of survival of sorts. But during the course of that position, he'd developed ulterior motives—unpleasant ones—for her. And now…now she felt a return to that childhood camaraderie, but could she trust it? No insight offered itself, so she moved on.

Japheth, another enigma. He'd seemed to be Aven's right-hand man. But twice, she'd felt a sense of doubt concerning his loyalty to the dictator. Why? What about Japheth made her think he might be on her side? While his attack earlier today had caught her unawares, looking back, she did believe he'd staged it. If he'd wanted to force himself there had been plenty of other times—when she wouldn't have had rescuers so nearby. He'd known they'd be interrupted, even welcomed it.

She opened her eyes, a decision about that, at least, made. Meeting with Japheth was risky, but she'd do it. It was vital to remove her father's notebooks—and herself—from this place, and if Japheth wasn't her ally, perhaps she could use him to get back to Josiah.

Not that he'd want to see her. She'd been responsible for Manaen's injury or possible death. Her eyes filled with tears. Would he believe the worst about her? Or did he somehow know she'd followed the only course possible? She swiped the moisture from her face. Now wasn't the time to think about it.

She pulled the small pad she'd smuggled from the lab out of the pocket of her tunic. There'd been no way to get the notebooks out, but she'd transferred some of her father's gibberish to this so she could work with it in private. His research wouldn't help any of them if she couldn't figure out the key.

Josiah's heart echoed the pounding of his boots on the flagstone corridors. This had to be the answer he'd been praying for.

He stopped a few feet from the door of an interrogation room in the temporary holding area. The sentry saluted and opened the massive steel door. Josiah nodded at Bezek, who rose to salute. The room had no windows, and the stonework had aged to a dark gray. The lighting grates were concentrated over the metal table, which was bolted into the rockcrete floor. There were four chairs, three on one side of the table and one on the other. The prisoner sat silent, facing the door, the plascuffs shackles on his wrists attached to a ring on the top of the table.

Josiah took all this in as a matter of course, but his attention centered on the rebel. He was a big man, not as massive as a R'hoban, although head and shoulders above the average Sintuen. Even that anomaly retreated in the face of an almost tangible aura of calm waiting which radiated from the man. Not what one would expect from a captive.

"You wanted to speak with me?" Josiah sat in the center of the three seats and nodded at Bezek who took up a position against the door.

The prisoner spoke, "I carry information you need." He tilted his head. "I believe you'll recognize my designation. I am Japheth."

Adrenaline surged through Josiah, but he gave no outward sign. "That is an interesting name. What does it mean?" The rebel's answer to the coded message would determine whether he truly was whom he claimed.

His calm didn't waver. "It means wide-spreading. I've been designated to help spread the truth of the One."

Bezek blew out a breath and relaxed his stance. "About time you showed up."

"Although it wasn't his place to say so, his comment is accurate." Josiah turned and gave Bezek a look. "Why have you waited so long to contact us?"

"My cover was deep, and I couldn't risk discovery. The stakes are too high."

"Are you joining us permanently then?"

"That had been my plan, but now, it won't be possible." Japheth glanced at his hands. "Can you release me?"

Josiah nodded at Bezek who pulled the key from his belt and unlocked the shackles and took a seat.

The former prisoner rubbed his wrists before meeting Josiah's eyes. "You know who you battle, right?"

"If you mean a traitor from our own ranks, then yes." Josiah frowned at the hard look on Japheth's face. "Is there someone else involved as well?"

"The Prince is the ultimate manipulator behind all this." Japheth looked from one to the other. "I prayed you would know — or at least suspect this was the case."

"Manaen was right." Josiah exchanged a quick look with Bezek, even as his gut twisted. "What name is he using this time?"

"He's calling himself Aven. And his plans reach beyond this planet. His goal is to destroy the One's chosen people." Japheth sighed. "With the girl — and the secret she carries — he has the power he needs if he can only find the key."

"And how do you come to such intimate knowledge of what the Prince plans?" Under the cover of the table, Josiah's hand loosened the pistol from its holster. More than one man had been turned from the service of the One to serve the dark Prince.

"You'll have no need of your weapon." Japheth smiled. "I speak not from changing allegiances. I have been his second for many years now, protected by the One so I might be ready for such a time as this."

"Who are you?" Bezek rose and stumbled back against the wall. "What are you?"

Josiah forced himself to stay in his chair. "Is there something I'm missing here?"

"There is one thing you need to know. That is who the enemy truly is." Japheth's face sobered. "You are not only fighting his soldiers from outside, but several within your own ranks."

"Elder Mahalah?" Josiah hadn't doubted the answer to this one. "They have reported the traitors found and apprehended. Are there still more?"

"It is as you suspect." Japheth nodded. "But fear not, others are aware of what has transpired. The Elders are once again winnowing out those who do not serve the One. They are equipped for the battle within. Your fight is with Aven."

Josiah turned to Bezek. "See that this man's weapons are returned immediately."

"Yes, sir." Bezek bolted out the door.

"We may have already kept you too long if you are to return without suspicion." Josiah rose and gestured for Japheth to precede him out the door. "What else can we do for you?"

Japheth reached into an inner pocket of his vest. "You'll have need of these." He handed a tiny message tube to Josiah. "This contains the layout of the enemy's stronghold, along with routes which you'll find unguarded."

Josiah took the tube. "Will you be safe?"

Japheth clasped Josiah's upper arm. "I am in the service of the One. I couldn't be safer anywhere else."

Bezek returned with Japheth's accelerator pistol and sword. "Here they are." He presented them and half bowed.

Japheth turned to Josiah. "Bezek can see me on my way." He nodded at the message clutched in Josiah's hand. "You need to get your plans made quickly. The night of battle is nearly upon us."

CHAPTER FORTY

The usual group, minus Japheth once again, gathered in Aven's rooms. Simon found it odd to see Aven without his second, but Delaina flitted about, offering refreshment and filling the area with her tinkling laugh. "Okay, everyone." She clapped her hands for attention. "Let's bring this gathering to order." She put a finger to her chin and threw an impish look in Aven's direction. "That is, if you're ready."

He gave her an indulgent smile and nodded. "Yes, even though we're missing one, we still have much to cover."

"Where is he?" Baanus swiveled his head, searching, as if he'd just noticed the absence.

"Japheth will return shortly." Aven waved a dismissive hand. "His errand was personal and fully sanctioned."

"Does it involve a certain young woman?" Salisa turned a sly wink at Simon.

Simon returned the wink and added a smirk, ignoring the bile rising in his throat. He'd die before he'd allow the hag to know the depth of his feelings for Bethany.

Salisa cackled at his response. "You're not fooling me one wit."

"Quit teasing the man." Delaina took the chair to his right and patted his arm. "How could he be interested in that child when he has others around with so much more to offer?"

"Come now, children." Aven gave them all an indulgent look. "I have serious matters to discuss."

"Hrumph." Baanus glared in Simon's direction. "It's about time we got down to business."

Aven steepled his fingers and leaned forward, his expression solemn. "It's come to my attention that we may have a traitor in our midst."

Salisa and Delaina immediately turned toward Baanus.

"See here now." His face blotched an angry red, and he swallowed hard before looking back at Aven. "You know where my loyalty lies." He gestured to Simon. "I say look to the newest members of this group."

Simon ignored Baanus and looked to Aven, keeping a carefully neutral expression. "Do you know the identity of the traitor?"

"I have a team working on that even as we meet." He grimaced. "It's such a sad business, extracting this kind of information."

"I'm so glad you are on top of this." Delaina gave a little shiver. "Extraction is always so messy."

"You're just not practiced enough." Salisa gave a self-deprecating cough. "There are ways to get what's needed without all the gore."

Aven clicked his tongue. "But, Salisa, if they don't have what we need, it's important to the cause to keep the brain intact."

She gave a bark of laughter. "Infants, that's what you all are. Just a bunch of babies."

A servant entered the room and passed a note to Aven. He scanned it before returning his attention to the group. "It appears I'm needed to help with the…" He looked at Delaina and laughed. "How did you put it? Ah yes, information extraction." He strode toward the door, still chuckling.

Bethany glanced at the chrono on her wrist. Iddo would be rising soon. She needed to decide whether or not to meet Japheth. There was something about the encounter with him that made her almost certain he meant no harm.

She went to the clothing chest in the corner of her room and exchanged her light-colored tunic for one of a deeper shade. The last thing she wanted was to draw attention to herself. She tapped the designation of Pod six on her cuff and hurried down the hallway.

As she walked she tried to come up with a plausible reason for wandering around alone, although none of those she passed challenged her—or, for that matter, appeared to give her a second thought. She moved past several hallways that ended at what she assumed were outside doors, each presided over by at least one sentry. Surely Japheth wouldn't send her to a guarded entrance. He'd gone to too much trouble to arrange the meeting in the first place.

The amber light on her arm blinked at an ever increasing rate, assuring her she was on the right track. There were fewer people about as she continued to pod six. One final turn found her in short corridor ending at a massive steel door, indicative of an outside entrance. She glanced back over her shoulder, but there were no sentries in sight.

She gave the door a slight tug, and it slid open without effort. An immediate smell of dirt and cooling rocks assaulted her. She looked down at her feet and found a small rock, about half the size of her thumb. It fit perfectly in the door track, and would keep it from latching when she exited. She inserted the pebble, took a deep breath, and stepped into the night.

Iddo was just visible over the horizon, and she stopped for a moment to take in the beauty of its rising. How she'd loved to watch the evening sky with her father.

"It is a sight to inspire, isn't it?"

She jumped back at Japheth's words. "I didn't hear you come up."

"I wasn't sure if you'd show up or not." He took her arm carefully and led her a ways from the doorway. The flat, rocky ground made walking easy, but she didn't pull away from his gentle grasp.

"I wasn't certain either. But I decided to trust you." She looked up to face him. "Did I make a mistake?"

"No, you did not." His white teeth shown in the moonlight. "I am honored you chose to trust me." He stopped when they came to several large boulders and he perched on one, bringing his head almost even with hers. "I have much to tell you."

She gazed back at the sky, trying to pinpoint her location without being too obvious. Knowing where she was put her one step closer to freedom.

Japheth took her wrist and studied the silver cuff. "As long as you wear that device, you'll not be able to escape."

She jerked her arm away. "If you don't mean to help me, why did you arrange this meeting?"

"You need to know the things that lie ahead of you." His eyes focused somewhere in the distance. "And what's at stake."

"I know what's at stake." She shook her head. "And what's coming can't be any worse than the things I've already lived through."

"I have to disagree." His expression was serious. "If the R'hobans are not victorious, all the evil you've experienced will be a but a fond memory."

She studied his face. "It's the future I read about in the Book of Truth, isn't it? It's here. Now."

He shook his head. "The Book of Truth states that no one knows the time of the end."

"But you're not just anyone. And it states that no *man* shall know. She brushed the hair back from her face as the wind picked up.

"What a thing to say." The grin was back. "I think you're comparing me to a certain giant with commander's bars on his collar."

She folded her arms and gazed at the dark landscape. Would she ever see Josiah again? No, she mustn't dwell on the might have beens. She knew better than to let the past engulf her. Bethany sighed and turned back. "What do want from me?"

"When the R'hobans come after you—" He held up a hand to stop her protest. "And they will. I need you to gather your father's research and stick close to me. It's imperative that Aven not have access to your father's research."

"His notes are indecipherable. And beyond that, the R'hobans believe I betrayed them." She gave a harsh laugh and walked a little away. "At least their commander does."

Japheth was beside her in an instant. "No, he does not." He took her by the shoulders and turned her so she faced him. "The love you and Josiah share has been ordained by the One."

Bethany fought the tears that gathered in her eyes. He couldn't know. How could anyone guess her feelings for Josiah? "No." She twisted out of his grasp. "He believes I betrayed and abandoned his sister. No one could ever forgive that." She held her head in her hands. "For all I know, Manaen didn't even survive."

"She survived, little one."

At the endearment given her by Josiah she turned, still blinded by the tears. "What…what did you call me?" She grabbed his arm. "And Manaen survived? You know this for sure?"

"Yes, I'm certain." He led her back to the boulders. "And I'm also certain they are coming. It's imperative you're prepared." He turned and spoke to the shadow of the doorway. "And you'll need to be ready as well."

CHAPTER FORTY-ONE

Josiah had loaded the message tube into the large reader in his briefing room. He studied the massive underground complex detailed in the schematics. How had something this huge escaped their notice? He leaned back and rotated his head, trying to ease the ache in his shoulders. Only someone with the authority of an Elder could have erased such information from the intel they'd been given. He glanced at the chrono readout. He'd ordered Bezek to bring Jael back with him. The three of them could get a head start on the plans.

Right on cue, he heard the outer door open, followed almost immediately by the appearance of the three. He gestured them to seats around the table, the schematic suspended in the air as a three-D representation of the underground complex.

Bezek whistled through his teeth at the gigantic installation. "Wouldn't have thought we'd have missed something so large."

Jael studied the layout. "We didn't miss it. It was purposefully hidden, wasn't it?"

Trust Jael to get right to the heart of the matter without mincing words. "We know Elder Mahalah and at least six other Elders were involved to some degree." Josiah focused on Bezek. "Have you briefed him?"

"I have." Bezek took a seat and began entering notes on the nearest keypad. "And I've given him the overview of our objective."

Josiah turned to Jael. "Any thoughts?"

Jael leaned in to peer deeper into the complex. "How confident are you of the intel?"

"I couldn't trust it more if I'd gathered it myself." Josiah still hadn't admitted aloud who or what he thought Japheth was, but he trusted him implicitly.

"Good enough." Jael returned to his study of the installation. "I assume the standard codes apply?"

Josiah nodded. "Yes, we'll be looking for entrances marked in amber. Those will be unmanned." He pointed to a map key, loaded with the information they needed. "From what I've seen, this includes up-to-date intel on everything we need to get us in undetected."

"Does this tell us where Bethany is being held?" Bezek faced Josiah square on.

Josiah grinned. "My assumption would be in the set of rooms marked 'Bethany's lab.'"

After another restless night, Bethany trudged back through the corridors to the lab. Her mind kept swinging between what Japheth had told her and memories of her father, especially how they spent hours watching the stars in the sky. As she turned the last corner, the flashing lights on her cuff pulled something to the surface of her memory. *Could it be that simple?* She rushed to the door and palmed her way in.

Once inside, she took a deep breath, forcing herself to move naturally. Japheth had warned about surveillance, and if she was onto something, she couldn't afford for it fall into Aven's hands. This time, she'd think first and act later.

She'd just finished fixing her qua when Dr. Stanos appeared. "Good morning, my dear." He began assembling his own beverage. "Did you sleep well?"

"Not really." She feigned a yawn and picked up her cup, moving with deliberate indifference in spite of the adrenaline coursing through her veins. "But I need to get to work."

"I was considering something last night." He leaned back against the cold storage cabinet. "Amariah did love his puzzles. But he kept them simple, obvious even. That's what made them so hard to see. The rest of us over-complicated matters." He sighed. "It was the true genius of your father—his elegant simplicity."

"Unfortunately, I've already looked at the simple solutions." Bethany laughed and headed toward her office, even as her palms fairly itched to get back at her father's notebooks. "I'm afraid Daddy made this one a bit more complicated."

"Such a shame it's been so long." He followed her to the doorway. "But give me a shout if you think of anything."

"Thank you." She palmed open the door, slipped inside, and set the qua on the desk. It would be odd if she didn't retrieve the notebooks, but she hated to have them out in the open. Someone else might discover the same clue she had.

"I'll leave you to it." He disappeared back into the main room, and Bethany squatted down to open the research.

She pulled the notebooks from the safe and placed them on her desk. She ran her hands over the worn covers, trying to appear as someone deeply lost in memories. She couldn't have been more alert. Her fingers searched for the tiny symbols in the upper left quadrant of each book. If they were present, she'd have the key to the chaos. There, looking to all the world like a dot or two of random ink, were the keys. Immediately, the order she'd been searching for crystalized in her mind.

Instead of taking the first one, though, she pulled a later one toward her and opened it. *Let it fall into place…and help me keep it hidden.* Sure enough, there before her lay the answer, mapped in the night skies of Sintue.

The summons flashing on his personal plasscreen must have been keyed to his chrono settings. Simon would have sworn it wasn't there when he'd entered the bathing unit. But it was there now, an invitation to break his fast with Aven. He grunted. A polite invitation—at least as long as he complied. He had no illusions about what would happen if he ignored such a summons.

He finished dressing, taking special effort with his uniform before he set off for the meeting. Only minutes later, a servant ushered Simon into Aven's morning room. The odor of Jakan's fabulous culinary creations wafted around him.

"Welcome." Aven, already seated at a small table in the alcove, waved him toward the chair opposite him. "I'm pleased to see you are continuing to be punctual."

"I can't imagine any who would be tardy to one of Jakan's feasts." He seated himself and a servant poured his qua.

"Do you hear that, Jakan?" Aven called to the chef who was entering with another steaming dish. "Your mastery holds even more appeal than mine."

Jakan just grunted and uncovered the dish of sautéed Turnish hens. The aroma hinted at a subtle nuttiness balanced with a citrus tang. In all the time Simon had spent with Aven, he'd never once heard Jakan do more than grunt. He studied the man as he busied himself arranging dishes and noticed the old scars around his face and neck. His twisted left leg was obviously the cause of his limp, but Simon wondered if there were other injuries that left him unable to speak.

"Thank you." Simon tried to test his theory.

Jakan didn't even grunt this time or bother to meet his eyes, just finished his duties and quit the room.

"Does he ever talk?' Simon took a bite of the hen and savored it. Jakan was a master artist when it came to cuisine.

"He cannot." Aven shook his head. "He worked for an enemy of mine, and we required some information. Delaina was still perfecting her technique…and there was an accident." He sipped his juice.

The fowl turned to dust in Simon's mouth as he considered what the man had endured. He swallowed hard. How could Jakan stand to remain in Aven's employ?

"It's not as bad as it seems." Aven must have caught the look on his face. "I called in Salisa, had her erase the memories of what had transpired." He gave a slight smile. "I'm not a monster, you see."

"Of course." Simon did his best to make his response as natural as possible. "Unfortunate business."

"So true." Aven set down his fork and pushed his plate away. "And now, we must discuss some other unfortunate business."

Simon reached for his qua and leaned back. *Here it came.* "I'm always ready to serve you."

Aven stood and began to pace. "As I mentioned last eve, we do have at least one traitor in our midst. We're ferreting out how deep the infection goes with the help of Elisheba. Her assistance is proving invaluable." He turned back to Simon. "She has an uncanny knack of being in the right place at the right time."

"I suspected as much." Simon took another sip. "Do we know yet how many of our people are affected?"

"No." Aven resumed his seat across from Simon. "But I must admit I have my doubts about your little Seeker."

Simon choked on his drink and took a moment mopping up what was spilled. This gave him time to present the façade he desired. "I'm truly shocked. It was my understanding that she was hard at work on her assignment."

Aven watched him with hooded eyes. "So it appears. But she's not been open to resuming her relationship with Elisheba, and that troubles us both." He pursed his lips. "It's this behavior I find suspect."

"I've sensed nothing but her gratitude at being rescued." Simon schooled his features into a look of concentration. This needed a careful touch. It wouldn't do to jump to her defense too readily. "Japheth and I have been keeping close tabs on her."

"Yes, I've noted how concerned you both are for her welfare."

Simon gave him a sharp look, but Aven didn't allude further to any possible conflict between he and Japheth over Bethany. "I will continue to stay on top of the situation."

"That is all I ask." Aven leaned back. "She is a most important part of my overall goal."

"Sir?" Could this be the information he'd been waiting for?

Aven carefully refolded the napkin at his place setting. "My plan is not just for the liberation of Sintue, but for the entire galaxy."

Simon nodded, willing Aven to continue.

"It seems Bethany's father was in possession of research that would allow us to re-energize the microscopic organisms here on Sintue." He gestured to the sky. "Or any world, for that matter."

"I had heard as much." Simon crossed his ankle over one knee. "But I'm not certain how that could help us wipe out the R'hobans."

"That's because I hadn't yet shared that part of the plan with you." Aven leaned back and smiled. "I've hints that this process can also be reversed, destroying everything on any planet."

"I see." Simon sat for a moment, letting the implications of this monstrous plan seep in. "In essence, you would hold the key to life and death—everywhere."

"Yes, yes, you understand now." Aven nodded. "But it is critical to get the exact formula from the girl. I am counting on you to make this happen." He narrowed his eyes. "One way or another."

Aven rose, and Simon joined him. "I have several pressing matters, but I want you to be aware that the entire key to my success lies in that one girl. Bring her knowledge to me, and you can name your price—and your position. Fail me, and…" He looked toward the food preparation area where Jael had gone. "Well, I think we understand one another."

CHAPTER FORTY-TWO

This morning, Manaen met with them in the large briefing room as they finalized their battle plans. She sat in her accustomed seat, to the right of Josiah. He hadn't demeaned her by speaking with the corps before her arrival, but his stern expression kept any who doubted her capabilities from sharing their concerns by overt comments or even sidelong glances.

Josiah glanced once more around the room of expectant faces before launching into the briefing. "As you are aware, we have come into possession of a detailed map of the enemy complex." He nodded toward the 3D representation. "With this information, the One has given us far beyond what we could ever hope or ask." A cheer erupted as faces celebrated the provision of the One they served.

He let the celebration die out before he continued. "But with this has also come the knowledge of whom we face." He shook his head. "And for the first time, we count some of our very leaders among those we must defeat." There were several audible gasps, and he nodded to Jael to continue.

Jael stood, his expression stony but composed. "We face an enemy who'd been against us from the beginning of time. The Prince of Evil has seen fit to wage war yet again, this time here on the soil of Sintue. Beyond that, some of the chosen have shared intelligence with our enemies, and even now, the Elders are meeting to clean up their own ranks." He held up his hand at the murmurings that broke out. "But the One has sent help from on high. And I believe we will be victorious—not just here, on Sintue, but throughout the galaxy."

Again, cheers resounded through the room, and Josiah held up his hands for order as Jael took his seat. "We've been at this all night and have devised a battle plan." He motioned to Bezek. "We'll give you the overview, then divide you into teams. The leaders will have your individual assignments."

Bezek stepped to the place Josiah vacated and outlined the scope of the plan. "We'll enter on three fronts." He illuminated three entrances in violet. "These are either not guarded at all or are held by minimal personnel. They also have the added advantage of being the most direct routes to the equipment magazine, the command center, and the largest vehicle bay." As he spoke, he illuminated the referenced paths and sections in amber. "We are uncertain at the number of personnel we'll encounter, so full stealth is required." He exchanged a look with Josiah. "We know they have no trouble bringing down a highly trained unit, so be ready for anything."

Josiah keyed a sequence on his own personal plasscreen that fed to the main viewer. "Jael will lead the raid on the equipment magazine. Bezek will direct the squads assigned to the command center." He took a deep breath and avoided Manaen's eyes. "And Calamus commands the team focusing on the vehicle bay." He nodded at each around the room. "You have your assignments and the rest of the day to prepare. Dismissed." Only then did he glance in Manaen's direction.

Her face was calm as she studied him. "And where am I assigned?"

"You're not." He broke eye contact first and glanced at Bezek who watched them both, even as he moved to brief his team. "I have been advised you're still healing."

She swiveled her chair, hands on the armrests, to face him more directly. "And since when has that stopped either of us from doing our duty?"

He took a seat beside her. "It hasn't—in the past." He ran a hand through his hair. "I know you can hold the same position as before. But you still need time to learn to compensate for the loss of your eye." He'd gotten it out. He could only hope she'd take what he said as a confirmation in her abilities and not as a slam on them.

She inhaled to speak, then stopped before starting again. "I agree. I cannot move back into my same position." She looked at him. "Not without a little time." She folded her arms. But I will *not* accept being left behind completely."

"I understand." He and Bezek had discussed this and had, hopefully, come up with a workable solution. "We need air support, even though this raid will take place mostly underground."

She bit her lip, and he could sense the battle she fought inside. After a long moment, she looked up. "Of course." Her smile held the promise of obedience and something else. "But I claim the use of your personal aircar."

The day had provided Bethany with one revelation upon another. She arched her back and the muscles complained after being in one position for too long. The hardest part was juggling all the information without recording any of it…anywhere. She sighed, but her confidence in her father's research knew no limit. It dovetailed perfectly with what she'd been working on when the cleansings began. And—more importantly—it explained the one green field she'd noticed. That had been her father's last planting, with her suggestions incorporated, before he'd been killed.

The knock on her office door brought her to her feet. "Yes. Who is it?"

"You've been in there all day," Simon said. "We're here to make certain you get a hot meal this evening."

She hated to stop now, but knew she needed to eat. She walked over and opened the door. "Just let me return these to the safe, and I'll be ready."

Japheth followed Simon into the office. "I'll help." He juggled some notebooks of his own and added two of hers to the stack.

"No." she put her hand out, desperate to pull them from his grasp, but something in his face stopped her. "Okay, I'll get the rest." She picked up the remainder from the desk.

"This'll make for faster work and get you fed sooner." He stooped down to opening and, with a slight of hand almost too fast to see, inserted his notebooks inside instead of her father's. His eyes held hers as he did it, trying to communicate a message she didn't quite understand.

"Oh, thank you." Bethany didn't know what he planned, but as long as the notebooks were still in this office, she wasn't budging. He'd just liberated two of hers, so maybe he'd do the same with the rest. She handed him the other four and watched him perform the same trick as before. Now he held her notebooks instead of his own. Was that really any better? Only time would tell.

Simon helped her to her feet and continued to hold her arm. "Let's get to it then. I'm starved."

CHAPTER FORTY-THREE

As they finished up the evening meal, a shrill tone came blasting over the intercom system, reverberating along Bethany's spine and drilling through the bones in her skull. This was followed almost immediately with a total blackout. *Not again.*

Japheth and Simon leapt to their feet, each grabbing one of her arms. As emergency lights flickered to life, they propelled her out of the food commons. Bethany checked to make certain Japheth still wore the side pack where he'd stowed her notebooks. Once she caught sight of it, she allowed herself to be bustled along the corridors. The lights flashed an odd counterpart to the shrill repeating tone, making her head ache and her eyes water.

She oriented herself and almost protested. Why weren't they heading to an exit instead of back to the lab? Japheth had her notebooks. There wasn't anything else of value left behind. How could Josiah find her there? Just when she thought she'd scream, the questions the noise cut off, the silence almost as disorienting as the warning system.

"Wait...stop." She managed to work her arm free from Simon and halted, facing him in the murky light, forcing Japheth to a standstill as well. "I'll not go another step further until you explain where we're going and why."

"It's the safest place for you." Simon reached for, and she evaded him. "I know you want to get out, but there'll be time for that after the fighting ends." He exchanged a glance with Japheth. "Besides, the R'hobans expect you to be in your lab. Nowhere else."

She turned to Japheth. "Is this true?"

He nodded, then forced her to one side as a squad of rebels rounded the corner and ran past them before disappearing from view. "Everything he said is correct, but we need to hurry." He looked around. "You must be there when they arrive."

Josiah had inserted himself and his personal team into the squads Calamus led. He hated to usurp the young warrior's first leadership position, but felt responsible for his safety. Besides which, the vehicle bay in his section really was the closest insertion point to Bethany's lab. They'd break off soon to rescue her.

So far, the attack was unfolding as planned. It was the first thing about this liberation that had gone as expected. Perhaps the worst was over. If things continued in this vein, he'd soon have Bethany safe beside him.

An explosion from their right rocked the corridor and the emergency lights flickered and died, leaving only their own headlamps to illuminate the obstacle. And obstacle it was. Enemy troops poured through a ragged opening in wall.

"Form up." The calm voice of Calamus echoed in Josiah's earpiece. "We expected an attack of this type. Engage and close the perimeter."

Josiah relaxed as he moved around the incursion, leaving command in Calamus's capable hands. He couldn't have done better himself. The troops responded well, and soon, the rebels were on the run.

"Stay focused." Calamus kept his men on track. "Our job is to secure the vehicle bay. No side trips allowed."

Excellent. This man will make a formidable leader. A flashing light on his helmet's screen caught his eye and reminded him it was time to veer off on his own mission.

"Sir." Calamus had engaged the private com. "This is where we part ways. Are you certain you have everything you need?" No worry in his tone, just a leader verifying readiness before moving forward.

Josiah toggled the com line with his tongue. "We're good to go." He gave the hand signal his team had been watching for. "I'm leaving the troops in excellent hands. We'll see you on the other side." He caught sight of Calamus's salute before he jogged down a corridor toward his own goal.

Bethany waited while Simon palmed open the lab door and entered. Almost instantly, he ducked to one side as he was met with the blast of an accelerator pistol, followed by Elisheba's screech. She and Japheth peered out as Dr. Stanos came into view.

"Woman, you will get us all killed." Dr. Stanos held the weapon in one hand and the arm of a struggling Elisheba in another. "My apologies." He shoved Elisheba toward Simon, who neatly pushed her out into the corridor and secured the entrance behind her.

"Nicely done." The smile in Japheth's voice was evident despite the erratic lighting. "Is there anyone else we need to be concerned about?"

"No, it was just us." Dr. Stanos set the pistol on a nearby counter. "This one's an extra. I thought we might need it."

"I take it she wasn't aware that you were on our side?" Simon retrieved the gun and stuck it in the waistband of his trousers.

"No." Dr. Stanos grinned. "And I took special delight in explaining it to her."

Bethany nodded toward the commotion coming from the outside lab door. "She doesn't seem to be taking it too well. Can she get back in?"

Japheth shook his head. "We had Dr. Stanos reprogram the entry codes today." He looked at Bethany. "It gave him something to do since you wouldn't accept any help."

"I wasn't certain whom I could trust." Bethany's face warmed as the blood rushed to her cheeks. *Good thing they can't see me in this lighting.*

"I hope you've managed to work out the code. I couldn't be sure, but thought you might have been on to something." Japheth pulled off the side pack and transferred it to Bethany's shoulder, adjusting the strap to keep it snug. "These are yours and need to stay with you—no matter what." He strode to the door. The banging had quieted, and he put his ear to it. "Looks like she's gone for some help."

"Where are you going?" Simon made a move toward Japheth, then looked at Bethany and stopped. "I thought you'd stay with us."

"I'll be back soon." Japheth eased through the entrance manually and peered outside. "I have one more quick task to accomplish." With that, he ducked out the door, and it whooshed shut behind him.

Josiah led the way through the corridors, confident in the map Japheth had provided. So far, no unexpected ambushes. The heat sensor suddenly blossomed dark red on his view screen and he pulled up, motioning those with him to halt. He focused its beam to bounce the invisible ray around the next corner and received the reading he suspected. A pod of enemy soldiers lay in wait, positioned to catch him unaware.

He grinned in his helmet, remembering lessons drummed into him by an elderly trainer. *An ambush is only effective when your enemies don't know it's coming.* Well, now his troops held the element of surprise.

Dividing his team into two, he sent half back down the corridor to approach from the other side. They'd catch the rebels between them and have them disarmed and unconscious before they knew what had happened. They were the last obstacle in his path to Bethany.

He glanced at his chrono. His men should be in place. He was about to give the signal to attack when the ceiling exploded above him, raining debris and laser fire down on them. A quick glance proved only one way out of this ambush. "Move forward, half take up rear-facing positions." Those could hold their flank while the rest moved out to engage the waiting ambush.

Explosions ahead assured him the rest of his team had the enemy's attention, and he led those with him into the thick of battle. Instead of a small rebel force, surprised by his team, he found himself looking down the barrel of a full-size laser cannon. "Evasive Point One," he ordered. The automatic response momentarily saved his life and that of his warriors. But he had to come up with a new option quick because they were caught between two larger forces.

Yet another wall exploded, this time directly across from his stranded team, and he felt his heart lurch. A third group of enemies would ensure their defeat. But instead of the enemy, he faced a lone man. He'd recognize that form anywhere. Japheth motioned them into the hole he'd ripped in the corridor, and Josiah held off enemy fire as the rest ducked into the opening. When all were safe, he backed in behind them and aimed his laser rifle up at a cross beam in the ceiling. His shot was true as debris rained down, blocking the recent escape route and making it impossible for the enemy to follow.

He pulled off his helmet and turned to Japheth. "What about the rest of my team?"

Before Japheth could answer, his remaining men jogged into sight. Josiah expelled a pent-up breath. "It seems I owe you our lives."

"Later." Japheth cocked his head, hearing something Josiah could only guess at. "You still have work to do before we're done."

Several minutes had passed since Japheth left, and from the noise at the door, it seemed Elisheba had returned with reinforcements. "Now what?" Bethany turned to Simon. "It won't be long before they get through." She didn't miss the look he exchanged with Dr. Stanos.

"Back to your office." Simon passed her the pistol Dr. Stanos had taken from Elisheba. "I hope you still remember how to use this."

She took the weapon and checked the charge. "If you recall, I'm a better shot than you."

"Were." He motioned her ahead of him. "I've had a few more years of practice now."

They barricaded themselves in the inner office and despite her bravado, Bethany's optimism began to ebb.

"Don't worry." Simon gave her a lopsided grin. "The One hasn't brought you this far to abandon you here."

"The One?" Her heart almost skipped a beat, and she grabbed him by the arm. "Do you know Him?"

He winked at her. "We've had some interesting discussions lately."

Before she could answer, she heard the outer door give way and a commotion erupted outside the inside door. The only familiar voice among the chaos belonged to Elisheba. "They're here. I know it. They must have retreated into her office."

Bethany exchanged looks with Simon and Dr. Stanos. Someone tried the door and it held. "They've got to be in here. It's secured from the inside," said Elisheba.

"They'll be in here with us in moments." Simon positioned himself in front of the door, and looked up at the ceiling. "Doc, do you know what's on the floor above us?"

Dr. Stanos squinted upward. "If my calculations are correct, I believe the large vehicle bay is directly above us."

"Not a good option." Simon examined the walls. "I don't think any of us want a couple of ten ton trucks sitting in here with us."

"With us would be fine." Bethany tried to smile. "But on top of us wouldn't work at all."

Dr. Stanos stared at the door, beginning to buckle under continued laser fire. "We may not have much choice."

Josiah and his team took the last turn and skidded to a stop outside the lab. Chaos reigned as several rebels held ongoing laser fire at an inner door. That had to be where Bethany was. But before he could act, the enemy spied them and fired at Josiah's team, forcing them to a defensive posture.

They returned fire and appeared to be gaining the upper hand when he saw the inner door give way. He caught a glimpse of Bethany and then an explosion rocked the room. Before his eyes, a large section of ceiling gave way and collapsed on the place where he'd seen her crouched.

The inner door disintegrated. Bethany saw what looked like a squad of R'hobans. Before she could be sure, the world above her fell in. She'd have been crushed if Simon hadn't shoved her out of the way. Coughing as the debris still filtered around them, she felt for the accelerator pistol, encountering an arm instead.

She swiped at her eyes and peered into the settling dust. Simon lay where she'd been only moments before, pinned beneath debris and unmoving. She tugged ineffectually at his arm, but he didn't move. He groaned, but she couldn't make out his words. Spying the accelerator pistol, she grabbed it and rose, hoping to go for help. Instead, her eyes met Elisheba, who gave a shout of triumph. Without a moment's hesitation, Bethany raised the pistol and pointed it straight at her. "Come one step closer and I'll shoot."

Josiah watched as Elisheba dropped out of sight behind the debris pile. He let his team secure the defeated combatants. His only coherent thought was to reach Bethany.

Before he could reach her, she dropped to her knees and began to work on freeing someone. "It's Simon. Help me get him out."

He joined her, but even with the help of his strength and that of his squad, it took several precious minutes to free the man. He was bleeding profusely from several shallow wounds and one arm was twisted at an impossible angle, but other than that, he seemed intact.

"My troops are in the bay above us." Josiah pointed at the long beam that made a ramp of sorts to the next level. "If we can get up there, we'll be safe." He could still hear fighting, but that was their point of extraction. He'd have to chance it.

Bethany turned to Simon. "Can you make it?"

He gritted his teeth. "I will."

Josiah sent half the squad up and positioned the rest around the room to keep them as safe as possible during the ascent. First up was Dr. Stanos, then Simon, then Bethany, and lastly himself, followed by his remaining troops.

As they ascended, the fighting escalated. Shouts of the enemy and his men mingled with explosions and small arms fire. He tried to use his bulk to shield her, but she was slightly ahead of him. Too late though, he saw a rebel sighting a laser rifle in her direction. Before he could react, Simon had thrown himself in front of Bethany. Red blossomed across Simon's chest as one of Josiah's squad pulled Simon to safety and another took out the sniper. They laid Simon carefully on the rockcrete floor, and Bethany collapsed beside him.

She worked to stop the blood flow, but Simon covered her hand with his. "Don't. I know it's my time." He coughed and a trickle of red appeared at the corner of his mouth. "Just remember me." He nodded at Josiah. "You'll be safe with him until we meet again in eternity." He gave a shuddering breath and lay still.

Bethany turned tear-filled eyes to Josiah. "We can't just leave him here." She was sobbing now. "He saved my life. I can't."

Josiah glanced around the wreckage of the room. He could see that the bay doors had been opened to the sky, and it appeared air support was close by. "Calamus, this is Red Leader checking in."

"Good to hear from you, Red Leader." The young man's voice came through the com strong. "We've got reinforcements from Yellow Leader just maneuvering into position. Copy?"

"Yellow Leader has you covered." Manaen's voice was a welcome addition to the battle. "Have you gotten the package out?"

"Affirmative." Josiah peered around a ground rover and saw his personal aircar hovering close by. "Ready to take it on board?"

At that moment, a small well-armored craft rocketed skyward, launched from inside another vehicle. It swooped past the aircar, gone too quickly for Manaen to bring it down. His gut clenched.

He'd seen a craft like that only once before. When he'd come close to capturing the Prince. Once again, his enemy had eluded him.

Manaen touched down in the main bay, and Josiah loaded Bethany, Dr. Stanos, and Simon on board. He turned to his sister. "Have the other teams reported in?"

"Everything's well in hand." She nodded at Bethany. "It's time to go home."

Bethany watched the woman with the amazing green eyes once again direct the craft that saw her to safety. The view of her world carried with it the perspective of the past few months. She sighed and leaned her head back.

"It pains me to think I ever doubted you." Josiah slipped into the seat beside her.

"I don't blame you." She glanced at him, his expression hard to read in the predawn light.

"I blame me." He drew her close to him. "And a lifetime won't be long enough to show you how much I love you." He gently put a finger under her chin and tilted her face up to his.

A sob caught in her throat. "I do love you."

His lips met hers as the sun's first rays touched the darkened sky. The long night was over. Her place in the light had begun.

EPILOGUE

"Are you certain I look good enough? For Josiah, I mean?" Bethany tugged at the neckline of her red gown. Although the style was simple, the rich fabric was woven with a gold thread in the warp, causing the garment to give off a delicate shimmer whenever she moved. The fitted bodice emphasized her small waist, and the sleeves ended in points that attached with a ring of twelve colored stones around each of her middle fingers. "Here on Sintue, we lean more to lace and ruffles for a joining."

Manaen laughed, an uncharacteristic girlish giggle. "We may be on Sintue, but we're celebrating as R'hobans." She peered over Bethany's shoulder at the reflection in the full length mirror. "And you look magnificent. Although I doubt he'll even notice what you're wearing."

Bethany moved aside so Manaen could adjust her own deep burgundy gown. Today, her unseeing eye was covered with a matching patch, giving her a rakish air. "Oh well, at least all eyes will be on you."

"I think you'll have Bezek's undivided attention." Bethany hugged her future sister. "Do you have a date for your ceremony yet?"

"We've just a few things left to finalize." Manaen returned the embrace. "We should have a time soon."

Josiah and Bethany stood close together as Elder Gemariah finished their joining ceremony. He laid his hand over the two of theirs. "I bless this lifemate union in the name of the One. May you go forth, sharing His love and His truth with all you meet. Amen."

The room erupted with cheers as he invited the newly joined couple to face the crowd.

ACKNOWLEDGEMENTS

No book can ever see the light of day without an entire team of people moving it forward. That's especially true of this book!

First and foremost, I want to give a shout-out to my long-suffering husband, Kirk Melson. Without his willingness to chip in with almost everything around the house, this would book would never have happened. And I would never forget my my precious sons—and their wives—Jimmy and Katie Melson, Kirk and Weslyn Melson, and John Melson.

I also want to thank those writers in my life who offer me almost daily support and encouragement, Beth Vogt, DiAnn Mills, Julie Garmon, Mary Denman, Vonda Skelton, Alycia Morales, Lynette Eason, Emme Gannon, and Lynn Blackburn. Additionally, I want to remember the writers' groups who have supported me and endured endless critiques from "that author who writes weird stuff," Cross N Pens, ACFW SC Chapter, My Book Therapy, and of course The Light Brigade.

A special shout out goes to my amazing (and in my opinion best) agent in the world, David Van Diest.

Of course I want to include everyone at Prism Book Group. You are the greatest group any author could ever hope to be blessed with. Thank you, Susan Baganz, for the editing eye you brought to this project. I and my words are better because of you.

I want to also give a shout out to my extended family, my sister and family—Katy, Kurt, and Ellery Schneider. Finally, I could never neglect to mention my parents, Jim and Monita Mahoney. You all have always believed in me and been among my staunchest supporters.

ABOUT THE AUTHOR

Edie Melson's motto is simple—*find your voice…live your story*. Her joyful spirit is contagious and has helped connect her with audiences across the nation and around the world. She's quick to remind those she meets about the practical and personal applications of God's infinite love. Her numerous books reflect her passion to help others hear from God and find His path for their lives.

She has loved science fiction since before she could walk. Some of her earliest memories involve being cuddled in her father's lap, watching Star Trek (yes, the original series). Edie's also a popular blogger, and her personal site, The Write Conversation, reaches thousands each month. She's the director of the Blue Ridge Mountains Christian Writers Conference, the social media director for Southern Writers Magazine, the Senior Editor at Novel Rocket and the Social Media Mentor at My Book Therapy.

She and husband Kirk have been married 35+ years and raised three sons. They live in the foothills of the Blue Ridge Mountains in SC. Connect with her on her website, www.EdieMelson.com and through Facebook and Twitter.

Thank you for your Prism Book Group purchase! Visit our website to enjoy free reads, great deals, and entertaining, wholesome fiction!

http://www.prismbookgroup.com

Made in the USA
Middletown, DE
10 May 2018